The Cinnamon Spice Inn

The Cinnamon Spice Inn

Harper Graham

bookouture

Published by Bookouture in 2025

An imprint of Storyfire Ltd.
Carmelite House
50 Victoria Embankment
London EC4Y 0DZ

www.bookouture.com

The authorised representative in the EEA is Hachette Ireland
8 Castlecourt Centre
Dublin 15 D15 XTP3
Ireland
(email: info@hbgi.ie)

Copyright © Storyfire Ltd., 2025

Written by Harper Graham

All rights reserved. No part of this publication may be reproduced, stored in any retrieval system, or transmitted, in any form or by any means, electronic, mechanical, photocopying, recording or otherwise, without the prior written permission of the publishers.

ISBN: 978-1-80550-214-2
eBook ISBN: 978-1-80550-213-5

This book is a work of fiction. Names, characters, businesses, organizations, places and events other than those clearly in the public domain, are either the product of the author's imagination or are used fictitiously. Any resemblance to actual persons, living or dead, events or locales is entirely coincidental.

For every reader who believes fall is the perfect season for romance, second chances, and a dash of spice.

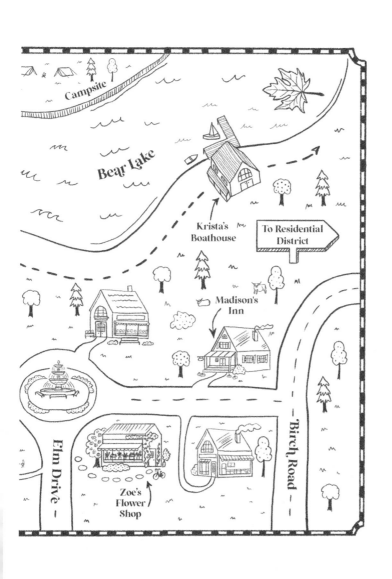

ONE

MADISON

October 11th

Madison Kelly squeezed her knees up tight to her chest. She could not believe what was happening to her. Just this morning, she'd been rushing down her New York street with a croissant and a coffee, heading to a meeting. Now she was back in her childhood home, the Cinnamon Spice Inn, with a mysterious letter under her pillow and a storm battering the windows.

The letter had arrived that morning. It was typed and unsigned, tucked in a worn envelope that looked like it had been carried around in someone's pocket for weeks. She'd known it was important the moment she'd picked it up.

She'd opened the letter, mind racing, hands trembling, the earthy notes of sandalwood and vanilla clinging to the page, stirring a memory.

Madison,

The Cinnamon Spice Inn needs you.
Your dad needs you.

Can you come home? Just for a little while?

—A friend

It wasn't from her dad; he'd never ask for help. And her maternal grandma, well, Gram had no problem telling Madison how it was.

Truthfully, it reminded her of her mother. But that was impossible. Her mom had been gone for the past three years.

It was a mystery. And Madison had a weakness for mysteries.

She loved a good puzzle, always had. Give her a locked-room murder, a crossword, or a half-finished recipe and she was in her element. Her brain liked order. Solving things, fixing them. So, as a secret mystery junkie with a competitive streak and a deeply unhealthy obsession with getting things right, well, she didn't stand a chance. She dropped everything and came back to the inn.

Back to Maple Falls. Back to the small lakeside town surrounded by forest-covered mountains and filled with quirky locals. Back to the place she had planned to never call home again.

Another crack of lightning flashed like a Polaroid, brightening her childhood bedroom. The Cinnamon Spice Inn seemed to groan as thunder followed, rattling the windowpanes.

Madison told herself to pull it together. She had survived NYC rush hour, disastrous first dates, and three chaotic wine-fueled Thanksgivings with her roommate, Jo. But nothing unraveled her quite like a Midwestern thunderstorm.

Only, it wasn't just the storm. Madison had been nerved up since she'd arrived that evening. The inn was in way worse shape than she'd expected. Back in the office, she'd found receipts from two years ago, a water bill from last summer, and a handwritten note from someone named "Tim" about "fixing the soft serve machine." She wasn't even sure they owned a soft serve machine.

Then Gram had let it slip that the twelve-room inn was mostly vacant, with only one couple remaining. It was heartbreaking.

The Cinnamon Spice Inn had once been the perfect spot for a fall holiday. Her childhood memories were full of the scent of her mom's famous cinnamon rolls and the terrace covered in dried leaves. The warm dining room with its vaulted ceiling and crackling fire. Nobody could come here and not feel like they were being enclosed in a big, warm hug. This was *the* place to curl up with a book and a coffee by the window, with a view of the gorgeous autumnal colors and the lake outside.

But now, it was clear her dad had stopped keeping up, and Madison's to-do list was longer than a French tasting menu.

But she'd fix it, she would. She'd get things back on track, hire a manager, and be back in the city by November 1st.

She just had to tackle one problem at a time. Make a list, stick to it. Madison was fabulous with lists.

Another boom rattled the inn. This time, she jumped so hard she kicked the tartan blanket off the bed.

She crossed her arms tightly and admonished herself. "Madison, you are a grown woman. You can handle this."

And she could. Now a popular food writer, she once rewrote a 1,200-word review of a Michelin-starred restaurant in twenty minutes flat after the editor changed the theme last minute from "culinary artistry" to "comfort food." This, in comparison, was nothing.

Even so, ever since she was little, Madison had been terrified of storms. And this one was so unexpected because it was fall—October 11th. Severe storms weren't normally a part of fall's script in the Midwest. It was supposed to be the coziest, most peaceful time of year.

Madison sank back against the headboard and tried to

ground herself. She remembered her mom comforting her in this very room, stroking her hair after a bad dream. She was the only one who knew what to say, how to calm her when her heart raced.

She closed her eyes and took a deep breath. It would all be over soon—the storm, fixing the inn. Then she could go back to her normal life, being the strong, confident woman she knew she was. The woman her mom would be proud of.

CRACK!

The sound of splintering wood shot through the house, followed by a crashing boom. Madison threw the blanket aside and scrambled to her feet. She tugged on the nearest sweater—a cranberry knit—over her checked jammies and grabbed her phone for a light.

Madison's thick wool socks slipped against the polished wood floor as she reached the top of the stairs and froze.

The dining room, her favorite part of the inn, usually known for its crackling fireplace and beautiful lake views, was destroyed.

The town's oldest maple tree, the one that was the hallmark of the inn's charm and a staple of Madison's childhood, had come crashing down right through the heart of the inn.

Rain poured through a gaping hole, soaking the hardwood floor and the overturned furniture below.

"Oh no, no, no, no," Madison said with each step as she jogged down the stairs.

The maple tree had been the backdrop of every family photo. She'd posed in front of it on the first day of school every year without fail, her mom pinning a different bow in her hair.

Now it was firewood.

"Alright there, Maddie?" came her dad's voice from the kitchen, lighthearted and entirely too calm for the occasion. His latest rescue, a puppy named Cocoa, was at his heels, barking in the darkness.

Madison turned toward the sound of his voice just in time to see George enter the room with a flashlight in one hand and, inexplicably, a cookie in the other. His striped pajamas were tucked into his slippers, and his gray hair stuck up in wild tufts.

"Well, I'll be darned. Will you look at that?" He shined the light on the ceiling.

Cocoa continued to bark, chasing the beam of the flashlight, oblivious to the toppled tables and debris.

"Alright, now. I got you," George said, scooping the puppy up. Cocoa was a small pup, weighing only a handful of pounds. She had a chocolate-colored curly coat and was wiggling all over, licking her dad's face, looking for cookie crumbs.

George continued fussing with the puppy while water rained down inside. "You don't like that storm, do ya? Madison is right there with you." Her dad chuckled as another bolt of lightning streaked across the sky.

"Dad, the roof," she pleaded, fighting for George's attention.

"Hmm?" He looked up from scratching Cocoa's ears.

Madison rubbed her temples. "This is serious."

"Yes, yes. Right. The roof." He cleared his throat, looked around, and then took another bite of his cookie.

Madison grabbed the paper towels from behind the registration desk and started mopping, but it was pointless. Her socks were soaked in minutes.

"You're alarmingly calm about all of this," she told her dad.

"Well, no use panicking. That never patched a roof."

Madison resisted the urge to throw her arms in the air.

"What time is it?" she asked aloud before glancing at her phone. "Two-oh-seven. Fantastic." She blew out a breath. "Okay. It's fine. I'll find a tarp, a bucket—"

George cut her off. "Don't go worrying, Honey Pie. It's not a big deal," he added, waving a hand like this was nothing more than a loose doorknob.

"Not a—Dad! Half the roof is missing!"

He nodded. "My guy'll fix it."

"You... have a guy?"

"Yep. Good one, too." He rocked back on his heels, looking quite pleased with himself. "Phone lines are down. I'll go fetch him."

"Fetch him? Now?" Madison grabbed his arm as he reached for his coat. "Dad, it's the middle of the night. In a storm!"

"Stay here and keep an eye on things," he said, handing Cocoa over. "The storm's about finished. Trust me. If your grandmother wakes up before I'm back, and I doubt she will, tell her I'm taking care of it." And with that, he patted Madison on the shoulder and was out the door, still in his pajamas, leaving Madison standing in the middle of a mess of fallen leaves and broken chunks of drywall.

Madison let out an audible groan and closed her eyes, which only made it easier to hear the rain dripping steadily from the ceiling. Cocoa whimpered in her arms.

"I'm sorry, little one. I guess I'm just feeling a bit overwhelmed." She held Cocoa tight to her chest and kissed the pup on the top of the head. "This isn't what we signed up for, huh?"

Madison willed away the tears that were threatening to spill down her cheeks and took a deep breath. She couldn't just stand there and wait. A bucket and tarp would have to do.

"Okay. We've got this." She pressed her cheek to Cocoa's soft fur for one last second of comfort, then crossed the hall to the inn's back office and gently placed the pup inside her crate with a fleece blanket.

In the lobby, Madison found an old raincoat in the front closet; it was stiff and yellow and had seen better days, like the rest of her dad's wardrobe. A pair of mud-caked boots sat below it and she carried them to the back door. Her dad had been right. The storm was easing, but the rain was still falling steadily.

"Alright, let's go," she said, giving herself a pep talk and stepping out into the rain.

In an instant, the wind blew her hood back, and rain pelted her face. Madison ducked her head and pulled the hood forward, but it was pointless, so instead of fighting with the raincoat, she made a run for the shed tucked along the back edge of the property.

The shed, like the rest of the inn, was well past its heyday. The white clapboard siding was supposed to match the inn, but the paint was peeling, and the hinges were practically rusted shut.

Madison's hair was soaked by the time she finally pried the door open. It groaned loudly like a banshee wailing in the quiet of the night.

"Yep," Madison muttered. "Definitely haunted."

She wrinkled her nose as she stepped into the damp and musty space. "Lovely."

The shed smelled of old wood, rusted metal, and motor oil. Her phone's flashlight lit up an assortment of forgotten tools, shelves full of cobwebs, and boxes stacked haphazardly in a corner. Madison shivered, pulling the raincoat tighter like it might protect her from whatever might crawl out from behind a toolbox.

"Okay," she whispered, glancing around. "We're looking for one bucket and one tarp. Preferably not covered in spiders." Madison hated spiders almost as much as she hated storms.

Focus, Madison. She searched through the clutter as quickly as possible. This was the kind of mess she hated. No labels. No order. No logic.

But still, her mom's old gardening trowels were right where she'd always left them, hanging neatly on hooks just above the shelf. That tiny bit of order made something ache in her chest.

"I should've come home sooner," she whispered.

But she hadn't, and now the inn was falling apart.

She shook her head. Now was not the time to wallow. She had a roof to fix.

"Ah, there we go," she said, reaching for a bucket. "Almost got it." Her hand was on the bucket when she heard it—footsteps. She froze. There was no mistaking it. Someone was coming up behind her.

Madison quickly tapped off the phone's flashlight app, plunging the shed into darkness, and set her phone down to look around for a weapon. It would've been easier to look for one with the light on, but she didn't want the killer to know where she was hiding.

Not a killer. Or probably not. Nice Midwesterners didn't normally kill people in sheds in the middle of the night.

Then again, it didn't normally storm in the fall.

Madison fumbled for a rusted trowel hanging on the nail above her. It was dull from use, but it was better than nothing.

The door creaked open, and Madison held the trowel up against the side of her head, ready to strike. She prayed she wouldn't have to use it, but desperate times and all.

She was greeted by a blinding, bright light.

"Mads? What the hell? You're back?" The man's voice was low and rough.

Madison stumbled back, the trowel clattering to the floor.

"Zach?" she breathed. Her stomach dipped, and her heart beat faster.

He stepped closer, the flashlight catching the rain dripping from his sandy hair and flannel shirt. His arms were crossed, his stance as steady and solid as she remembered.

It was him.

Her ex, her first love, her former best friend.

He was taller somehow. Broader. His jeans clung to his legs in a way that made her throat go dry. His eyes—deep hazel pools—held a look she couldn't quite decipher.

Appalled? Annoyed? Both?

The rain intensified, drumming on the shed's roof as her pulse hammered in her ears. Zach's brow furrowed, his gaze unwavering, the tension between them thickening. His eyes lingered on her, searching, hungry.

For a heartbeat they simply stood there—two ghosts from the past. Madison felt a powerful urge to close the gap between them. Her breath hitched, a strange thrill rushing through her veins.

As Zach held her gaze, a smirk tugged at his lips and her heart lurched. She steeled herself, dug her nails into her palms.

She could not let her memories take over. She could not let the feelings in. She wasn't the same girl who'd left Maple Falls all those years ago.

And yet, there was that magnetic pull deep in her chest.

A burning sensation.

Like she was a moth being drawn into the flames, ready to be set alight.

TWO

ZACH

Zach hadn't expected her to be here.

Not now.

Not after all this time.

But there she was, standing in the shed, looking like she'd stepped out of one of his half-forgotten dreams. And what had she been holding? She'd looked ready to pounce.

For a moment, all he could do was stare. Seeing her again hit him like a sucker punch to the gut. It had been six years since she'd left Maple Falls, six years since she'd walked out of his life without so much as a backward glance. And yet, here she was, standing in the shed like no time had passed.

One look at Madison Kelly, and he was twenty-one again, heart pounding, hands itching to touch her. He hated it.

Hated how her fiery hair was even more striking now, a mess of damp curls spilling over her shoulders. Hated how those bright green eyes, wide with surprise, still had the power to undo him. And most of all, he hated how his body instantly remembered every curve, every soft laugh, every moment they'd shared.

"What are you doing here?" His voice came out harsher,

rougher than he'd intended, but he didn't care. He couldn't afford to care.

"I—uh—" Madison stammered, clearly flustered.

Good. Let her feel off balance. She always had a knack for putting him on edge in a way nobody else could.

"I'm looking for a tarp and a bucket," she said finally, her tone sharpening.

Of course she was. Too bad a tarp and bucket weren't going to do much. No point in telling her that, not unless he wanted a fight.

"What are *you* doing here?" she asked, as if it wasn't obvious.

"Your dad called round." Zach leaned against the doorframe. "Said it was an emergency." Zach figured that had to be true. George wasn't one to ask for help; he was a lot like his daughter that way.

It didn't matter that it was the middle of the night with a storm raging. Zach had come right away. Helping people was what he did—it was what he'd always done. He was a good contractor, with his own business, and he cared about this town and the people in it.

More than Madison ever had.

Madison brushed a strand of wet hair from her face. "Still. I didn't think he'd go to you."

"Yeah, well." Zach's eyes narrowed. "It's what I do. I show up when people need me."

He didn't miss the flicker of hurt that crossed her face before she masked it. *Good.* She'd left Maple Falls and never looked back. She didn't get to act surprised that he'd stepped up when she hadn't.

"Zach, my boy!" George's friendly voice called from outside, breaking the tension. Madison's father popped in a moment later, rubbing a towel over his damp hair. "Guess who's back? I forgot to mention." He chuckled. "Isn't that great?" he said, drying his hair with a smile on his face.

Zach glanced at Madison. "Great," he repeated flatly.

"Temporarily," Madison amended.

"Even better," Zach replied under his breath. But he could tell by Madison's glared response that she had heard him.

"Well, I guess I'll go put the kettle on," her dad said, retreating into the night. "You two kids catch up!"

Zach watched him leave then turned back to Madison. She was standing perfectly straight, glaring at him like he was the source of all her problems.

"You didn't have to run right over in the middle of the night," she said finally, her voice defensive. "I'm sure you have better things to do."

Zach just shook his head. Madison didn't get it, and she never would.

"What's that supposed to mean?" Madison crossed her arms, posture defensive.

Zach ignored her, glancing back toward the inn. "Look, I've got work to do. The faster I can patch things up, the faster I can get out of here."

Madison's jaw set. "That won't be necessary."

His brows lifted. "Excuse me?"

"I've got it under control," she said. "I'll handle it."

Zach let out a slow breath, biting back the urge to laugh. Madison would seriously rather deal with a caving-in roof herself, with nothing but a bucket and a tarp, than accept his help.

Unbelievable.

He folded his arms. "Really? And how exactly do you plan to fix it?"

"I'll hire someone," she snapped. "There are other contractors in this town besides you, Zach."

Not very good ones, Zach thought. But the words didn't come out.

Madison lifted her chin defiantly before turning on her heel, boots squelching as she marched past him toward the inn.

Zach hated to admit it, but he needed a minute. There was so much electricity in the air, and not only from the storm. The tension between them fizzed. He leaned against the doorframe and rubbed his temple with his thumb, trying to make sense of it all. Trying to get her out of his head.

Mads.

He could never have seen it coming, the way she had shown up tonight like she so often did in his dreams. He spotted a rusty old trowel on the ground and realized that's what she had been clutching, ready to fight off an intruder. He almost laughed, remembering how fiercely stubborn she could be. How she never backed down from a challenge.

And what had she been wearing? Zach shook his head. A smile tugged at the corner of his mouth. He pictured her in her flannel pajama pants and a red sweater that clashed spectacularly with her unzipped yellow raincoat. It was so her—thrown together, unpolished, and yet, somehow, it worked.

Zach had forgotten the way her hair fell in her face when she laughed. The way her eyes could flash with mischief one second and burn with intensity the next. Tonight, her hair had been damp and her eyes full of annoyance—and a flicker of something deeper he refused to think about.

Zach exhaled slowly. How could his emotions be this raw after all these years? He didn't understand how they hadn't dulled even one bit. If anything, they'd grown.

For one crazy second, he considered going after her, but what would he have said? He shook his head. That way led to trouble.

Zach knew himself too well. The pull Maddie had on him, even now, was dangerous. He'd been reckless with her once before, following his heart instead of his head. When it had all fallen apart, it had nearly destroyed him.

He looked back at the inn. A flashlight looped in the window. Maddie was probably inside, stomping around, talking to herself as she tried to fix things. That was her way, diving headfirst into things, trying to do it all alone.

He needed to stop thinking about her.

He clenched his jaw, closing his eyes. But they were seared on the backs of his eyelids—Madison's dragon-green eyes.

Pulling him in, like the darkest magic.

THREE

MADISON

Madison lay awake in her bedroom. The storm outside had passed, but one was building inside of her.

Zach.

She couldn't believe how infuriating he still was. The way he said her name—Mads—in that low calm voice of his. It was a mixture of gravel and honey, all rough and yet sweet, like the way he used to make love to her.

What?! Where did that come from?

Madison groaned. This was impossible. Zach shouldn't have had any power over her anymore, and yet it was going on 4 a.m. and she was still wide awake.

Madison was determined to get a couple more hours of sleep; otherwise, she would be best friends with the coffee pot come 8 a.m. Not that they weren't best friends already, but one probably shouldn't drink more than six cups of coffee in a day—or so she'd been told.

She wasn't sure when reality ended and the fantasy started. But one moment she was staring at her bedroom ceiling, and the next, she was transported to a different time.

A different place...

. . .

She was in the honeymoon cabin down by the lake, still on the inn's property, but reserved for couples who liked a little more privacy. Zach and Madison had taken advantage of that fact many a time back in their early twenties, before everything had changed.

But that didn't matter. Not now, not in this fantasy.

The honeymoon cabin, with its oak floors and log interior. The fireplace blazed, filling the room with a soft, dreamy glow. A soft rain fell outside, but in here it was warm and dry.

Zach stood across the room, leaning against the doorframe, arms crossed over his flannel-covered chest. Only this time, his shirt wasn't soaked and clinging. It was open all the way down, his stupidly defined abs on show.

She felt herself move toward him in the dream, barefoot, wearing nothing but her favorite cranberry sweater and black panties. His gaze dropped, darkening as it trailed down her legs and back up again.

"You came back," he said, his voice low and rough.

"I couldn't stay away," she replied.

Zach reached out and pulled her to him, one hand wrapped around her waist as the other slid up her bare thigh. His touch was hot, electric, and achingly familiar.

"You always knew how to drive me crazy," he said.

"Do I still?" she whispered.

His answer was a kiss. It was slow, deep, and all-consuming. It was the kind of kiss that left her breathless.

Zach broke away just long enough to lift her by the hips and set her down on the edge of the kitchen table.

The old wood was cool beneath her thighs, but Zach's hands were hot. They slid up beneath her sweater, fingers rough with calluses, but moving with a gentleness she hadn't expected.

"Do you still think about me?" he asked, voice barely above a whisper.

"All the time," she admitted, her throat thick.

He kissed her again, then slowly dragged the sweater over her head. She was bare before him, flushed and already trembling. The heat in his gaze scorched her.

"Beautiful," he murmured, like it was a secret.

His mouth found her neck, then her breasts, tongue flicking, lips teasing. She arched into him, panting as her hands gripped the table's edge.

He kissed lower, down her stomach, before kneeling between her legs and tugging her panties down.

Then his fingers were there—just one at first, then two, slow and deliberate.

"Don't stop," she begged.

Now he was kissing the inside of one thigh, then another. His lips met his fingers at her center, and his mouth made love to her as if he could never taste enough—

A sound outside broke through and dropped her back to reality.

Cocoa. Barking from the next room.

There was no Zach, no honeymoon cabin. No life-altering orgasm just minutes away. There was just Madison, flat on her back, in her childhood bedroom, tangled in too many blankets and completely, utterly mortified. Like someone had thrown a bucket of cold water right over her head.

"Oh my God," she whispered, throwing a hand over her face. Her body still pulsed with the frustration of her unfinished fantasy, heat flushing every inch of her skin.

Madison sat up, yanked the sheet higher, and stared at the ceiling.

What in the actual hell?

It had been years since she'd seen her ex. And yet she'd had the world's most vivid, full-body fantasy about him on her very first night back.

She hadn't even been able to finish the dream, although that was probably a good thing.

But it had left her more frustrated than she'd ever been in her life.

She groaned. Loudly.

How was she ever going to survive the next three weeks?

FOUR
ZACH

October 12th

That storm last night was a wild one, Zach thought as he assessed his farmhouse in the breaking daylight. Zach didn't think he'd been rash when he'd thrown his life savings into renovating his grandparents' apple orchard and the house on it. The place had sat vacant for a generation. But if anyone could fix it up, it was him.

What he hadn't counted on was last night's storm frying the wiring and knocking out his power.

The entire house needed to be rewired.

Zach didn't require much, but electricity sure as hell was useful.

He knew Madison must've been terrified last night, but he also knew she would never let it show. If she was mad enough seeing him, she would've been even madder if he'd asked if she was okay.

Living through a tornado did something to you, especially when you were a kid and had to take shelter while a twister tore up the ground around you.

Zach remembered it like it was yesterday. A perfect spring afternoon, the kind where you barely thought about storms because—well, there was always a chance of storms in the Midwest.

But that day there had been no tornado warning.

Later, that would matter. But in that moment, they were just kids on their bikes, riding the lake trail, when the sirens went off.

At first, they figured it was just a test. Until Zach remembered tests only happened on the first Saturday of the month at 1 p.m. And it wasn't Saturday.

Within seconds, the sky turned an eerie green, and the winds picked up. They pedaled their bikes as fast as they could, heading for the 76 Station on the other side of the lake near the campground. Its orange and blue sign summoned them like a beacon.

They got inside just as the tornado touched down, ripping the roof off the convenience store and scattering chips and candy in the air like confetti. They hid behind the counter with Gary, the store owner, as he tried to keep them safe.

The sound was like a freight train barreling toward them. They linked arms, covered their ears, and leaned against one another. Zach would never forget the tears streaming down Madison's face as he tried to calm her. But it was pointless. The storm swallowed his words. Madison trembled beside him, holding on tight, eyes squeezed shut.

Zach had been terrified, too. But afterward, the high of surviving it felt like nothing else. The adrenaline rush had been out of this world. Thankfully, the tornado only skipped across the lake, touching down at the convenience store and a cabin or two, flipping over pontoons and destroying a dock before disappearing into the sky.

But Maddie had been petrified of storms ever since.

Zach didn't want to think about her, but he just couldn't help himself.

Maddie. It was always Maddie.

Zach gritted his teeth and shook his head.

Last night, after he saw her standing there, wide-eyed and soaked from the rain, he told himself he was done, that she and George could find someone else to do the job. He wasn't about to get dragged back into whatever fresh hell Madison brought with her. Been there, done that. And he had gotten burned for it, too.

But George had asked him and he couldn't let him down.

He told himself it had nothing to do with the fact that last night, Madison had stirred something deep inside of him he could've sworn had been gone for years. Or the way she'd stared at him like she wasn't sure what to say. Madison *always* knew what to say. She was decisive to a fault.

And it was nothing to do with the fact that despite every reason he had to stay away, he still hated the idea of her sitting in that inn with a busted roof.

No, it was because he owed it to Edith, Madison's grandma, and George.

But Madison had dismissed him, hadn't she? A flicker of irritation passed through him. Screw her and her stubbornness. He'd call George, tell him he was on his way.

First, he just needed a run to clear his head.

Zach took a quick, cold shower—another downside of losing power. At least it helped with his growing frustration. Madison had twisted up his usually laid-back self into a ball of tension. Made him think of things, want things, cravings that he'd buried a long time ago.

Not that he wanted to take a cold shower every day.

He could go to his mom's for a few days. She'd been renting a small apartment around the corner from her café ever since he and his younger sister, Emily, had moved out.

Or his best friend, Liam, was an option, but he knew Zach too well. One look and he could read Zach's mind. As he should, seeing as they'd been best friends since third grade. But there were some things Zach wanted to keep to himself. Like his feelings about a certain someone who was back in town.

His mom's it was.

Mind made up, Zach gathered his tool belt and all of his equipment and loaded it in the back of his truck, along with a duffel bag.

Fifteen minutes later, Zach pulled into Water's Edge Park, by Bear Lake.

The park was connected to the lake's walking trail and housed two pavilions, a playground, and a set of public restrooms. It was the go-to spot for summer birthday parties, church potlucks, and family reunions.

It was also the home base for the Walleye Festival that would kick off in April, when fishermen would come from all over the state to try their luck at the spring walleye run.

Bear Lake wasn't massive by any stretch of the imagination, but it had an outlet to the Silver Valley River, which meant a fresh stream of fish migration.

The sunrise glinted off the water, casting streaks of orange, pink, and gold across the surface. Wafts of mist rolled across the lake, low and thin, making only the tops of the trees on the other side visible—their branches ablaze in fiery reds and pumpkin-colored oranges.

The air had that familiar crispness to it, carrying the earthy sweet smell of fallen leaves and woodsmoke from the nearby campground. Somewhere above him, a loon called out, breaking the stillness, a sharp note against the hush of the morning.

Zach took a moment and watched as the light climbed higher, setting the whole shoreline aglow, a final burst of color before winter came to strip it all away. It was a moment of peace before the day fully began.

Zach loved it here, and he needed this headspace. He had a feeling today was going to be a long one. Especially if Madison's temper last night was any indication. She'd give him hell, of course she would. He wouldn't expect anything less.

But even if she tried to toss him out again, Edith would have the final say. Madison's grandma respected him. She knew he was the best man for the job, and so did George. And at the end of the day, it was their home, their inn. Not Madison's. Not anymore.

Zach pulled off his sweatshirt and threw it in the truck. It was cold at first, but he knew he'd be sweating in no time. He grabbed a water bottle and slipped on his AirPods, kicking up the music to help motivate him.

He started with a light jog to warm up. He'd run this route hundreds of times—if not thousands. The paved trail looped around Bear Lake, a six-mile stretch lined with flaming red maples and thick oaks. Today, he'd have to cut it short. He wanted to get to work before Madison woke up.

He was running at a steady pace now, his feet hitting the paved trail in a rhythmic slap. Zach waved to Mrs. Humphrey, who regularly walked her black schnauzer, but other than that, the trail was pretty empty, which didn't surprise Zach. It wasn't yet 8 a.m.

Early morning in Maple Falls belonged to the dedicated few—the dog walkers, the farmers, and the ones like him who needed the miles to think straight. Liam, for one. The man hit the trail harder than Zach did, but not in mid-October. Not when he had his hands full at the farm, gearing up for his family's annual pumpkin patch opening. The weekends were nonstop for Liam. Zach didn't know how he handled the crowds trampling all over his property day after day. Zach would take the quiet solitude of his apple orchard any day.

Zach hoped things would lighten up for Liam when his brother, Jackson, came back from the military. Maybe Liam would finally get a chance to open that farm shop he'd been preparing. It was so nearly there, and Zach would help finish renovating the retail space, stock inventory, whatever Liam needed.

Zach was about halfway through his run when he spotted his mom, Anita, power-walking ahead of him. She was hard to miss in her purple windbreaker, black leggings, and a thick white headband, her short pixie-cut hair spiked up around it.

Zach saw her before she saw him, but the moment she recognized him, her face lit up.

"Morning, son. You look tired—Mrs. Bishop isn't keeping you too busy?"

"Not when I have to keep re-ordering her cabinets," Zach said, coming to a slow stop.

Mrs. Bishop was indecisive—that was a nice way of putting it. Zach preferred to do commercial construction, with its poured concrete, steel beams, and a clear set of plans. Residential work meant emotions. Arguments over paint swatches. Endless second-guessing. At least in commercial jobs, no one cried over countertop samples. Mrs. Bishop only had herself to blame, and all of her home décor magazines that she kept referencing whenever Zach went over. They'd ordered the cabinets twice, and he had already repainted the kitchen once, and she still wasn't sure if that was the color she wanted. They hadn't even gotten to the hardware yet.

And yet, he still took on Mrs. Bishop's kitchen renovation because that's what you did in Maple Falls. You helped your neighbors, even if it meant repainting the same kitchen three times because "eggshell white" somehow looked "too white."

Zach wouldn't have it any other way. Maybe it was because of the way he'd been raised, or rather, the way the town had stepped up after his dad left. He'd been nine—old enough to understand the heated conversations and slamming doors, but too young to do anything about it.

Zach had learned quickly that family didn't always mean blood. Sometimes it was the people who showed up without being asked. It was the ones who mowed your lawn, dropped off casseroles, or taught you how to fix a broken furnace because you were the man of the house now. Those were the lessons that stuck.

The whole town had raised him and Emily. His grandparents had helped, but they had their work on the farm, running the apple orchard. After they passed, it was Mrs. Bishop, Mr. Jensen at the hardware store, and half the church ladies who made sure Zach and Emily never went without birthday presents or winter coats, especially those first couple of years. He owed them everything.

Which was why leaving Maple Falls had never been an option for him. Not like Madison.

So, yeah, Zach was happy to help even the most infuriating clients, like Mrs. Bishop. But right now, they were waiting for her latest order to arrive before he could keep going.

"Good, I was hoping to hear you had some time," his mom said, pumping her arms as she marched in place.

Zach unscrewed the top of his water bottle. "You were?"

"I heard about the roof at the Cinnamon Spice Inn."

Zach narrowed his eyes. "How? It happened—what—five hours ago?"

His mom smiled. "I have my ways. You going to fix it? See, the thing is, I got a letter." Anita looked around as if making sure they were alone. "An anonymous one, asking if I could help out with the inn. Sounds like it's from a concerned local, you know how we are. Just like you know George isn't going to take charity, and that inn hasn't been bringing in any money."

The Cinnamon Spice Inn had always just been there. It was as much a part of Maple Falls as the town square. But everyone round here knew how much George had been struggling since Madison's mom, Meredith, had died. The inn just wasn't the same as it used to be.

"Anyway, I wondered if this roof might be a way to get George to accept some help. You could start with that, then see what else needs doing. Plus, they've got that extra cabin on the property..." she continued.

Anita was talking about the honeymoon suite down on the lakefront—a rustic cabin with one bedroom, a kitchenette, and a bathroom. He and Madison had snuck off there more than once in their early twenties. Not that he was about to tell his mother that.

"That cabin needs work, like the rest of the place," she continued. "And you need somewhere to stay—"

"What? How do you know that?"

"Betsy called me from the electrical company. She put in an order for breakfast sandwiches for the call center," she said as if that explained everything.

"Of course she did." Zach knew what it was like living in a small town. He didn't usually care unless it was his business everyone was talking about.

"Well, there you go. You need a place to stay, George has an inn that needs fixing up. So he won't think it's charity. Problem solved." Anita beamed while still marching in place. Her face was brighter than the sunrise.

Zach exhaled, rubbing a hand over the back of his neck.

Staying in the inn's cabin made sense. It had power, running water, and more privacy than his mom's apartment. It would put him close enough to the inn to get started on the roof first thing.

And, if he was being honest, it was the only way he could help without George insisting on shelling out money he didn't have. A full roof repair job would normally cost more than the Cinnamon Spice Inn had to its name these days.

Still, it irritated him that his mom had maneuvered him into this.

"And you think sticking me in the cabin is going to fix all the inn's problems?" he countered.

"I think," Anita said, stepping forward and poking him lightly in the chest, "that you're the best shot they've got at buying time, without George feeling like he's taking a handout. And Madison..." She trailed off, her smile softening. "Madison can't fix everything on her own."

Before Zach could say anything, Anita kept on going.

"I'm going to do my part, too. Once the inn's been fixed up, I'm going to offer a free meal at the café for every two-night stay at the inn. Just for the first month," Anita amended, seeing the look on her son's face. "We'll advertise it at the café and online, pull in some tourists. Every bit helps."

She didn't wait for a response, just waved a hand dismissively and started back on her power-walk. "You're welcome!" she called over her shoulder, already moving ahead.

Shaking his head, Zach took another swig of water before capping the bottle and tucking it under his arm. He didn't need his mother meddling in his life, even though this time she had a point.

But how would he get used to being so close to Madison Kelly again?

The girl who once made him forget every reason he had to be careful. The woman who still made it impossible to think straight.

He shouldn't have noticed the way her wet, red hair tumbled down her shoulders. Or the fire behind her eyes, making his mouth go dry. Or how her voice, low and exasperated, had settled back under his skin like an itch he couldn't scratch.

Madison would hate him being around. Which only made Zach smile.

Not that it meant anything. Not a damn thing.

Zach picked up his pace, setting his sights on finishing his run in record time. He no longer noticed the falling leaves or the light wind that blew off the lake. He tuned out the birdcalls and the sound of a boat motor in the distance. The sooner he got started on the work, the sooner he could put all this—his mother's scheming and Madison's flashing eyes—out of his mind.

And maybe, if he ran fast enough, he could outrun the memory of Madison too. Outrun the way she smelled faintly of apple and ginger when she curled into him, the heat of her body against his, the way she used to say his name as she fell asleep.

Zach clenched his fists and ran harder.

He needed to keep Madison out of his head.

Fix the inn. Stay the hell out of trouble.

And under no circumstances fall for Madison Kelly all over again.

FIVE
MADISON

Madison woke up hours later to the sound of banging below her. She squinted and rubbed her temple with two fingers, feeling very much like she was hungover, but not from drinking too many martinis at the Village Vanguard. No, this was an emotional hangover fueled by exhaustion, stress, and a vividly inappropriate, unfinished dream.

No amount of caffeine could fix this.

Madison groaned, flopping back against her pillows for a second. She had absolutely, positively not needed that dream. It wasn't enough that he'd barged into her life again looking unfairly good. Her subconscious had decided to serve up a full-body, heart-racing, orgasm-teasing fantasy just to torment her.

THUMP. THUMP. THUMP.

She sat up.

Zach.

Hadn't she explicitly told him she didn't need his help? Hadn't she made it perfectly clear that she would handle this on her own?

Madison willed the memories of last night, the dream, to go

away. But no matter how hard she tried, they flooded in. Uninvited. Unabated.

Zach, waiting for her in the cabin, their cabin, with his taut abs and broad shoulders, standing there drinking her in. The way his touch burned. His kisses left her breathless. His fingers. His mouth. The way he worked her body, so close to the edge...

She squeezed her eyes even tighter, trying to stop the flood of delicious images.

She clearly hadn't had the same effect on him.

His loss, she told herself, ignoring the twinge of pain in her chest at his fiery reception. It wasn't like she'd expected him to wrap her in a hug and spin her around like she'd returned from war. And she'd hardly been thrilled to see him. But still, there was something about the heat in his expression. The bite of his words. Like he hated her guts, like she was the last person on Earth he'd ever want to see. And now he was downstairs banging around like he owned the place.

Her place.

Although... it didn't feel like hers.

When she'd arrived last night, the wide-covered front porch, with its stately pillars and wooden rocking chairs, had been entirely empty. One of the rocking chairs was even missing. It was practically a crime.

Madison's mom had always decorated the porch. This time of year she would've had swooping boughs of autumn garlands and bundles of cornstalks tied to the pillars. There would've been pumpkins. So many pumpkins. And chrysanthemums—white, yellow, orange, purple, any and every color. And bales of hay. There'd always be hay.

Guests would trample it in on their feet, their luggage. Gram would complain about always having to pick up hay halfway down the hallway, but Mom loved it.

Her wreaths too. She had such a collection. There'd always been one displayed front and center on the main door.

Meredith would switch it out every season. Right now it should've been the brown wicker wreath with orange ribbon and golden sunflowers.

It wasn't just the decorations outside.

Inside, the wooden floors had always gleamed, and the scent of apple cider and cinnamon lingered. Madison supposed it still did a little, but it wasn't the same. Her mom had had a way of making sure every guest felt at home. She'd set out a tray of her freshly baked apple scones by the coffee station, swap out the throws in the sitting room, and decorate the mantel with candles and knickknacks. It had always been warm, inviting, effortlessly beautiful.

And now, the reality hit her like a cold gust of wind off the lake. The inn wasn't the same. The warmth was missing.

Madison took a steadying breath.

All wasn't lost. Gram had promised to make her legendary shortbread. It was the same recipe she'd taught her daughter, and which Madison's mom had taught her. And maybe Maurice, the inn's chef, would make his famous pecan French toast.

Not to mention the views. They were still there—thank God.

The inn's two-story great room, which you entered as soon as you walked through the front doors, still took her breath away. It had a stone fireplace mantel and soaring windows that framed the lake beyond. This time of year, the lake would shimmer in golden sunlight filtered through the fiery red and gold maple leaves.

Just thinking of seeing that lake again made her heart ache in a way she hadn't expected, as if some part she'd thought she'd outgrown was still here, waiting for her to come home. She couldn't wait to get out for a walk around it.

Behind the inn, a cobblestone path wound toward the lakefront, creating a walkway perfect for weekend strolls with takeaway coffees. Madison used to walk it as a girl, pretending she was off on some grand adventure.

Now, she just wanted to bring that magic back.

That was her first priority.

THUMP. THUMP.

Or make that her second priority. She had an annoyingly attractive contractor to deal with first.

But just as she swung her legs off the bed, her phone buzzed. She smiled at the hearts flashing across the screen.

"Tell me you've come to kidnap me," Madison said to her best friend.

"Well, good morning to you, too. I see all is well at home sweet home," Jo said with a throaty laugh.

"You don't know the half of it."

Jo waited on the other end of the line for Madison to elaborate.

"A massive storm rolled through here last night, and a maple tree crashed through the roof."

"Oof. I know how much you love storms."

"Yeah. That and... everything else. It's a lot."

Hammering continued in the background.

"At least someone's fixing it?"

Madison hesitated. "Uh. Yeah."

Jo caught the hesitation instantly. "Wait. That's not a good thing?"

Madison sighed. "Do you remember Zach?"

Jo gasped so dramatically that Madison swore she could hear her clutching imaginary pearls. "Sexy carpenter Zach? The guy who could melt your panties with a single look?"

"How do you remember that?"

"I remember all the good bits. Now tell me everything."

Madison rolled onto her back and stared at the ceiling. "He's the one fixing the roof."

Jo squealed loud enough to make Madison yank the phone away. "Things just got interesting."

"Doubt it. He looked more annoyed than anything."

"Mm-hmm," Jo drawled. "And yet you're lying in bed thinking about him. Interesting."

"You are deeply unhelpful."

"Oh, I am your most helpful friend. I'm just waiting for the inevitable. The sizzling chemistry. The heated arguments. The eventual panties removal."

Madison whipped off the covers. "Okay, I'm officially done with this conversation."

Jo snickered. "Fine, fine. But don't think I'm letting this go."

Madison laughed. "I know you won't, but I've got bigger things to worry about."

Jo sobered instantly. "Like the letter?"

For the first time since she'd woken up, her thoughts drifted back to the moment she'd walked through the front door, Gram's gasp of surprise, the way her dad had teared up as he'd pulled her into a hug. The way she'd had to swallow the lump in her throat.

She hadn't meant to arrive so suddenly. Hadn't even given them a heads-up. She hadn't wanted her dad to tell her he was fine, that he didn't need her help, when she knew he did. It had been three years since she'd been home, six months since she'd seen them in New York, but the minute she'd read that letter, she'd just... come home.

"Madison?" Jo prompted, pulling her back. "What's going on?"

Madison exhaled, rubbing her forehead. "I haven't told my dad the real reason I came back."

"Why not?"

"Because it would hurt his pride," Madison admitted. "I told him I needed a break from the city. But the truth is, he's been struggling so much, trying to handle everything on his own. Gram can only do so much..."

Gram had lived at the inn ever since Gramp passed away when Madison was a little girl. Gram didn't have an official title; she always just helped with things. Half of the time, you didn't even need to ask. But still, the woman couldn't do everything Madison's mom used to, and it wasn't fair to expect her to.

Jo's voice softened. "That's a lot."

"Yeah. And last night, we stayed up for hours, drinking hot chocolate by the fire, just talking. I can't even remember the last time any of us relaxed like that."

"Yeah, no clue," Jo agreed. Life was hectic like that.

"He's happy I'm here. I can tell. Just like I think he's secretly relieved, even though he keeps telling me they're getting by just fine. But I know better."

"So, you're making it seem like you came back for *you*, not for him," Jo said.

"Exactly."

"And have you figured out who sent the letter?"

"No. I haven't had time to think about it."

Jo gasped. "Excuse me? Madison Kelly, lover of all things mystery, hasn't investigated something thoroughly?"

"Hey now, I've been a little busy with tree damage and unexpected run-ins with ex-boyfriends."

"Mm-hmm. Priorities, darling. Priorities."

Oh, Madison knew all about priorities.

Priority number one was downstairs right now, wielding a hammer with a tool belt slung across his waist, and she was about to confront him.

SIX
MADISON

Madison stepped off the staircase only to come face-to-face with Gram, who was refilling the coffee station while whistling a tune.

Madison looked into her grandmother's eyes. They were the same rich green as hers, with gold flecks around the irises. Though Gram was well into her seventies, she carried herself with the confidence of someone half her age. Her silver hair was pinned up into a twist, though a few wisps had already escaped, much like her frequent opinions.

"Morning, Gram," Madison greeted her, ready to confront Zach, but a second later, all rational thoughts left her brain.

Zach was there, alright, working on the dining room ceiling. His head was through the hole, leaving only the lower half of him visible.

And oh, what a view.

Perfectly fitted jeans. Strong, muscular legs. Firm backside —and exactly at eye level, too. His flannel rode up just so, revealing a sliver of his lower back.

For a second, Madison lost herself as she stared up at him.

First the sex dream, now this. As if she needed a real-life

encore to last night's thoroughly inappropriate fantasy. She needed an ice-cold coffee, stat.

Madison tugged at the collar of her sweater, feeling like it was suddenly a hundred degrees in the lobby. The worst thing about being a redhead was the instant blushing. Otherwise, she was proud of her hair—it reminded her of her mother's Scottish roots.

People said don't mess with redheads for a reason. And normally, Madison liked to think she lived up to that fierceness.

But right now? She was one hot, flustered mess.

She blinked. Swallowed. Looked away. Looked back.

"Nice view, isn't it?" Gram quipped.

Madison nearly choked on air. She whipped her head toward her grandmother, who was smirking knowingly.

"I... What... I have no idea what you're talking about."

Madison's phone pinged and she looked down, avoiding eye contact just as Zach joined them in the lobby.

"Who was that, love?" Gram asked as she made her way back to the inn's front desk.

"Jo," Madison said, forgetting the text message entirely. Her throat was suddenly dry. Very, very dry as she watched Zach use a worn red rag to thoroughly dry off his hands before tucking the lucky piece of fabric into his back pocket.

"And how is your lovely Jo?" Gram asked.

"Perfect. Missing me already, but, you know..." Madison, still flustered, turned and poured a cup of coffee to keep her hands busy and her eyes from wandering.

At that moment, her phone vibrated again.

Madison glanced down at the text, only to nearly choke again at the message. It was the combination of an exhale and a cough that did her in. She laughed to try and cover it, but the noise came out more like a strangled wheeze.

It was three emojis: eggplant, sweat droplets, saucy wink. Followed by: *Send a pic.*

No way. Madison was not about to sneak a pic of Zach for Jo.

She clutched her phone to her chest in case he saw it. She went so far as to cover the back of the camera with her hand.

Zach look at her oddly, which only made her nervous laughter worse. It was possibly the most unnatural sound she'd ever made. Why couldn't she just be cool?

Zach's brows lifted. "Something funny?"

"Hmm?" Madison shook her head.

"You okay?" Zach asked.

"What? Yes. I'm fine. Thanks," she said far too quickly.

Madison cleared her throat, forcing her voice into something resembling normalcy. "Thought I told you we didn't need your help." She motioned toward the dining room.

"Actually..." Gram smiled. "Zach has already had a chat with me and your dad. He's going to be staying here a while, fixing up the old honeymoon cabin."

Madison glared at Zach. "You're *staying* here?" Her brain short-circuited.

She could practically feel the amusement radiating off him. Yep, that stupid smirk was back.

Madison inhaled sharply through her nose, grasping for words, but her grandmother was already looking at her like she dared her to make a scene.

Madison forced a tight smile. "I see," she said, her voice dangerously even.

Zach's grin widened.

She was going to kill him.

Zach bypassed Madison and moved to pour himself a cup of coffee before joining Gram at the registration desk. "You sleep okay?" he asked Edith with easy charm. He looked so relaxed in the lobby, as if he took coffee there every morning.

"Like a dream," Gram replied honestly. "It'll take more than a tree crashing through the roof to disturb my sleep."

"We could all be so lucky." Zach took a slow sip of his coffee. "Still, I'll have it fixed in no time."

Madison spoke up. "Hold on. Do we have a quote yet?"

"Madison!" Gram scolded.

"What? You don't expect me to agree to work without seeing a quote first." Madison's eyes widened with mock innocence.

Gram scowled. "Don't mind my granddaughter. She's been in the city for far too long." She shot Madison a look.

Zach chuckled as if Madison amused him.

Madison pursed her lips and tightened her fists until her nails dug into her palms.

"I don't mind. I can get you a quote," Zach said, with far too much ease for Madison's liking. It was infuriating how calm and relaxed he was. And she hated how she suddenly felt like the outsider in her own family home.

She would find somebody else to take on the project, someone who didn't make her feel like she was twenty-two again, with a heavy dose of frustration pumping through her veins. She was about to tell Zach to get his toolbox and get the hell out of there—that she didn't care about whatever agreement he, Gram, and her dad had shaken on—when a tiny blur of fur charged into the room.

Cocoa ran straight for Madison and jumped up on her, pushing her backward with more force than one little puppy should be able to manage.

If Madison hadn't been holding a coffee cup, she might have caught her balance, but unfortunately, that wasn't the case. Her woolen socks slipped on the hardwood floor, and she started to fall—until warm, steady arms caught her.

Zach's hands wrapped around her waist, keeping her upright with an ease that made her stomach flip.

For a second, the world narrowed to the space between them.

Madison's breath hitched. Zach was close. Too close. She could feel his body—solid and warm—against hers, his grip strong enough to steady her, but he didn't let her go.

His thumb brushed the hem of her sweater, barely grazing the skin beneath, and she swore she felt the heat of it straight to her core.

Zach's gaze flickered over her face; his brows pinched like he was checking for injuries, but his hands hadn't moved.

Neither had hers. Her fingers had instinctively gripped his forearms and now, she was hyperaware of the firm muscle beneath her palms, the way his flannel was rolled to his elbows, exposing tanned skin and strong wrists.

Her mind betrayed her, flashing hot and fast to the fantasy last night.

His hands on her hips.

Lifting her onto the kitchen table like she weighed nothing.

His mouth on her skin, leaving a trail of kisses that made her toes curl.

A slow, desperate ache unfurled low in her belly.

For one wild second, Madison imagined sliding her hands higher, fisting his shirt, tugging him closer until there was nothing between them but heat and memory.

Until reality blurred into fantasy, and this time, she could actually *finish*.

Zach's throat bobbed. His fingers flexed at her waist, digging in slightly, like he wasn't entirely immune either.

Then, with visible effort, he let her go.

She barely had time to process before Gram scooped up Cocoa. "Here, I'll take the little rascal."

Zach brushed his hands off on his jeans, but Madison noticed how he flexed his fingers, like he still felt her.

He looked back at her. "You sure you're okay?"

Madison swallowed, willing her voice to sound as normal as possible when she responded, "Yeah. It was nothing."

She was not about to admit that her entire body was still tingling.

Zach nodded, slipping back into his normal cool, calm self. "Alright then, I'm going to run to the hardware store and pick up some drywall. I have a patch on the roof that will hold for now. I'll work today cleaning up the dining room, and then I'll be in the rafters dealing with the structural end of things. That part's going to take a few days."

"Take however long you need," Gram said. "You know where to find us." She beamed at Zach.

"Mind if I store my tools in the back?" Zach motioned to the inn's office.

"Um, you better not," Gram replied with an apologetic smile just as Madison was about to tell him he could take his tools with him. "But I'm sure you can leave them in the dining room," she added.

Madison was confused again. There was no way Maurice would want a bunch of tools in his way. What did Gram know that Madison didn't?

"Alright, then. I'll be back in a bit." Zach grabbed his coffee and left them with a nod before heading toward the kitchen.

Gram waited exactly three seconds after he walked out the door before turning on Madison.

"You should take it easy on Zach," she said, shaking her head. "He's doing us a favor, you know. They'd charge us ten times as much if we had to call one of those fancy contractors in Merrillville."

Madison sighed, staring into her coffee. "I know."

"He's a good man," Gram continued.

"I know," Madison repeated, still not looking up.

She was about to make an excuse to disappear upstairs when the smell of smoke reached her. "Is something burning?"

Madison didn't wait for Gram to answer before tearing across the lobby, through the dining room, and into the kitchen.

Madison had heard that toasters could catch fire, but she'd never actually seen it with her own eyes.

Her dad was standing in the kitchen, too, his back to the appliance, examining something. He didn't even notice anything was wrong until Madison came running over.

"Dad, the toaster!"

"What now?" He turned. "Ope! That would be breakfast." Her dad looked to the left, then the right, for something to help.

Madison quickly raced to unplug the toaster and then covered it with hand towels to smother the flames. She searched the cupboards for a box of baking soda just in case the towels weren't enough but came up empty. In fact, most of the cupboards were empty.

He looked up at her with surprise, holding what looked to have once been an egg between his fingers. "Sorry about that. It's just... are hard-boiled eggs supposed to be powdery?" he asked, genuine curiosity in his voice.

She momentarily froze. "What? No! What is happening here? Where is Maurice?"

For years, the inn had had a brilliant French chef, Maurice, who was one of the biggest reasons Madison fell in love with food in the first place.

Maurice and her mom had baked treats for the inn from old family recipes, the pair of them filling the kitchen with laughter and the most delicious of scents.

"In Bordeaux, I suspect. Or was it Lourdes? I can't remember where he was retiring to." Her dad scratched his chin.

Madison's stomach dropped in shock. "Maurice is retired? Since when?" Madison had assumed he had simply gone home for the evening when she'd arrived last night.

"Oh, I don't know... the past four, maybe five months? But don't you worry, I've been managing the kitchen." Madison's dad waved his hand in front of him. "Nothing fancy. I put a stack of plates out and let guests serve themselves."

"Stack of plates," Madison mumbled.

She couldn't imagine the inn without Maurice. Most chefs would've kicked an overly curious eight-year-old out of their kitchen, but not Maurice. No, he'd pulled up a milk crate, handed her a spoon, and put her to work.

"A good chef knows how things should taste," he'd say, plopping a dollop of sauce onto the back of her hand. "Not guess—know."

Maurice had taught her how to tell if peaches were ripe just by their scent. How to pick the best bread by the feel of the crust. How to whisk eggs until they turned the perfect shade of pale yellow.

He also had zero patience for laziness.

"Why are you chopping like a sad little bird? Use confidence, Madison!"

"No, no, no—your béchamel is too fast. Slow down!"

Madison had worshipped him. The first time he'd let her carry a plate out to a guest, she'd felt like she'd won an Olympic gold medal.

Now, she was standing in the same kitchen, staring at what could only be described as a culinary crime scene. And here she'd been hoping for Maurice's butter pecan French toast.

Madison's gaze swept over the disaster in front of her. In addition to burnt toast, her dad had managed to serve up something that once used to be eggs, along with undercooked bacon and overripe fruit with a side of watery yogurt.

Her dad, completely oblivious, smiled at her proudly. "Sometimes I add donuts from the Stop 'n' Go."

"The gas station?" Madison asked incredulously.

"Guests seem to really like them," he said with a shrug.

It was worse than Madison could've imagined. Maurice was probably somewhere in Bordeaux, sipping a fine Chablis, blissfully unaware of the culinary crimes being committed in his absence.

If he saw this, he would weep.

"Course, I know it's not forever..." George said, correctly reading his daughter's expression. "I just didn't know how to find someone to fill Maurice's shoes. I put out an ad in the paper, but the only person who interviewed was an out-of-towner who didn't like animals. Aspen was put off his food for a day when I told him. Can you imagine!" George shook his head.

No, Madison couldn't. George loved animals and had an addiction to rescuing them. Cocoa was only one of the inn's latest pets. Honey and Biscuit, a pair of miniature Highland cows, were a destination in their own right, given to Gram on her seventieth birthday. They also had two goats—*They can't live all by themselves! They'd be lonely!*—and Aspen, her father's white pony, rescued from a circus.

The animals were some of the many additions her parents had made to the historical inn over the years. Now, the inn had no chef, no money, it was falling apart, and yet her dad couldn't seem to stop rescuing animals. Heaven help her.

"I've got to go," Madison said, her thoughts snapping back to the present. Her habitual fight-or-flight response had kicked in hardcore, and she needed space. Needed to think. Or not think. Everything was all too much.

She just needed to go.

Madison turned on her socked heel and made for the exit.

"Wait! You're not going to stay for breakfast?" he called after her.

"Sorry, Dad, not hungry!" she replied without looking back.

"I can get some donuts if you'd like?" he added, but Madison was running away.

She tugged her boots on and wrapped a knit scarf around her neck before quickly stepping outside. She didn't think; she just escaped.

She had avoided Maple Falls ever since her mom's funeral a few years ago. It had been too painful, too full of memories.

But even before then, Madison had mostly stayed away since leaving home in her early twenties. Sure, she'd visit her family over the holidays. But every time, she'd keep herself hidden away at the inn, away from the town she'd once loved so much. The guilt had been too much.

It wasn't just the way she had left for the internship, when she and Zach were still together, and how they'd started to talk less and less often as work and city life consumed her.

No, it was what came after. When she'd come home on the anniversary of when they first started dating, to surprise him. She wanted to tell him about how amazing New York was, how a whole new world had opened up to her, and maybe, just maybe, persuade him to move there with her. This wasn't the type of conversation to have over the phone. Oh no. This was a big, life-altering conversation, and she'd wanted to have it in person. In her mind, she pictured them celebrating their anniversary before asking him the question that could change everything.

But instead, she'd found him at the bar, playing pool and laughing with another woman, the girl leaning too close, smiling in a way that made Madison's stomach twist. She'd turned around and walked out before he even saw her, her heart splintering in a way she hadn't let herself think about since.

A few days later, Madison had called him, saying she could feel something was off between them and asking if there was anything he wanted to tell her. He hadn't said anything. Only silence, an awkward pause.

So, Madison did what she had to do. She told him she was going to stay in New York for her career and that maybe it was better if they broke up since the long-distance thing clearly wasn't working.

Zach didn't argue. That fact still hurt all these years later.

Deep down, she had hoped he would stop her, admit what was going on with that other girl, say he still wanted them, that he would try. But he hadn't fought for them at all. He had just let her go.

After that, it hadn't taken long for her to lose touch with all her friends. They were all so connected to Zach, from his sister, Emily, to his best friend, Liam, and it just felt like there was no space for her anymore.

All the same, their friendships had been real, deep, and important, and she had pushed them away. Now, she wasn't sure if she'd be welcomed back.

She could still turn around. Run back to the inn, to coffee, to comfort.

But standing on the porch, the leaves whipping around her feet, it was like a cool breeze was stirring in her heart too. Whispering that it was time to come home. Madison stepped off the porch.

Maybe she'd walk down to the lake first. Let the cold air clear her head.

Or maybe she'd just wander. See how the town had changed. See what was new.

Maybe—just maybe—she'd run straight into the person she was trying so desperately to forget.

SEVEN
ZACH

Zach pulled into the hardware store. The air was brisk, and the sky was that bright, cloudless blue that only seemed to show up in the heart of fall. Any remaining low-lying fog would disappear within minutes.

The shop was easily within walking distance from the inn, but he needed his truck to haul the drywall. He cut the engine and stared out the windshield for a moment, trying to clear his head. A gust of wind sent leaves fluttering down from the maple trees that lined the sidewalk, scattering them across the wooden benches and the brick walkway.

On the sidewalk, Mrs. C. and Mrs. Bishop strolled past, arms linked, with their knit scarves and tweed coats, on their way to the bakery, no doubt, talking about last night's storm. There were a few branches down, more leaves scattered in the road. Nothing a few helpful neighbors wouldn't have cleaned up by lunch. The inn had taken the brunt of it in town.

The women waved. It took Zach a second to realize it was directed at him. He replied with a head nod, forcing a smile he didn't feel.

"Get the drywall, fix the inn, and keep away from her,"

Zach told himself with as much conviction as he could muster. It was self-preservation at its finest. Even after all these years, the sight of Madison did something to him. He was convinced she'd have that pull on him until the day he died. She would forever be the love of his life. He didn't deny that.

But he couldn't let those feelings take over; he couldn't fall for her again. Wanting Madison had never been the problem. Surviving her leaving was.

Zach got out of the truck and walked up to the entrance. Old Man Perkins was relaxing out front in one of the wooden rocking chairs placed there for locals to socialize. He had a Styrofoam cup of coffee in one hand and was just polishing off the rest of his glazed donut when Zach approached.

"Morning, Zach," Perkins greeted, chewing the last of his donut. "That tree falling through the inn's roof got you already working?"

Zach slowed his stride. "Morning, Perkins. Yeah, gotta grab some drywall."

"Heard all of Popple Lane lost power." He took a sip of his coffee.

"Doesn't surprise me. It was a hell of a storm."

"Yep. Sure was. Hey, do me a favor."

"What's that?" Zach paused, waited to hear what errand he'd be adding to his list.

"Tell Edith she still owes me for that blackberry jam from last summer," Mr. Perkins said, rocking back in his chair. The motion caused the chair to creak under the weight.

"Will do," Zach said, pulling open the glass door and stepping inside.

The hardware store in Maple Falls was more than just a place to get a few nuts and bolts; it sold everything from paint and lumber to dishware and winter gear, mixed in with a selection of local goods, including Zach's apple butter.

The recipe had been his grandmother's. Zach had found it

in the back of a kitchen drawer while demoing the old kitchen. The first time he'd whipped up a batch, it had tasted like his childhood when he'd had sleepovers at Nana and Pop's house. Nana would serve freshly baked biscuits and apple butter for breakfast before Zach and Pop would head out for a morning of fishing.

Without thinking, he walked over to the display of his spread and rearranged the glass jars. He took a mental inventory, noting he'd have to restock soon. His bourbon apple butter was always the best seller, and by the looks of it, he'd need to bring in more in the next day or two.

Just as he was finishing up the display, a voice behind him purred, "I sure do like that butter of yours," and Samantha Weiss sidled up next to him.

Zach hadn't even seen the recent divorcée come up behind him. "Thanks, I appreciate it."

Samantha was all smiles as she leaned toward the apple butter, feigning interest in the glass jars, but in reality, she was showing off her impressive cleavage. It might have been fall and only fifty degrees out, but Samantha was wearing tight black jeans, a low V-neck tank top, and an oversized cardigan that she let slip off her shoulder just so.

She ran a manicured nail along the glass jar. "Of course, maybe I could afford some of your apple butter if I wasn't spending all my money trying to fix my back door," she said, eyes flicking up at him.

Zach barely registered her words. "Uh-huh," he replied, jotting down a reminder on his phone to restock the bourbon one.

He was about to wish her a good day when she reached out and squeezed his forearm.

"You know, Zach..." She lowered her voice, making it softer somehow, silkier. "You're so good with your hands..." She trailed off suggestively.

Zach blinked. "I guess. I mean, it comes with the job," he said, clearly not catching on.

Samantha let out a soft laugh. "They're so strong and capable." Her eyes flickered up to his. "And my back door just needs a bit of work. I was thinking maybe you could come by and... take care of it?" She cocked her head playfully.

Zach was staring off in the distance, trying to remember everything he needed to pick up. There was the drywall, screws, seam tape. Probably should grab a new sanding sponge.

Samantha cleared her throat.

"What was that?" He looked back at the woman.

"My back door. Will you take care of it?" Samantha looked up at him with innocent doe eyes.

Zach still missed her point entirely. "Oh, um, sure. No problem. I'll grab my toolbox and stop by this weekend. Maybe tomorrow afternoon?"

Samantha clapped her hands together in front of her chest. "Perfect. I'll make us a nice dinner as a thank you."

Zach looked genuinely confused. "Oh, you don't have to do that. I'll be in and out quick."

Samantha laughed again, slow and teasing. "Promise?" She trailed her fingernail down Zach's shoulder before squeezing his forearm one last time and sashaying out of the hardware store.

"Bro, that was painful to watch." Zach's best friend, Liam, emerged from the next aisle, grinning.

Zach turned away from the apple butter display and started heading toward the drywall. "I have no idea what you're talking about," he muttered.

Liam fell into step beside him, their strides and height almost equal. "You do realize she just invited you over for more than handyman work, right?"

Zach frowned. "What are you talking about? She needs her back door fixed."

Liam snorted and scratched his beard. "Oh, she definitely wants something fixed."

Zach shook his head, realization dawning a second too late. "Oh, hell."

Liam cracked up, his dark eyes sparkling. "Man, I forgot how awful you are at this. It would almost be too painful if it wasn't funny as hell."

"I'm just a bit..." Zach trailed off, unsure how to finish.

"A bit preoccupied with the fiery redhead who's back in town?" Liam prompted.

Zach shot him a look. Liam held up his hands.

"If looks could kill—I'm gonna let it slide and use Madison as the excuse for why you haven't wished your best buddy a happy birthday yet."

Zach blinked. "Sorry, man. You're right. It is the twelfth. Happy birthday."

"Wow. When you say it like that..." Liam laughed. "You sure know how to make a guy feel special. But that's okay, you can make it up to me tonight."

"Tonight?"

"The Kettle. Seven o'clock. Be there."

The Kettle was short for the Copper Kettle and was the only place in town to grab a cold beer and play a round of billiards, darts, or keno—patrons' choice. Zach was pretty sure they even had pull tabs.

"I don't know... I've got a lot of work going on. There's a bunch of projects. I don't even have power—"

Liam cut him off. "No excuses. You owe me."

Zach glanced past the pegboard full of power tools. "I fixed your porch last year for free."

"Different situation. This is a social obligation."

Zach sighed. "You won't be alone. I'm sure you've got the entire town lining up to buy you drinks."

"True, but none of them are as fun to mess with as you."

Zach weighed his chances of getting out of it.

Liam grinned. "Just agree to show up and get it over with."

"I don't know, man. The house, the orchard..." Zach tried one last time.

"What, harvesting apples on a Friday night?" Liam smirked.

Zach shot him a look. Liam damn well knew he didn't need to harvest apples tonight. He knew how it worked. They'd both helped Pop with the orchard back when Liam didn't have his own farm to manage. Now, though, Liam had an entire produce operation, a fall harvest to oversee, and way more land than Zach.

Zach's was more of a hobby farm, focusing on small-batch apple butter and supporting a few local businesses, like his mom's café and the bakery. The rest he bagged up as deer feed, selling that too at the hardware store.

Zach liked it that way, simple, relaxed. Ten acres, an apple orchard, and views of the lake. He couldn't ask for better—well, maybe a house that wasn't about to fall apart.

"No, but if I'm ever going to fix the house up, I'm going to have to work on it nights and weekends," Zach said, rationalizing.

"I'm all for that. I'll even lend a hand," Liam offered. "But you're not getting out of this, man. It's my birthday. Shake on it." Liam stuck out his hand, the same way he had since they were nine years old.

Zach shook his head but reached out anyway. "I'll stop by. Promise."

It was only when he walked away that he realized Madison might be invited too.

EIGHT

MADISON

The cold, fresh air stung Madison's cheeks. It was almost cold enough to see her breath in front of her face. A light fog floated through the streets, but the bright morning sun was quickly dissipating it, casting everything in a warm, golden glow.

She was wearing her old, worn leather hiking boots, a black woolen coat, and her mom's emerald knit scarf, which she touched with a soft smile. October mornings in Maple Falls could be downright chilly. She didn't know where she was going exactly but she needed this: fresh air and a chance to clear her head.

Maple leaves crunched underfoot as she walked. The inn was set along the spring-fed lake, with a walking trail that wrapped around its entire perimeter. The downtown area curved around the lake and housed all the independent shops and restaurants. The other side of the lake was a residential district, home to the school, police department, post office, and bank, along with neighborhoods nestled among the trees. A stretch of forest separated the two areas, with a small campground between them.

Now smoke drifted in the air from the handful of brave

souls who still camped, even though nighttime temperatures were dipping into the forties.

Madison smiled, remembering the time she and Zach had spent a chilly night in a tent. It had been his best friend Liam's idea—a party at the campground to celebrate his and his twin brother Jackson's twenty-first birthday. Of course, the memory of what they'd done to stay warm made her cheeks flush. She gave her head a little shake. If only things hadn't ended the way they had.

Madison continued down Oak Way, the town's main street. All the surrounding streets were named after local trees—Elm Drive, Popple Lane, Birch Road—which seemed fitting for a town named after a hardwood.

Shops were on either side of the inn along the lakefront. And now, Madison caught her first full glimpse of the lake since returning home.

She stood there, between the inn and the Little Lantern Bookshop, and gazed at the lake between the trees. It had been dark by the time she'd arrived last night. Now, the morning mist was nearly lifted and the sight was breathtaking.

A few boats were out fishing for early-morning walleye, and a pair of loons floated nearby. The birds would be heading south soon, but for now, Madison enjoyed hearing their calls, even if they had a tendency to wake the town up at six in the morning. Thankfully, the lake had a no-wake zone until 11 a.m., allowing nature, the fishermen, and the townsfolk to enjoy the tranquility without motorboats zipping around.

"Morning, Madison," Dolores Humphrey called as she walked by, her little black schnauzer trotting along in front. The dog wore a red sweater and a matching bow tie, looking very dapper, and judging by the way he held his head high and swished his tail just so, he knew it. "Edith said you were back in town. Didn't think I'd run into you first thing, but happy I did."

Mrs. Humphrey had been Madison's first-grade teacher,

and she looked the same as she had twenty years ago. Madison wondered how that was even possible, but it was. The retired teacher carried a takeaway coffee in her hand, and the sight alone was enough to make Madison know exactly where she needed to go.

"Morning," Madison replied with a smile. "Nice to see you too." Just the simple act of greeting someone on the street made her think about how different things were in Maple Falls compared to the city. It might have only been three years since she'd been home for the funeral, but it felt much longer. Even then, she'd kept her head down and avoided people. Losing her mom had been hard enough without adding everyone's sympathy on top of it.

Madison never knew what to say when people expressed their condolences. Sometimes, it felt like she ended up comforting them instead of the other way around. The whole thing had been exhausting, serving as a constant reminder of how much she had lost. Madison shook her head, unwilling to dwell on the past, but she couldn't deny how much being home stirred up old memories.

Still, as she walked toward the bakery, she smiled, taking in the seasonal storefront displays. It looked like the storm had knocked over a couple of planters, broken a few branches, and toppled a scarecrow or two, but she was glad to see no one else had any structural damage.

That was a relief, since the Maple Falls Pumpkinfest was next Friday. Businesses were already gearing up, and it showed. On the day of the festival, Oak Way would be shut down, turning the downtown area into a street fair with the festival spilling over to the community park along the waterfront. All the downtown businesses participated, from a bouncy house in front of the bookstore to a hay bale maze sponsored by the Kettle. There was face painting, pumpkin bowling, a kids' craft table, and so much more.

The hardware store's window featured a scarecrow dressed like a fisherman, complete with a flannel shirt, overalls, and a toy fishing pole. In front of Harvest & Hearth, the culinary shop, a rustic wooden sign invited festival-goers to their cider-tasting event, boasting flavors like honey crisp, spiced pear, and mulled cranberry. The chocolate shop, the Cocoa Corner, made Madison stop and smile. The owner, Rita, had made a massive hollowed-out chocolate pumpkin, with a contest to guess how many candy corn pieces were inside. The winner would take it all.

Down the street, the hay bale maze was under construction in the town square, where children would soon race through tunnels of straw. The pumpkin-carving contest was scheduled for next Friday afternoon, and if memory served, the winner always walked away with a fall-themed gift basket complete with a cozy blanket, spiced candles, and locally made treats. The scarecrow-making competition was another festival favorite. Businesses and families alike participated, crafting everything from traditional hay-stuffed farmers to elaborate, themed designs.

And, of course, the food. Madison's stomach rumbled just thinking about it. There would be fresh caramel apples, spiced cider served steaming in paper cups, hot kettle corn, and Maple Falls' famous cinnamon donuts, served warm from the fryer. The bakery always sold out within the first few hours, and people lined up early to get their hands on a dozen before they were gone.

Throughout downtown, bright orange pumpkins, stacked bales of hay, and chrysanthemums in deep burgundy, sunny yellow, light purple, and soft white decorated the streets. Madison instinctively glanced over her shoulder at the front of the inn and sighed. It's not like she expected someone to magically decorate the porch overnight. Still, the lack of decoration was a glaring reminder of just how much still needed to be done.

Thankfully, she reached her destination before she could spiral into further frustration. She pulled open the door to the Pumpkin Pie Bakery and stepped inside.

The bakery had a vintage farmhouse charm, with worn wooden floors and cream-painted shiplap walls. The chairs were black wrought iron with natural wood seats, and greenery filled the space—lemon and orange trees soaking in the abundant natural light from the windows.

The air was warm and filled with the scents of cinnamon, vanilla, and freshly brewed coffee. Madison's stomach rumbled as she caught sight of the display case—cranberry-orange scones and mouthwatering cream cheese danishes lined the first row. The second case was dedicated to gourmet cupcakes, everything from devil's food cake filled with chocolate ganache and raspberry jam to yellow cake iced with vanilla cookie buttercream, and lemon cake with cream cheese icing and a lemon curd filling.

But what caught Madison's eye the most were the sugar cookies. They were easily the size of her palm, if not larger, and cut into adorable shapes like oversized leaves, acorns, apples, and pumpkins. Each was topped with a thick layer of fluffy, smooth buttercream frosting.

Madison's mouth watered. She couldn't deny it. If she had a vice, it was an addiction to coffee and buttercream.

"Madison Kelly, is that you? Oh my gosh, you're really back!"

Madison froze for half a second before turning.

Emily Whitaker, Zach's younger sister by eighteen months, was rounding the bakery counter, wiping flour from her hands before pulling Madison into a tight hug.

Madison was surprised by the sudden, familiar aroma of warm vanilla and fresh bread that clung to Emily's clothes. It tugged at old memories of lazy Saturday mornings, splitting muffins and gossiping about boys before life had gotten so complicated.

She hadn't planned on running into Emily today, and she honestly wasn't sure what to expect. They hadn't seen each other since her mother's funeral. And even then, they hadn't talked much. That day was a haze, but she remembered Emily had hugged her, said she was there for her if she wanted to talk. But Madison hadn't spoken to her in years. When her mom was sick, she hadn't been able to reach out to Emily in the way she would have once. Because things could never again be the way they were before Madison and Zach split up.

Now, this long hug was definitely unexpected. A knot deep inside her stopped Madison from softening into it, a resistance, a fear. She couldn't help wondering if Emily would suddenly pull away. But Emily only hugged her tighter, and the knot in Madison's chest loosened just enough for her to hug her back.

"Hey, Emily... It's good to see you. I didn't know you were working here now?" Madison said, stepping back once she caught her breath. She glanced around, expecting to see the owner, Mrs. Myers, pop out from the kitchen, scolding them for sneaking extra cookies after school.

"Work here? Heck, I own the place. Took over after Mrs. Myers retired." Emily leaned in and lowered her voice as if sharing a secret. "Still can't make pastries as good as she does, but don't tell anyone."

Madison laughed, and warmth spread through her chest. "Your secret's safe with me."

For a moment, she wasn't Madison Kelly, food critic and city girl. She was just Maddie, standing in the bakery that had once been a second home.

"I just can't believe you're really here. It's been way too long." Emily stepped back behind the counter.

"I know, it has," Madison admitted. She half expected

Emily to continue on, guilt-tripping her for never coming home, for breaking her brother's heart, but to her surprise, she didn't. The tension in Madison's shoulders eased, just a little.

"Coffee?" Emily asked, already poised to start making it.

"You know me." Madison hadn't had nearly enough this morning. Only one cup, and she'd ended up nearly wearing half of it. She would've too, if Zach hadn't caught her.

Her face warmed at the memory—his firm hands gripping her waist, the rough brush of his calloused fingers against her soft skin.

His hands had always undone her.

It was bad enough she'd practically melted under his touch, but worse was the fact she couldn't stop thinking about it. Couldn't stop thinking about him.

Not after that blasted dream. One innocent brush of his hand, and suddenly all she could think about was Zach lifting her onto the table, his body pressed tight against hers. The way he'd made her tremble, desperate for release.

Madison shoved her hands in her pockets, trying to push the images out of her head before she burst into flames right there on the bakery floor.

She looked up at the chalkboard menu instead, scanning the impressive selection. So many new options since she was last here—gingerbread iced coffee, brown sugar oat latte, and the classic pumpkin spice.

Madison had become a flat white kind of girl—straightforward, strong, no nonsense. But still, something about being here made her crave the cozy indulgence of the past.

She worried her bottom lip with her top teeth as she fought to make up her mind.

"I could always make you an apple cinnamon vanilla latte. The apples are locally sourced," Emily said with a knowing smile.

Madison's head jerked up, her lips parting in surprise. "You remember that?"

"Of course I do." Emily's grin widened. "You and I used to come in after school, sit in the window seat, and talk about how we were going to travel the world. You always got that latte, even in the summer."

A rush of nostalgia hit Madison square in the chest. She could practically hear their teenage voices filling the bakery. Back then, everything had felt wide open and possible.

"It's not on the menu," Emily added, "but I have everything right here."

Madison felt a lump form in her throat, but she swallowed it down and forced a smile. "That would be perfect. Thank you."

Emily nodded, already getting to work, but Madison could tell she wanted to say more. So did Madison. There were a thousand things she wanted to ask—about life here, about the bakery, about how Emily had stayed while she had left.

But before she could, the bakery door chimed, and a steady stream of customers bustled in.

"Hey, maybe we can catch up soon?" Emily asked, handing over the coffee a few minutes later.

"I'd love that," Madison replied and felt something that might have been tears in the back of her eyes.

She ended up caving and getting one of the frosted sugar cookies, too. "Surprise me," she had told Emily when asked which one.

Emily had chosen an orange pumpkin, and it tasted heavenly —a perfect mixture of buttery soft shortbread and sweet frosting. Was there anything more perfect than coffee and cookies?

Madison took her sweet treat and coffee and sat by one of the windows for a moment, letting her thoughts wander.

It wasn't that she'd ever stopped caring about Emily or her other friends, or even Maple Falls.

It was just... after she'd left, after her heartbreak over Zach, it got so much harder to bridge the distance. She'd felt like she was worlds apart from her old friends. They didn't understand her new life, but even when they were all teenagers, she had talked non-stop about moving to the city one day. Becoming a writer, traveling, seeing the world.

Zach had known this—he'd encouraged her dreams—and Madison had hoped from the beginning that he would go with her. But his life was rooted here, and it wasn't until after Madison received the internship offer that she realized she'd be going to NYC alone.

She told herself they could figure it out, that they'd talk it through when she came home. They hadn't been talking as much as she'd thought they would. She'd been so busy for those months of the internship. But she still loved him, and she thought he loved her enough to move to the city when she told him she needed to stay.

So she had come home, ready to surprise him on their anniversary. Only that's when it truly fell apart.

That woman he was flirting with, the way she leaned into him and he let her. The undeniable spark between them, when he had no idea Madison was right there watching.

It had shattered her heart, the pieces crumbling inside her as she walked away.

Still she'd hoped there was a chance for them, until that phone call a few days later when his silence had told her everything she needed to know.

In the end, she hadn't just ended things with Zach. She'd ended them with Emily, Liam, and the rest of Maple Falls, too. Every missed call and delayed response was another brick layering up into a big wall between them.

And then her mom died, and that wall felt too high to climb.

For a second, she let herself imagine an alternate version of her life. One where she never left. One where she still popped in here every Saturday, where she and Emily still split cinnamon rolls and swapped stories about terrible bosses, crazy customers, dreams they weren't sure they were brave enough to chase.

Madison exhaled slowly.

It was foolish to mourn a life she had walked away from. And yet, here she was. And she had missed this place so much.

Outside, locals and tourists continued to walk down the sidewalk. They were bundled in their woolens with shopping bags swinging from their wrists. It was nice to see that the downtown area was busy. Well, except for the inn.

She pulled out her to-do list. Picking up a box of baked goods and a potted mum from the hardware store would be quick wins.

Enough daydreaming. Madison had work to do, an inn to save.

NINE

MADISON

Madison waited until there was a break in customers before heading back to the bakery counter. "Hey, Emily, when you get a minute, can you box up a dozen of your danishes and muffins? They're for the guests at the inn." *The two that remain,* Madison added to herself.

"Sure, I have some coming fresh out of the oven. Give me about fifteen minutes."

"Thanks, Em. You're a lifesaver." Madison smiled. It felt so natural somehow, back here in the bakery, talking to her oldest friend. Like the years they'd been apart just didn't matter.

"I meant to ask, who's your new chef? I heard Maurice retired," Emily said while refilling the drip coffee pot. She offered free refills on her house blend, and several regulars took her up on it, sitting eating cookies, drinking coffee, and gossiping for hours.

"That's just it—my dad hasn't hired anyone," Madison confessed.

Emily's eyes widened. "But your dad can't cook." She clapped a hand over her mouth as if she couldn't believe she had just blurted that out.

Madison laughed. "I know!"

"It's just... I remember all the sleepovers we used to have. Your mom always did the cooking because your dad..." Emily hesitated, struggling to find the right words.

"It's okay, you can say it—my dad can't even boil water. You should've seen the kitchen this morning. There was smoke coming out of the toaster."

Emily winced.

"I know I obviously need to hire someone, but I'm not even sure where to start." If Madison were back in New York, she'd have a dozen chefs ready to jump in and help, but her contact list in Maple Falls was nonexistent. "Maybe we could do a daily pastry order until I can figure something out?"

Emily snapped her fingers in excitement. "I know someone you have to talk to. She's a bit crazy... but in a good way," she added quickly when she saw Madison's skeptical expression. "Like, in a culinary genius sort of way," she clarified.

"Uh-huh," Madison said, unconvinced there was anyone in Maple Falls who could fill Maurice's shoes.

"You know Norma Steigler?"

"Norma Steigler, the seamstress?" Madison thought back to the old lady who walked around town with a pincushion always strapped to her wrist.

"Yes, that's her. Her great-niece just moved into town. She finished culinary school out west not too long ago, but she wasn't having much luck landing a job. Norma offered for her to stay here for a while and save up before trying her luck in the Big Apple. Anyway, I had her fill in here at the bakery a time or two, and she's a genius. Her flavor combinations are out of this world. I wish I had more work for her, but I just don't. I honestly think she'd be perfect for the inn. Here, let me give you her number."

Madison pulled out her phone, and Emily AirDropped the chef's contact information.

"Kit Riker," Madison read aloud.

"Call her. You won't regret it. Tell her you and I go way back, and I'm sure she'll jump at the chance."

Madison thanked Emily again and went back to her table to wait for the pastries.

"Ms. Madison, it is so good to see you, honey." Madison looked up to see Mrs. Bishop walking over. The petite older woman wore a deep plum cardigan with tiny, embroidered pumpkins at the hem. She had a matching one on her turtleneck and pumpkin earrings dangling from her ears. It was as if she'd been waiting all year for the season to arrive.

Her friend Mrs. C., short for Copplehagen, fell into step beside her, ever the leader between the two. Where Mrs. Bishop dithered, Mrs. C. had the sharp, no-nonsense authority of a retired librarian, capable of silencing an entire room with a single arched brow. Today, her gaze was just as assessing, though there was warmth in it, too.

"Welcome back," Mrs. C. said with an assessing head nod. "Your mama would be so proud you're helping your dad." She took a measured sip of coffee, her expression unreadable.

Madison barely had a chance to respond before Mrs. Bishop spoke up again, her tone shifting. "And we can expect to see you at the Pumpkinfest committee meeting, can't we?"

Madison blinked, caught off guard. "The... Pumpkinfest committee?"

Mrs. C. let out a long-suffering sigh. "Your father has missed the last two meetings, and we don't want another scene like last year."

At this, the two women exchanged a knowing look over their coffee cups.

Madison had absolutely no idea what they were referring to, but she also wasn't sure she wanted to ask. "Of course," she said, plastering on a fake smile. "I'll be there. Just tell me where and when."

"Good." Mrs. C. nodded approvingly, already reaching into her bag to retrieve what Madison was certain would be a notebook filled with meticulously outlined festival plans. "It's at Anita's café tomorrow at eleven o'clock."

Madison opened and closed her mouth, not sure what she was going to say. She hadn't planned on running into Anita if she could help it. Zach's mom and hers had been best friends. There had been a time when Madison couldn't walk into Anita's café without getting wrapped in one of Anita's tight hugs or hearing stories about how proud her mom was of her.

She hadn't seen Anita since her mother's funeral, and it was one reunion Madison wasn't ready for.

Madison barely had a chance to respond before Mrs. Bishop added, "Have you seen Zach yet? He's such a good boy. He's remodeling my kitchen!"

At that comment, a young woman's ears two tables over perked up. Madison didn't know who she was, but she seemed interested in any conversation that revolved around Zach. Madison tried to ignore her and turned her attention back toward the older ladies, who kept right on talking.

"It'll never get done if you don't make up your mind," Mrs. C. chimed in, giving Mrs. Bishop a condescending look.

"It's a big investment. Can't go making the wrong choices, now can I?" Mrs. Bishop looked to Madison for support.

Madison took a careful sip of her coffee, working on keeping her expression neutral. She barely registered the sweetness of the vanilla and warm cinnamon, watching the two women bicker.

"She has the poor boy repainting her kitchen every five minutes." Mrs. C. hooked her thumb in Mrs. Bishop's direction.

"Now, it's not every five minutes. It's only been twice... Might be a third time, but that's it! These things are important," Mrs. Bishop pleaded.

"Well, if you get tired of yanking him around, send him my

way. I have a busted cupboard I need fixed," Mrs. C. said with a nod.

"Didn't he just fix your cupboard?" Mrs. Bishop asked.

"No, that was a shelf I needed hanging. He wouldn't accept a cent, either. I had to pay him in cookies! I made the good kind, too, double chocolate chip," Mrs. C. added.

Madison forced a smile, though her stomach dipped. That sounded exactly like Zach. He preferred his own company and could come across as grumpy, but he was always there for anyone who needed him.

The younger woman, two tables over, sighed. "It's too bad he never seems interested in dating."

Madison coughed, her coffee going down the wrong way. "Sorry," she replied as her eyes watered. She looked away and cleared her throat.

Mrs. C. leaned forward, eyes twinkling with mischief. "Well, you were always the only girl for him, Madison." She winked.

Madison froze, fingers tightening around her coffee cup. She could feel the heat creeping up her neck, and it had nothing to do with the coffee. She forced out a light laugh, but even she could hear the slight edge to it. "I highly doubt that." If Madison's memory served her right, Zach had no problem striking things up with women, especially when his girlfriend was away in New York City.

The younger woman's ears perked up. "You and Zach?" She suddenly studied Madison with newfound interest.

Madison wasn't sure what to say or how much to reveal. Thankfully, she didn't have to say anything at all.

"Oh, those two lovebirds go way back," Mrs. Bishop declared. "I lost fifty bucks when you left town. I thought for sure you two would end up walking down the aisle."

Madison's polite smile faltered for a second before she caught herself.

She shifted her weight, trying to shake the sudden feeling of being on display. "I'm sorry to disappoint," she said with a practiced smile. She needed to change the subject, but her mind refused to cooperate, spinning in place instead.

"It's okay. I won that plus some in bingo a week later. It all worked out in the end!" Mrs. Bishop declared. The ladies chuckled, sipping their coffee as if they hadn't just casually thrown Madison's love life under the town microscope.

"Glad it all worked out," Madison said briskly, standing and taking a step back from the table. "It's been lovely to chat with you, really, but I should... Uh, I have a couple more errands to run. Nice to meet you," she added to the younger woman. Madison waved goodbye and popped back up to the bakery counter. "I'm just going to step out. I'll come back for the pastries soon," she told Emily.

"Perfect. I'll have them here and waiting. And don't forget to call Kit!"

"Don't worry. I won't!" Madison called over her shoulder before escaping out the front door.

But even once outside, thoughts of Zach refused to leave her alone. His flannel shirt clinging to his broad shoulders. His hands gripping her waist.

It was a sinfully delicious fantasy. It was also never going to happen.

She just hoped he couldn't read her mind.

TEN

ZACH

The Cinnamon Spice Inn's honeymoon cabin looked out across Bear Lake, and it was the coziest place. Almost like something you'd stumble across in a fairy tale. Surrounded by trees, its wooden roof was now coated in red and gold leaves. Zach could hear the water lapping as he walked up to it, the crunch of acorns and dry leaves under his feet. Something chattered up in the trees, a squirrel perhaps, and the soft smell of rain and damp earth lingered. The air had a gentle bite to it, the breeze a whisper.

The cabin was only a short walk from the inn, and it had been a getaway spot for Madison and Zach when they were young lovers. It was imprinted with memories, of nights talking out under the stars, of skinny-dipping in the moonlight. Of burning hot night after night, devouring each other in uncontrollable ecstasy.

Zach hadn't been here for years, not since Madison left. He took a deep breath, his chest strangely tight. Slowly, he opened the creaking door, half expecting to see her there with his younger self. She'd be wearing his flannel shirt, and nothing else. Her hands clutched around the coffee he'd just made for her. She'd take a slow sip, and smile at him like there was nobody else in the world, just the two of them, and that was enough.

But there was nobody here. Just Zach and his memories. And it looked like nobody had been inside the cabin for years. The disrepair was way worse than he had expected.

Zach sighed, dropped his duffel by the door with a heavy thud and surveyed the space, distracting himself from his thoughts about Madison by cataloging the work that needed to be done. It was one room, with a small kitchenette and a four-poster bed pushed against the wall. The bathroom was tiny, but the water worked. The knotty pine ceiling had started to separate, allowing water to seep through and drip onto the hardwood floors, which probably meant the roof needed replacing, too. There were broken windows, a dripping faucet, the faint scent of mildew.

Even the hearthstone on the fireplace had cracked clean down the middle, causing the entire mantel to pitch into a crooked V. He'd have to reseal the roof, caulk the seams, maybe tear half the place apart. He'd need to go back into town shortly to get some more materials. It would take a bit of time, but still, he could make it livable. He could make it look like it once did.

The place where he knew he'd fallen in love and nothing would ever be the same again.

Zach's eyes landed on the windowsill. That was the spot where he and Madison had carved their initials all those years ago. He forced himself to stay rooted to the spot. To not go over and trace the indent, relive the moment.

He couldn't help it. His mind pulled him back to the last time they'd stayed here. They were celebrating and he'd brought a bottle of champagne, the expensive kind, which was saying something, considering he and Liam had been splitting rent on a crappy two-bedroom apartment.

Madison's New York internship was only supposed to be

for the summer, after all. And hell, he was proud of her, so proud. He knew she had big dreams of travelling the world and launching her career in the culinary world. But he also knew she loved Maple Falls as much as he did, and it seemed impossible to him that she wouldn't soon find her way back here. She was brilliant, she was full of ideas and creativity and worked harder than anyone. She just needed to spread her wings for a bit, and then she'd be able to build her perfect life here. With him.

So, they celebrated her internship thinking she'd soon be back. They'd spent it paddleboarding on Bear Lake with Liam, Jackson, Emily, and some other friends, then headed back to the inn for a cookout. They'd all felt so young, so free, the world full of endless possibilities. It was a summer that seemed like it would stretch out into forever.

Zach grinned, remembering how badly George had burned the hot dogs. Flames had shot out the bottom of the grill. He hadn't even known they could do that. Meredith had nearly called the fire department before Edith doused the whole thing with a bucket of water.

They'd ordered pizzas after that, eaten them around the campfire. Followed by s'mores, cold beer, and plenty of laughs.

It wasn't until later, much later, when the sky was dancing with shooting stars and the slice of silver moon was high in the sky, that they'd found a moment to sneak away.

Madison had popped the champagne, the cork flying across the room with a satisfying *THUMP*.

She'd then tipped the bottle right to her lips to keep it from spraying everywhere.

Zach smiled, recalling the memory.

He had quickly run over with coffee mugs from the cupboard, and she'd poured two oversized toasts.

"To the future," he'd said.

"To us," Madison had replied.

They'd clinked their glasses, kissed, and Zach had felt so ridiculously happy.

He'd then lit a fire while Madison put on some music. They'd danced together, right in the center of the room. Zach's eyes landed on the spot as if it were yesterday. The warmth from the fire. The softness of her curves, the way she'd leaned into him. The love, fierce and loyal, that had flashed in her eyes.

"Shit." Zach shook his head, trying to keep all the emotions, memories, from rushing back at him.

The night she left, she'd promised to call every night. She said she would visit over the coming months. She said she'd be back after the internship.

But the calls got shorter. The gaps between them grew longer. The visits never happened.

Zach hadn't said it aloud, not even to himself, but he'd known the moment things shifted that summer. She'd started talking about the restaurants she was writing about, the chefs she was shadowing, the new apartment she might take.

And suddenly, it wasn't about coming home anymore—it was about making it there.

He didn't blame her, not really. He was still proud of her, and he always would be. At the end of the day, Zach and Maple Falls were just not enough for her.

He just wished he'd at least tried to tell her how much he loved her and that he wished she'd come home. She'd asked him if something was wrong, all those years ago on the phone, the day after she forgot their anniversary. He'd tried to call her that day, but her phone went straight to voicemail, over and over.

He'd tried to tell himself she was just busy, that she'd call back. But as the hours ticked by, he couldn't move past the hurt. It felt like she'd forgotten him, forgotten *them*.

Bitter and angry, he'd cancelled the flower order he'd sent to her New York apartment. Then he'd gone to the Kettle, downing cheap whiskey, letting the noise of the bar drown out the hurt clawing at him.

That was when Tara Miller, a girl he barely knew from high school, had slid onto the stool beside him. She laughed too loud, leaning in, clinging to him. He remembered the way she looked at him, expectant, like she thought he wanted this, when he clearly wasn't interested. Not in her, not in anyone else.

He spent the whole night staring into his glass, hardly listening as she talked about things he didn't care about, his mind wrapped up thinking about Madison.

The final straw was when Tara had tried to kiss him next to the pool table. He thought playing a game of pool would give him some space, but she'd followed right along, taking it as her cue to make a move.

Zach had been surprised and slow to react at first, but then he stepped back, shaking his head, muttering something about it being late. He'd gone home alone, crawled into bed with the scent of whiskey clinging to him, and stared at the ceiling until dawn.

The next day, Madison finally called, her voice clipped and careful, asking if he had anything to tell her.

And he didn't know what to say.

Because what was there to say? Wasn't he the one who should ask her that question? He was the one she'd left behind, the one she'd called after ignoring him on their anniversary. He was the one expected to make it easy for her to leave.

The truth was, Zach had never chased anyone in his life. Not his father when he'd walked out. Not Madison when she'd stopped calling. Because somewhere deep down, Zach didn't believe he was the kind of guy people stayed for.

So, he'd let her go. And now, here he was, six years later, sleeping in the same cabin where they used to plan a life together.

And she was back at the inn just a few steps away.

Zach sank onto the edge of the bed and let his head fall into his hands.

Maybe this was his chance to finally let go.

Or maybe fate was giving him one more shot.

ELEVEN
MADISON

Outside Emily's bakery, Madison held tightly to her latte, the warmth seeping into her fingers but doing little to distract her from the thoughts swirling around her head.

Had Zach really never moved on?

It sounded like something out of a romance novel—small-town boy holds a torch for the girl who left. But life wasn't a movie. And she wasn't that girl anymore.

No, if Madison had to bet, Mrs. C. was just romanticizing the past. People loved a good love story—especially if it was hard fought. It gave them something to root for. Happily ever afters were even better when they were tied up neat and tidy with a little bow.

But real love was never tidy. And Zach hadn't loved her enough to come with her, or even to keep away from another woman on their anniversary.

Madison knew it had been hard for him when she left. It was hard for her to leave him too, but the internship in New York had been everything Madison dreamed of. She simply couldn't have turned it down.

The thing is, she'd hoped he would've at least asked her to

stay. Or better yet, offered to join her. But he hadn't; he'd just let her go. No big fight. No sad goodbye. Nothing. Not even when she'd given him the chance to come clean about that girl.

That silence had stuck with her. Twisted itself into doubt over the years. If he hadn't fought for her then, why would he still want her now? And why should she want him, why should she forgive him, after what he'd done to her?

She took a slow sip of her coffee, letting the familiar taste of apple, cinnamon, and vanilla mix in her mouth. It was fall in a cup—like fresh orchard air, golden afternoon light, and the crunch of fallen leaves beneath her boots.

Madison took in the scene around her. Across the street, a group of kids wearing blue and red puffy jackets and knit scarves clustered around a street vendor. The older man stirred an iron kettle full of hot caramel, dipping apples into the melted candy before rolling them in crushed peanuts and setting them aside to harden.

It was so peaceful and cozy, the rhythm of small-town living. She needed this, she realized, being back home. Being grounded in the comfort of her childhood. It soothed something inside of her that she hadn't realized had been frazzled to begin with.

Madison let out a breath and forced herself to focus.

She wasn't going to think about Zach. She couldn't. Not his maddening half-smile that used to undo her in seconds. Not his steady hands and quiet presence. Not how he'd filled out over the years with broad shoulders, those ripped forearms, the way his jeans fit like a temptation she didn't need and made her forget how to breathe.

Nope. Not thinking about any of that. He did not deserve even a fraction of her thoughts.

And she couldn't afford the distraction, anyway. Not if she wanted to get things checked off her list and stop the inn from collapsing physically, financially, and in every other possible way.

Refocusing, she tapped her phone screen with her thumb, pulling up her messages. At least one thing had a clear solution—she needed a chef. And Emily had given her a name.

Madison: Hi, this is Madison Kelly. Emily Whitaker gave me your number. My family owns the inn in town. She said you might be looking for work? We need a new chef. Do you have time to chat?

Madison felt her phone vibrate not two minutes later.

Kit: Would love to. I'm free today if that works for you?

Madison couldn't believe how quickly Kit had replied. In New York, things took longer. Sure, the city never slept, but people's schedules were jam-packed, and nobody would just drop everything at a moment's notice to meet up.

Things worked differently here. People in Maple Falls weren't rushing from one meeting to the next, checking emails at red lights, or scheduling lunch two weeks in advance. There was time here—time to pause, time to breathe, time to just... exist.

For so long, Madison had craved the city's frantic pace. She needed the endless work, the jam-packed schedule. It filled the space where the loss of everything she'd left behind, and then grief over losing her mom, would have crept in. Her city life gave her something to chase instead of something to feel.

But now maybe the quiet was just what she needed.

Madison replied to Kit that today would be great and suggested they meet at the inn at 1 p.m. She was still looking down at her phone when she nearly walked straight into Liam.

"Well, look what the wind blew in! Madison Kelly, back in town."

Madison's smile was wide and immediate. "Hey, Liam. I see you're still here stirring up trouble."

She hugged Liam with one arm, careful not to spill her coffee, while still holding her phone in the other hand. He squeezed her back, grinning, with what looked like a sketch book tucked under his other arm.

Madison wondered if liking Liam's social media posts counted as keeping in touch. She'd rarely commented, but she admired the work he'd been doing on the family farm and he'd posted about the new farm shop he was getting ready to open in town.

He'd stayed and built something here. Something substantial. His family must be proud. He must be proud. She wondered if Zach felt the same. Did he have something that satisfied him, made him happy?

"Me, trouble? Never. That's Zach's job." Liam pulled back, flashing her a knowing grin. "Speaking of, I heard you two already crossed paths."

Madison sighed dramatically. "Gotta love living in a small town."

"You know it." Liam cracked a grin. "Seriously, though, now that you've got that awkward first meeting out of the way, we can all hang out like old times, no?"

"I don't know." Madison looked down at her coffee cup. "It's been so good seeing you, Emily, everyone, really. But... I think it's best if Zach and I keep our distance."

"Nah, where'd be the fun in that?"

"You and I have very different ideas of fun."

Liam rolled his eyes. "You two are both so stubborn, you know that?" He nudged her shoulder.

Madison let out a soft laugh. "Gee, thanks."

"You free tonight?" Liam asked.

Madison hesitated. Because it wasn't just about grabbing a drink and catching up. It meant stepping back into a world she wasn't sure she still belonged to. As much as part of her missed the town, missed these people, another part worried the feeling might not be mutual.

"I'm not sure," Madison said, forcing a casualness she didn't feel. "What's going on?"

"Just a couple of friends getting together down at the Kettle for my birthday. It would mean a lot to me if you could join us." Liam rocked back on his heels.

Madison smiled. "Is it the twelfth already?" She glanced at her watch, then back at Liam. "It is. Happy birthday."

In Madison's experience, most men tried to shrug off their birthdays, but Liam loved any reason to get together and throw a party. It was just his personality. He was outgoing and funny and kind-hearted. Nothing like his twin brother, Jackson, who skipped half the parties and joined the military as soon as he turned eighteen.

Madison had never been very close to Jackson. But Liam had been a good friend to her. Even after she'd broken up with Zach, he had been the last connection to let go.

Liam had always believed in her, too. He said she could do anything, if she put her mind to it. Even launching a career all alone in the big city.

And she really did. She had helped transform the food scene; people knew who she was, and they respected her. If you were opening a new restaurant, you cared about her opinion. Sometimes, Madison wanted to pinch herself with how fortunate she had been. She had worked hard to get there, but she knew it was a privilege to do a job she loved so much. She was passionate about food, about finding the stories behind every dish, and writing about it. But despite all the business accolades and professional success, part of her heart still felt hollow.

She sometimes wondered what Zach would think of New

York, and she missed talking to Emily. She wanted them there with her.

She wanted the impossible.

Madison swallowed hard, pushing the thought down the way she always did.

She hadn't just left Maple Falls; she'd cut it off. Cut off friends who once felt like family. Cut off memories too bittersweet to revisit. Because once she started missing it—truly missing it—she was afraid she'd never be able to move forward again.

Anyway, this wasn't the time to get sentimental.

She was here to help the inn get back on its feet, nothing more. Then she could leave again, clean and simple.

"So, does that mean I'll see you tonight?" Liam asked, already turning to walk up the street.

"I'm not sure. I'll see what I can do," Madison replied.

"Uh-huh, and then something will 'come up,' and you won't be able to make it." Liam smirked. "Just think about it, okay? I'll be sure to keep Zach in line. If he even shows up," he added.

Madison frowned. She refused to chase after Liam for gossip about her ex. But seriously, why wouldn't Zach come to his best friend's birthday party? Surely, it wasn't because of her... was it?

Madison shook off the thought and headed for the hardware store.

"Well, if it isn't Miss Madison! So good to see you," the older gentleman behind the counter greeted.

"Thanks, Mr. Alders. It's good to see you, too. I see you have a lot of mums still in stock. I'd like to get four of them for the inn's front porch, please. And I'll take the jumbo pumpkins, too."

Mr. Alders nodded, punching the numbers into the register.

"Do you have any hay bales left? I didn't see any up front," Madison asked, scanning the store.

"Tommy's picking up a fresh order right now. They should be in this afternoon."

"Great! Can I put in an order for two? I'll pick everything up later."

"How about I have Tommy deliver everything?" Mr. Alders offered.

"Oh, I'm sure you need Tommy for other things."

"Trust me, he enjoys being out and about. Expect to see him sometime after one."

Madison thanked him and tried to tip Mr. Alders a twenty.

"Not necessary. Happy to do it. And happy to see you back in town."

She smiled, grabbed her receipt, and headed for the door.

After a brief pop-back to the bakery, Madison headed back toward the inn, feeling better than she had when she'd left it. Maybe the caffeine had finally kicked in. Maybe it was the endorphins from catching up with old friends. Or maybe it was the high from checking things off her list.

Whatever it was, Madison had a smile on her face, her third cup of coffee in one hand, a box of fresh baked goods in the other, and the day was just getting started.

There was a lot to do, but instead of feeling overwhelmed, she felt energized. It was time to get things done. The wind lifted her hair, blowing it back, and she breathed in deep. She'd missed this—the rhythm of a small town, the way people stopped to chat, how every street and storefront held a memory.

It had been so long since she'd let herself slow down and just be. She'd been so afraid of coming home. But now she felt something shift. Perhaps because she wasn't here to wallow in the past. She was here to rebuild.

There was still a bubble of nerves pressing at her ribs. Would she be able to pull this off? Could she really transform the inn and successfully avoid her ex even while he worked on the roof and lived just yards away?

She only had until November 1st. She couldn't stay away from the city for very long after giving everything to build her carefully curated New York self. Her career was at its peak; she didn't want to mess it up now.

She pushed the doubt down. Of course she could do it.

She was Madison Kelly. She thrived under pressure.

And then, of course, there was the letter. She hadn't let herself dwell on it much, not yet. There had been too much to do.

But as she neared the inn, she felt that letter nagging at the back of her mind. Who had sent it, and why now?

A dozen faces swam in front of her eyes—Anita, Mrs. Bishop, Mrs. C., even Mr. Alders at the hardware store. The truth was, a lot of people cared about her dad—about her whole family, really.

The Cinnamon Spice Inn was more than just a place to stay. It was a piece of the town's history. And people around here tended to look out for their own.

Still... something about the letter tugged at her. It wasn't just the words themselves; it was the feeling behind them. Like a thread deep inside. Madison wanted—no, needed—to know who had sent it. Because whoever it was hadn't just asked her to come home. They had *known* she would. And she couldn't shake the feeling that if she found out who it was... she'd also find the part of herself she'd left in Maple Falls all those years ago.

That was the last thought she had before she slammed into something tall, firm, and unmoving.

"Oof," she said as the air left her lungs. The lid of her cup popped off, sloshing hot coffee over the rim and straight onto a broad, flannel-covered chest. The bakery box she'd been carrying completely smashed between them.

Madison's eyes went wide as Zach steadied her with one

hand while the other grabbed the crumpled box before it could hit the ground.

Zach's jaw tightened, and his grip remained firm. "Madison," he said, voice low and unreadable. He let go of her arm and handed her the box.

Madison stared at the mess—the crumpled box and the stain spreading across his shirt. The pastries were squashed beyond saving and forget her coffee.

Fantastic. Just fantastic.

She couldn't bring herself to meet his eyes. Not yet.

"That makes two catches in one day," Zach mused. "Must be some kind of record." He chuckled.

Her eyes darted up.

There it was. The smirk.

As if this was all some great, hilarious joke.

Madison narrowed her eyes. "Listen, I'm sorry. I obviously wasn't looking where I was going."

Zach shook his head. It was that infuriating, silent, dismissive shake of his head he'd mastered.

Like she was ridiculous. Exactly the same girl he used to know—the one who rushed headlong into things without thinking.

And that annoyed Madison to no end.

Her fingers curled around the mostly empty coffee cup.

Madison straightened her spine, determined to salvage whatever was left of her dignity.

"I'll replace the pastries," he offered, motioning back to the bakery.

"Don't worry about it. I can do it," she fired back. She did not need his help.

"Just let me fix it, Mads."

Madison clenched her teeth. That name again, as if they were still both who they used to be.

Like she hadn't left. Like he hadn't let her go.

She stepped back, needing space. Needing to breathe. "I have to go."

She turned on her heel, but before she could take two steps, Zach called after her.

"You always have had a habit of running away, right, Mads?"

Madison froze, just for a second. So what if she had a tendency to run? She was here now, wasn't she? Facing him, despite how much he'd hurt her and how angry she still felt.

Madison forced herself to keep walking. To leave before she did something she'd regret.

Like throw the rest of her coffee in his irritatingly handsome face.

TWELVE

MADISON

"Aha! You're back!" her dad called out as she stepped into the lobby, a swirl of leaves blowing in with her.

George was tossing a tennis ball for Cocoa, who bounded through the room, yapping excitedly. Cocoa's nails scratched against the worn runner, the center almost threadbare in spots. Even the sunshine filtering in through the front doors couldn't brighten the room.

"Careful now—she might trip you up. Cocoa's got a bit of energy today."

"I see that," Madison said, the tension from her encounter with Zach melting away. She laughed as she had to sidestep quickly to avoid Cocoa pouncing on her instead of the ball. Madison slid the baked goods, a second box, onto the side table next to a vase of dusty artificial sunflowers. She unwound her mother's scarf but didn't hang it up. Not yet.

Across the room, the front desk bell dinged as a man in a fleece jacket and jeans leaned over the counter, glancing impatiently at his watch.

Gram came out from the back to assist him before George could.

"The Grants, checking out early," her dad said to her under his breath. "Something about the heat being finicky in room four."

Madison winced. Weren't they their last guests? That wasn't good. She added "radiator inspection" to her mental to-do list.

"Don't worry, I'll get to it," George said, correctly reading his daughter's expression before changing the subject. "So, tell me, what did you think of downtown? That storm rough it up a bit?"

"Not really. Looks like we're the ones who took the hit," Madison replied.

"Well, glad it wasn't worse then, huh?" Her dad grinned, scooping up the ball before Cocoa could sink her tiny teeth into it.

"I suppose that's true." Madison exhaled, letting herself relax into the familiarity of home. "Speaking of which, I saw all the decorations downtown. It looks great; thought we should do the same."

He blinked as if the thought had never crossed his mind. "Oh, you're right. Your mom used to fix up the porch for the holidays." A frown crossed his face.

Madison softened. "I figured I'd go through the attic and see what decorations are tucked away up there."

"Knowing your mom, there will be bins full of them." Her dad smiled.

"That's what I'm thinking, too. I also stopped by the hardware store and ordered a few things for our porch. Tommy's going to deliver them this afternoon."

"Ah, just like your mom. She used to order dozens of pumpkins every fall."

Once again Madison was grateful that her dad and Gram had understood how hard it was for her to come home. They had never pressured her once in the last few years, never made her feel guilty. They knew Madison felt her mom everywhere, from the cinnamon-scented halls to the soft quilt draped over the couch.

Being here meant facing everything she had lost.

The funeral was three years ago. But even before that, Madison had kept her distance, especially from the town, ever since leaving when she was twenty-two years old.

The few times she had come back to Maple Falls—Thanksgiving, an occasional birthday visit—she had kept to the inn. She hadn't felt ready for the inevitable small-town welcome, the questions, the reminders of how much she had missed. And, if she was being honest, she hadn't been ready to bump into a certain someone, either.

But now there could be no staying away, no more running. Dad and Gram needed her. The Cinnamon Spice Inn needed her.

Madison chose her next words carefully, not wanting to hurt her dad's feelings. "I ran into Emily at the bakery. When I told her you were handling the cooking since Maurice retired, she offered to have the bakery deliver breakfast pastries to take one less thing off your plate."

"Did she now? I don't know, seems like that might be a bit expensive."

Madison tried to keep her voice light. "Not at all. Emily gave us a great deal. Plus, your time is probably better spent taking care of the animals and the grounds, and being front of house, right? You're so good at that."

"I have been spending an awful lot of time in that kitchen," he admitted grudgingly.

"Exactly. And you're the heart of this place, Dad. You belong out front, not stuck behind a stove."

That earned a small smile from him. "I suppose that's true."

Madison pressed on, still careful not to push too hard. "Emily also said that Norma Steigler's great-niece is staying with her. She's a chef looking for work. I'm going to chat with her this afternoon and see if she might be a good fit. It might not come to anything, but if we can get someone cooking here full time, it could be a real draw for new guests."

She paused, hoping he'd come to the same conclusion. While she waited, Madison couldn't help looking around the lobby with a critical eye. Without her mom's touch making everything feel warm and inviting, the oak trim and wainscoting, a hit in the 1990s, now looked dated. So did the threadbare green carpet with its miniature rose pattern, worn from years of foot traffic. Madison avoided looking directly at the faint cracks in the drywall around the windows she knew were there. Just like she tried to pretend she didn't hear the radiators rattling to life.

"And Dad..." She hesitated. "I think I should take a look at the finances. Just to get a better idea of where things stand."

Her dad stiffened, his back going straight. Cocoa let out a sharp bark, echoing his sentiments. "Things aren't that bad. Guests will probably pick up in time..."

Madison walked over and patted his shoulder. "I know. And you've done a great job holding everything together. Truly. But I really want to do this. As a project. For me. Please?"

"Well, now..."

Madison knew he was softening. "Just think, once we get this place all spruced up, word will get around, and we'll have to turn people away."

Her dad chuckled. "Now you sound like your mother. She could always see the possibilities in any situation."

"I'll take that as a compliment." Madison leaned in and kissed his cheek. "Now I'm off to the attic to see what treasures I can find. Wish me luck!" She waved over her shoulder and headed upstairs.

. . .

The alarm on Madison's phone went off, startling her. She blinked down at the screen—her interview with Kit was in ten minutes. How was that even possible? She had been organizing the totes in the attic by holiday. So far, she had only made it through Easter.

Madison stood up and walked toward the oval-shaped attic window, which had been her favorite as a child. Dust motes floated lazily through the sunlight streaming in from the window, turning the cluttered space into something magical. The inn had always been bustling with guests coming and going, but the attic had been her own secret spot—a place where no one could bother her. It smelled just the same, too. It was a mix of cedar wood and a trace of cinnamon that seemed baked into the walls.

Madison could still picture the checkered fleece blanket she'd lay out in the sunlight from the south-facing window and the tea party she'd have with her dolls and stuffed rabbit. Gram never seemed to mind that her shortbread went missing at an alarming rate.

She'd had her first kiss with Zach under that window. It had been so soft and innocent. They were only twelve. She'd been showing him the best hide-and-seek places around the inn, and the next moment, they were entirely alone. For the first time in their lives, it had been just the two of them. No Liam. No Jackson. No Emily. Just them.

Zach had held both of her hands, and they'd leaned in, like they'd watched people do in the movies. Madison still remembered Zach holding his breath. The whole thing had probably only lasted two seconds. But it had sealed their fate. From then on, they'd been inseparable.

The wood creaked under her footsteps. The attic was full of hidden memories and treasures. The paintings her dad had collected from garage sales, extra furniture for the rooms, nightstands stacked against the walls, and an antique desk she was fairly certain hadn't been used for decades—yet the space still felt warm and cozy.

It was organized up here, her mother's doing. The decorations would've been too, if she hadn't gotten sick...

"Madison, are you up there?" Gram's voice called out.

"Yes, I'll be down in just a second!"

"Oh, good. There's someone down here who says she has an interview with you. I'm not sure who's more excited—her or Cocoa."

"She's here early," Madison muttered as she left the totes and headed down to the lobby.

The first thing she saw was Cocoa—rolling over onto her back, her tail wagging wildly as an unfamiliar woman scratched her belly.

Kit was petite, with dark hair cut into a bob that fell forward while she leaned down. She wore a red wool coat over dark jeans and a plain black t-shirt, a pop of color against the muted tones of her outfit. Her black high-top Converse peeked out beneath the cuffs of her jeans, giving her a playful edge.

"Aren't you a gorgeous little girl?" Kit cooed, laughing as Cocoa squirmed with delight. She leaned in, letting the pup lick her chin. "Oh, I know what you're after. You want some kisses? Is that what this is about?"

Kit must have been a dog lover, or she never would've been able to handle the amount of slobber Cocoa was dishing out.

"You must be Kit," Madison said, striding across the lobby.

"I am! It's so good to meet you." She grinned, extending her hand. "Hope you don't mind a little bit of puppy love."

"Not at all," Madison replied, accepting the handshake.

"I love dogs," Kit continued, bending to give Cocoa one last scratch before standing up again. "Is this the only one you have? My aunt has two—Labradoodles, so quite a bit bigger than this little gal, but just as affectionate." She barely took a breath before adding, "Oh! Before I forget, I made you some apple pie tarts with a little bit of ice cream, and I've got some recipes to show you in action. I figured instead of just talking about my cooking, I'd let the food speak for itself. Sometimes, my mouth gets me into trouble. I mean, if that's okay. If you don't want me to cook, I don't have to. I just thought, well, you should see what I can do. Does that make sense?"

Madison blinked. The woman was a whirlwind. She hadn't even had a chance to get a word in before Kit was already moving, gesturing toward the insulated bags she had brought.

"I can get started right away, well, after I wash my hands. Hygiene is super important, don't you think?" Kit asked.

"I do. How about we head to the kitchen?" Madison suggested.

"I'll be sure to keep Cocoa out," Gram added. "Or give her to George."

Madison glanced around. "Where is Dad, by the way?"

"Out feeding the animals, I suppose." Gram waved a hand then muttered something under her breath about "that son-in-law of mine" before shuffling back to the front desk.

Thankfully, the burnt smell from the morning no longer lingered, and the kitchen was back to smelling of roasted herbs with a hint of nutmeg, though it was missing the fresh warmth it had when her mom ran things. The copper pots hanging from the rack gleamed under the soft glow of the overhead lights, and the butcher block counters had seen years of flour-dusted mornings and simmering soups.

Kit wasted no time getting to work in the kitchen. Before even unpacking all her ingredients, she plated one of her tarts. It was a golden, flaky pastry topped with a scoop of vanilla ice cream, drizzled with caramel, and finished with a dusting of cinnamon and sugar.

"Normally, I'd serve the tart warm, but I just took it out of the oven before coming here," Kit said, watching Madison's reaction with an eager expression. "So it shouldn't be too cold—but hopefully, you get the idea."

Madison took a moment to admire Kit's plating. Despite throwing it together in haste, she had done a marvelous job. She cut into the tart, letting the ice cream melt slightly as she scooped up a forkful, making sure to capture as many flavors as possible.

The moment the dessert hit her tongue, a soft moan escaped her lips.

"Oh my goodness, you weren't lying. This is heavenly. The tart apples, the flaky crust, the sweet caramel, the cold ice cream—it's the perfect balance of sweet, creamy, and tart."

She'd be a fool not to hire Kit on the spot.

"I'm glad you like it. Hopefully, you'll like this too," Kit said.

Madison barely had time to process what she meant before Kit was already using a mandoline to julienne Honeycrisp apples, which she quickly tossed in lemon juice. She did the same with Manchego cheese, adding it to the apples along with chives, shallots, and olives before gently tossing everything together and seasoning it with salt and more lemon.

It was clear—Kit was a wizard in the kitchen.

"You don't have any dietary restrictions, do you?" Kit asked.

"No, I don't."

"And what about seafood? Love it, hate it, could live without it?"

"I love it. I'm a food writer based in New York—I've pretty much eaten a little bit of everything."

"Well, I wish you hadn't said that. Now you're gonna make me nervous, and I was already nervous before I got here."

Madison laughed. "You have no reason to be."

"Well, I hope that's true," Kit said, winking. "Either way, my crab croquettes are to die for. Doesn't matter if you're a food critic or not."

Madison watched as Kit moved around the kitchen, pulling out ingredients, her energy infectious.

She glanced down at the tart and took another bite. When she was working, she typically only took a couple of bites of each course to pace herself and keep her palate clear. Not today. She was going to eat every last bit of this tart.

"I've eaten here before," Kit said while working.

"You have?"

"Mm-hmm, my great-aunt brought me a time or two," Kit continued, barely slowing down. "I know your previous chef was French-trained, and he was amazing, but I'd love to lean into something even cozier than I remember. Farm-to-table, seasonal, nostalgic flavors—things that feel like home."

Madison nodded, already imagining the transformation.

"Although there's one thing I remember that I would love to bring back. Your mom's cinnamon rolls. One time I stopped in for a visit, and your mom gave me one. Talk about heavenly." Kit threw her head back and laughed at the memory. "I was thinking... what if we brought it back with a twist—apple butter in the center."

Madison felt something catch in her chest. Her mom's cinnamon rolls were legendary, the kind of thing that made guests return to the inn year after year.

"There's this guy, Zach. He makes the best apple butter in town," Kit added casually, continuing to work.

Madison cleared her throat. There was no way Kit could know about her history with Zach. "I love it. We'll make them the signature breakfast dish."

"Perfect. I've got more ideas, too," Kit said, brimming with energy. "Wild mushroom soup, maple-braised short ribs, butternut squash risotto. Think cozy, comforting, but still special."

"Yes." Madison's voice was firm. "That's exactly what the Cinnamon Spice Inn should be."

Madison leaned against the counter, picturing it. The dining room, refreshed. Warm lighting, mismatched stoneware mugs, tables set with sprigs of rosemary in Mason jars. Candles flickering, cinnamon rolls fresh from the oven.

The kind of place that didn't just serve food but wrapped you in warmth. Her mother had created that feeling once. Madison was going to bring it back.

She took another bite of the tart and smiled. "We have a lot of work to do," she said.

Kit grinned. "Good thing I love a challenge."

THIRTEEN
MADISON

Kit and Madison spent the rest of the afternoon experimenting with different recipes and developing a menu. When Kit left just before five, Madison felt energized.

Working in the kitchen made her feel alive. She could already picture the menus—printed on thick linen paper with gold leaf accents. The menu would always be seasonal, and Kit planned to rotate offerings monthly, plus daily specials offered with a variety of diets in mind. Madison loved where Kit's heart was—just like Madison, she wanted to make sure everyone felt welcome at the Cinnamon Spice Inn.

"Alright there, Madison?" her father asked as he walked into the dining room just as Madison was reimagining the space.

"There you are. I was hoping you'd pop in so you could meet Kit. She's an amazing chef and has some brilliant ideas for the menu that are going to be a hit. We're going to turn the Cinnamon Spice Inn into a dining destination—you have my word on that." Madison could see it all, and she was ready to run with it.

"I don't know, that seems like a lot of work."

Madison knew her dad cared about the inn; he just couldn't see the future the way she could. He'd been in survival mode for far too long.

"Not more than we can handle. We just need to remodel a few things, redo the ceiling, obviously. Some fresh paint, change the lighting a bit. I can see it, Dad, and it's beautiful. And besides, it'll be fun."

Or, at least, it would be if Zach Whitaker wasn't going to be involved in every last stroke of paint. Madison ignored the heat that thought triggered. She didn't want him stroking *anything*. And she definitely didn't want to see his frustratingly handsome face every time she turned around.

She didn't need to be reminded of what they'd once had—and lost. And she sure as hell didn't want to be reminded of that fantasy.

But the inn needed her.

"Trust me, Dad. I want to do this. Mom would have loved it," Madison added.

That softened him just a bit.

"You think so?" he asked.

"I know so. We're just going to need a little bit of help," she added, refusing to keep thinking about Zach. "Speaking of which, where is everybody? I know Maurice retired, but where's Barry? Monica?"

George looked away. "Had to let them go. Money... Besides, Monica wanted to spend some time in Florida with her sister, and you know Barry spent half the day napping."

Madison smiled. That was true. Barry had been "retired" when Madison left, but he still worked around the inn, napping in the corner chair and assisting guests with their luggage when they needed it. "True, but guests loved him. Does he want to come back?"

"Well, now, he might've said something about it at the hardware store last week." George put his hands in his pockets.

"Alright, ring him up. See if he'll start back next week. I know we only have two rooms booked—"

George sucked in a breath.

"Wait, we do have rooms booked, don't we?"

"Not right now. But I'm sure it'll pick up with folks coming into town for Christmas," George said.

There it is, Madison thought, *that Kelly family stubbornness.* She knew exactly where she got it from. But now wasn't the time for pride. Now was the time to get things done.

"Or it might not, and you know that. I know you do." Madison softened her voice. "You've worked too hard to have the inn go down like this."

"I suppose that's true..."

"It is true. Just let me fix it up a bit, make it shine again. For Mom, for all of us."

George stared at her for a long moment, the proud stubbornness in him warring with the quiet pride he still had in the inn.

Finally, he exhaled and cracked a smile. "Alright then. What do you need me to do?"

Madison grinned. "You get to keep doing what you do best, making people feel at home and taking care of the animals our guests will love. Now, it'll take a couple of weeks to get the dining room up and running with our new chef and menu launch." Madison was mentally targeting Halloween. "In the meantime, I have pastries being delivered and I'll stop by the café to see about offering food that guests can order on demand for the time being."

Madison mentally added creating a menu for the guest rooms to her growing to-do list. She pictured a little chalkboard by the front desk, listing the day's pastry flavors—warm apple turnovers, buttery croissants, thick frosted cinnamon rolls—free for guests to grab with their morning coffee.

She was going to make the inn feel welcoming again—one cozy bite at a time.

"Right-o. Guess I'll leave you to it, then."

George turned to leave just as Madison got another idea. "Actually, Dad, there is one thing I could use your help with right now."

"Oh?"

"Outside, the fencing, around the animals. It's a bit loose in some places. I'm worried Honey and Biscuit might get out." Highland cows running down Oak Way would be a very bad thing.

"Oh?" Her dad perked up. "I'm sure Cocoa and I can tackle that."

"Perfect." She leaned forward and kissed her father's cheek.

It had been quite a day, but Madison was too keyed up to go to her room and crash. It was only five-thirty on a Friday evening, and she was itching to go out and do something. She'd call Jo, but her best friend would give her an earful—weekends were the busiest time for restaurants.

She could go for a walk around the lake. The leaves had turned a magnificent display of reds and oranges as if they were on fire, and she knew there'd be the sweet scent of cinnamon-roasted almonds in the air from the street vendor. But when she glanced out the window, she realized it would be a rather short walk. The sun was already sinking low, painting the horizon in striking golds and rich purples.

And honestly, relaxing wasn't what she wanted. She needed to fill up every minute with activities so she wouldn't end up replaying every charged glance, every accidental touch, every memory of Zach that seemed determined to break through her defenses.

"You keep biting your lip like that, and you won't have much left," Gram said, entering the room.

"Sorry, I think I'm just a little restless," Madison confessed.

"And I think you need to get freshened up and hightail it to the tavern. That's what I plan to do," Gram said.

"You're headed to the Kettle tonight?"

"Sure am. Got a hot date with Hank."

"Hank? You mean Mayor Bloomfield?" asked Madison, her eyes widening.

"Don't look so shocked. He's been sweet on me for years. Besides, I promised Liam I'd buy him a drink."

Madison shook her head. She wasn't about to stay home while her grandmother went out.

"If you hurry and get cleaned up, you can come with me. I'm heading down around seven."

Madison debated for a few moments longer.

"Stop thinking about it and just go get ready. Put something nice on. Hank's got a grandson I might be able to fix you up with," Gram teased.

Madison hurriedly shook her head and Gram chuckled. "I kid. You should see the look on your face. Honestly, I think you need to go out more than I do."

Promising she'd be quick, Madison went upstairs to get ready. It wasn't going to be easy to go to the tavern, given the last time she'd been there all those years ago, she'd taken a blow harder than she could ever have imagined and left with a broken heart. But Zach's comment about her "running away" had stuck in her mind. How dare he judge her, how dare he make fun of her? He was wrong. She wasn't afraid of him, of the pain in her past. She was different now, stronger, more confident. And she deserved to go and have a night out with her old friends.

Don't overthink it. Just get dressed and go, she told herself.

But of course, she did overthink it and she did get cold feet.

Which was why she found herself standing in the middle of her room, staring at her phone like she didn't fully trust it.

She hadn't texted Emily in... years. Sure, they still technically followed each other on social media, trading the occasional like on birthday posts or pictures of pets and new jobs. But it wasn't the same. Not like it used to be.

Back then, Madison could walk into Emily's kitchen without knocking. Emily and Zach had been a package deal. Her best friend for years and her boyfriend for just as long. They'd grown up together, then Madison had left and let it all slip away.

Emily should have been furious with her. But she hadn't been. And if Emily could hug her in the bakery like no time had passed, Madison owed it to her, and herself, to try.

She took a breath and tapped out a quick message.

Madison: Any plans tonight? Thinking about heading out, but not sure.

Emily: Liam's birthday. Didn't he invite you?

Madison: He did. Just wondering if you were going to be there.

Emily: Me and the rest of the town. It would be great to see you.

Well, that settled that.

Madison would be heading to the tavern.

She slipped into a pair of high-waisted jeans and an oversized cream sweater. Running her fingers through her hair, she fluffed out her curls, then went light on her makeup—just a touch of blush and a swipe of lip gloss. To finish the look, she pulled on a pair of brown ankle boots.

Tonight, she was going out.

. . .

Madison wasn't sure what to expect when she walked into the Copper Kettle, but it certainly wasn't this.

The place was packed. Laughter and chatter filled the air, mixed with the scent of pizza and all things fried—cheese sticks, French fries, and chicken wings. It was louder and livelier than she ever remembered.

Gram ditched her the moment they stepped inside, disappearing into the crowd like she owned the place. Madison barely had time to process it before Gram reappeared at a long table near the back, surrounded by more familiar faces than she would have thought possible.

Zach's mom, Anita, was there, deep in conversation with the ladies from the bakery, while Mrs. Humphrey was laughing about something Mr. Alders from the hardware store had just said. Their table was already half-filled with drinks and plates of appetizers, with empty seats waiting for their various dates to arrive.

Good thing they'd claimed their spots early.

There was something about the tavern on a Friday night. Right now, it was packed with everyone from families loading up on pizza to singles meeting up at the bar and everything in between.

Kids stood in front of the kitchen's glass barrier, their hands pressed to the glass, watching the chef slide pizzas into the red-brick oven with a long wooden paddle. The fire flared with every pizza, lighting up their faces as much as the exposed brick walls. A guitar player sat in the corner, his voice almost lost against the current of conversation.

Madison walked forward, feeling the uneven cobblestone floor beneath her feet. While it might have added to the old-world charm, Madison knew from experience it became an obstacle course after a few cocktails. She'd have to keep that in mind with her boots—low heel or not.

She tried to take in the warmth of the place, the flow of conversation, the way people called out to each other. But as soon as her eyes drifted toward the pool tables, the memories came rushing back.

The last time she'd walked into this bar, she'd come to surprise Zach and found him flirting with another woman. On their anniversary.

The bastard.

"Hey! You made it." Liam's voice jolted her back, and she managed a smile as he gave her a one-armed hug. His other hand held a cold bottle of beer.

"Don't sound so surprised," Madison said, forcing her voice to sound light.

Liam leaned in slightly. "He's over at the bar if you're looking for him."

Madison raised a brow, feigning innocence. "I have no idea who you're talking about."

Still, Madison's eyes couldn't help but drift toward the bar top, where a familiar head of sandy-blonde hair and a worn red flannel shirt caught her attention. Zach leaned casually against the bar like he belonged there. *He does belong here*, she thought. *I'm the outsider.*

Madison tried to look away, but her gaze kept returning—drawn, despite herself, to the blue-eyed blonde chatting him up, just like all those years ago. The woman kept playfully pawing at Zach, trying to get her hands on him any way she could. To be fair, he seemed rather distracted himself, looking off into the distance, only catching part of the conversation. But the woman was definitely interested.

Madison smoothed her expression, not wanting to be caught shooting daggers their way. Her insides were another story. Madison's stomach twisted into a knot that she had to fight to unwind. *You have no claim to him now. It shouldn't matter who's talking to him.* And yet—

"Welcome to the wildest night in Maple Falls," Emily announced, looping her arm through hers and leading her to their high-top.

Madison smiled, welcoming the pull from her thoughts. "This town doesn't exactly do wild."

"Oh, just wait until the cinnamon whiskey starts flowing." Emily laughed. "Your gram is the one that usually starts it."

"I can believe that," Madison said, looking back over toward the table of seniors. Gram already had a drink in front of her.

It took Madison all of two minutes to realize she had walked straight into a high school reunion. It seemed like everyone from their old friendship group had come out to celebrate, including ones like Zoe, who Madison didn't think were back in town.

"Madison, so good to see you." Zoe came around the table and squeezed Madison tight.

"Zoe? What are you doing here?" Madison hadn't seen Zoe in years. Last she heard, she was working for the National Park Service somewhere in the Appalachians.

"Moved back about a year now. I took over Mom's flower shop, Cherry Crush," Zoe told her.

"Good for you." Madison nodded. Zoe had always loved the outdoors, flowers, plants, exploring.

"Ope, Mrs. C. is calling me over. I'll catch up with you later. Welcome home!" Zoe waved and walked away.

Madison's heart squeezed tight. Was this still her home? Or was she just a visitor now, someone who had traded small-town roots for big-city dreams and lost her place in the process?

"Hey! I didn't know you were coming out tonight. We could've walked down together," Kit said, sidling up next to her as if they were long-time friends. She wore a green and gold beret perched on her head that matched her gold loop earrings, creating a style that was unique to Kit.

Madison laughed. It shouldn't surprise her that Kit fit right in. She seemed to have made fast friends with the entire town already. And if Kit could do it, Madison could too. She looked away, drawn back to the bar again, and Kit's gaze followed.

"Ohh, who's the hottie we have our eyes on?" Kit lifted up on her tiptoes. "Wait, is that Zach?" She peered through the crowd. "Hey, now, what's the story there? You two have history, huh?" She bumped her hip into Madison's.

"What? I don't know what you're talking about," Madison said a little too quickly.

"Don't let her fool you; she knows exactly what you're talking about. She just won't admit it," Liam said, suddenly appearing at their table.

Madison shot him a glare, but he only smirked. "What can I get you to drink?"

"I thought we were supposed to be buying—it is your birthday, after all," Madison pointed out.

"True, true. I'd bet you'd love an excuse to saddle up at the bar right now," Liam teased.

Madison rolled her eyes. "I'll take an Old Fashioned."

Liam turned toward Kit. "And for you?"

"Tequila on the rocks," she said without hesitation.

Liam's eyebrows shot up. "Okay, I see how it's gonna be tonight." He grinned.

"I am celebrating a new job, after all," Kit said, flashing a broad smile at Madison.

"Is that so?" Liam looked to Madison.

"That, I will gladly raise a glass to," Madison replied.

She still couldn't believe how many people she recognized in the tavern—and how easily they fell into conversation. It was as if no time had passed. Old friends asked about her life in New York City, whether it was really as hectic as it looked on TV, and if she had ever been to Times Square.

"I don't know," Zoe said, shaking her head. "I got lost on the subway once. Scared me to death."

"It's not that bad, trust me," Madison said. "Once you get the hang of it, you learn to ignore people mostly and just do your own thing."

The conversation drifted to high school memories—like the time Zoe laughed so hard that chocolate milk came out of her nose, or when Liam danced to "Single Ladies (Put A Ring On It)" in the talent show.

All the while, Zach remained cornered at the bar, sleeves rolled up, forearms flexed, hand wrapped around his tumbler like he owned the room. He looked a hell of a lot sexier than was fair.

Madison couldn't stop her eyes drifting back to him.

The last time she'd been here, she'd witnessed how little he really cared for her. Devastated beyond words, she'd left this place, and him, behind.

But that was then.

Tonight, she had a chance, a shot at a little payback.

A reminder of everything he gave up when he ruined what they had.

FOURTEEN
ZACH

Zach knew the Kettle was going to be busy. The tavern was always packed on a Friday, but add in Liam's birthday, and it was guaranteed to be standing-room only.

Zach was counting on it. That way, he could stop by for a quick drink, a "happy birthday," and then get out before he had to socialize with half the town.

He walked in with his hands tucked in his jeans pockets and scanned the crowd. It was easy to spot Liam—he had a big, broad grin on his face and was shaking hands with nearly everyone, clapping the rest on the back, or leaning in for hugs. Zach couldn't help but smile. Liam had no problem being the center of attention.

Zach, on the other hand, would rather be renovating his kitchen, living room, or, heck, even the bathroom. Give him a power tool, wood, and silence any day over a party.

But he owed it to Liam to be here. Liam had been his best friend since Zach was the new kid in town. Liam had a way of making you feel like you belonged. Like you weren't just the kid whose dad bailed and whose mom was barely scraping by.

Zach had barely taken two steps when Mrs. Bishop sidled

up beside him, pretending to use his arm for support as they walked.

"There you are," she said, her voice full of warmth. "Mrs. C. didn't think you were going to show up, but I told her you wouldn't miss your best bud's birthday."

"Evening, Mrs. Bishop. How you doing?" Zach asked. He would always have time for a woman who had once shown up at their door with casseroles after his grandpa died.

"Oh, can't complain, except maybe about the color of my kitchen."

Zach inwardly groaned. He was hoping he wouldn't have to repaint the room a third time. "Are you sure? Thought you loved that color."

"Oh, I suppose I did at one time. But, well, maybe it'll grow on me." She patted his hand.

Zach was waiting for her to ask him to do another job for him when he realized she was leading him straight to a blonde woman standing at the bar.

A woman whose name, for the life of him, he couldn't remember. Was it Amy? Maybe Ashley?

That was the extent of what he knew about the woman—her name started with an A and she wasn't a local.

"Ah, here we go. Zach, this is Alyssa." Mrs. Bishop thrust a drink in Zach's hand and then stood behind him, pressing both of her hands on his shoulders, forcing him to sit down on the barstool. In terms of setups, it wasn't the most subtle.

"Hi," Alyssa said, smiling as she brushed a light touch over his arm. "It's nice to officially meet you."

Zach subtly pulled his arm away, using the hand to lift the drink to his mouth. It was bourbon and cranberry. At least Mrs. Bishop had gotten that part right.

"I've seen you around town," Alyssa continued, still smiling.

"... Right."

Zach didn't want to do this. Alyssa was sweet and pretty by anyone's standards, but he just wasn't interested.

Zach had tried dating over the years since Madison, but the relationships were doomed from the start. He wasn't built for easy charm or constant conversation. He was built for loyalty. For the long haul. And the only person he'd ever wanted to share that with had walked away.

He tried to catch Liam's eye across the room, but at that moment, Madison walked in, and Liam was giving her a hug while the rest of their friends welcomed her to their table like old times.

"So, Mrs. Bishop says that you're a contractor?" Alyssa tried again.

Zach looked back at the woman, remembering that he was supposed to be chatting with her.

"I am. I own my own business. Maple Falls keeps me pretty busy."

He knew it was his turn to ask a question, but honestly, he just wanted to finish his drink and leave.

Alyssa didn't seem deterred. "That's great! So, do you do mostly houses? Or do you work on businesses too?"

"Businesses, some houses," he replied vaguely.

She smiled, swirling her drink with her straw. "That must be really rewarding, seeing something come together like that. I bet you love it."

He shrugged. "It's work."

Her brows lifted slightly, but she kept going. "And you grew up here, right?"

"Yeah."

"I think that's so nice—small-town roots and all." She paused as if waiting for him to elaborate. When he didn't, she pushed on. "Did you ever think about leaving? You know, seeing the world?"

Zach took a sip of his drink, trying not to glance over at

Madison, who was laughing at something Liam had said. "No, figured I'd always stay."

Alyssa tapped her fingers against her glass. "That's really refreshing. A lot of guys want bigger things."

He forced a polite smile and nodded, hoping she'd take the hint.

"So..." She leaned in slightly, hand on his arm. "What do you do for fun?"

Zach exhaled quietly, then tilted his drink toward her. "This."

She laughed, but he wasn't joking.

No matter how much Zach tried to ignore Madison, he could feel her. He could hear her laugh and picture her expression when she rolled her eyes at something Liam said. It was infuriating how quickly he'd fallen back into sensing her, knowing her actions, even without seeing her face. It messed with his head. He should have been focused on the present—the woman in front of him. On moving the hell on.

Zach took two quick gulps of his drink. The whiskey burned his throat, and he coughed hard enough to draw a glance from a few tables over.

And maybe from Madison too, because when he risked a glance across the room, he caught her looking away too quickly.

Her cheeks pinkened from the blush rising and her expression made his heart stutter.

Hell. She could be blushing for anyone, laughing at anything.

But he knew that look. He knew her.

Alyssa leaned in and placed her hand on Zach's forearm again.

"You're always so busy. Maybe you should take some time off, and we could have lunch together?" she suggested.

Zach barely processed what she was saying. His eyes flicked back to Madison. He watched her tuck a stray hair behind her ear. She was pretending not to care, but there was tension in her shoulders and a fake smile plastered on her face.

She looked incredible tonight. Jeans that hugged her hips, that soft cream sweater that slid off one shoulder if she moved just right.

Realizing Alyssa was still waiting for a response, he turned back to her, clearing his throat.

"Sorry—what was that?"

"Lunch? You and me?" Alyssa laughed lightly.

Zach exhaled, then stood up. "I'm sorry, I don't think that's such a good idea." He kept his voice even. "But thanks for asking."

He stayed long enough just to watch the hurt cross Alyssa's face, and yeah, it made him feel like an ass, but leading her on would've been worse.

"You have a good night now," he added before striding toward Liam.

Zach tried to ignore Kit, who was nudging Madison again, whispering something that made her shake her head. And Mrs. Bishop, who was scowling at him from across the room. Although, he swore he heard Mrs. C. say, "I told you so," as she sat next to her.

"Finally, I see you've come to join the party," Liam said dryly.

"Blame Mrs. Bishop," Zach replied.

"Game of pool then?" Liam offered.

"Lead the way," Zach said, hoping to put some distance between him and Maddie.

"Girls versus boys, yeah?" Liam asked the group.

Zach's stony expression was answer enough.

"Yes!" Kit exclaimed. "You boys are going to go down!"

"I wouldn't get too confident," Liam told her. "Zach and I are an unstoppable duo. That is, unless Madison is playing."

Liam's words sent a ripple of amusement through the group

as they migrated toward the pool table. Madison trailed behind, fingers curled around her glass, her mind clearly anywhere but the game.

Her head jerked up. "What? I'm not playing."

"I guess Madison's lost her touch," Zach said, meeting her eyes in a challenge. He knew he was playing with fire but couldn't help himself.

Their gazes locked for a fraction of a second too long.

Zach swore the noise of the tavern faded—the clatter of glasses, the guitar player in the corner, all the conversations dulling into the background. It didn't matter that everyone was watching them—old friends, his mother, Mrs. Bishop. He couldn't look away. He wouldn't look away. Not even if someone had a buzz saw at his boots.

Oh yes, the fire was still there, anger flickering around the edges of her emerald irises, but at the center, her pupils were dilated. Deep black pools that Zach knew mirrored his own. He felt the release of endorphins pulse through his body, starting in his chest and rolling through his fingertips down to his toes. He simply had no control over the chemical reaction that took over whenever Madison was around.

"Alright, that settles it, then," Liam said, breaking the spell. "Girls break first."

Zach turned and tried to pretend they hadn't just devoured one another with their eyes.

He knew Madison had felt it too—by the way she took an overly hefty sip of her drink before setting it down and rolling her neck.

"So, what, are you like a pool shark or something?" Kit asked, bouncing on her toes next to Madison.

Zach overheard Madison reply, "Hardly. I haven't played since I left Maple Falls."

"Maybe it's like riding a bicycle," Kit said hopefully.

Liam clapped his hands. "Alright, ladies, let's see what you've got."

Madison picked up a cue and stepped forward. Zach was determined not to watch the way she lined up the first shot—or the way her sweater hitched up on the side, revealing a triangle of perfectly peach-colored skin.

"Might want to try not to stare so much, mate," Liam whispered.

Zach didn't bother to reply. He looked back just as Madison's break sent the balls scattering across the table, and he cursed under his breath. There was no denying it—it was a hell of a break. And by the smug look she shot him across the table, she knew it too.

"What did I say? Like riding a bike." Kit came over and gave Madison a high-five before turning her attention to the men. "You boys ready to lose?" She grinned.

"Please. We're just getting started," Liam replied.

But Zach knew he was screwed.

In more ways than one.

FIFTEEN
MADISON

Madison didn't know exactly when it happened, but sometime between the first break and her next shot, she started to have fun and relax like she hadn't in a long time. The tavern itself hadn't changed in years. The din of laughter and the clicking of glasses filled the air. In the corner, a TV shot off the keno numbers, and locals gathered around, trying to see if their numbers had been picked. Mr. Alders sat on his favorite barstool, waiting for the next person to saddle up and chat the night away.

Maybe it was the familiar weight of the pool cue in her hand or the thrill of the game. Or maybe it was the way Zach crossed his arms every time she sank another shot, his jaw set tight, his expression dark. She knew he was getting hard; she knew that look. It must be killing him. And it felt so good to wind him up, right here in this place where he'd broken her.

The feel of the pool cue sliding through her fingers and the slow burn of Zach's gaze following her every move shifted something inside of her. Soon, it wasn't just about getting one up on him because even though she still burned with anger, her little game of revenge was turning her on too. She couldn't help it; she liked this flirtatious game they were playing. The heated looks, the spiky banter. It was fun, addictive, and dangerous.

Madison leaned across the table with a practiced ease, one she didn't know she still had. Her sweater hitched up, exposing a sliver of bare skin above her jeans. She stretched out her arm, deliberate and slow, feeling the air tighten between them.

She drew out the moment. "You good there, Zach? You're looking a little... tense."

"Just shoot already," Zach shot back, pretending not to care. But oh, how he cared. Madison could read the desire in his eyes.

Then, with a quick pump of the cue, she sank the ball.

Gram whooped.

"Now that's a sexy shot," Kit said, raising her drink in approval.

Madison grinned and clinked her drink with Kit's, enjoying it all.

The bar had grown quieter, more eyes turning toward their game. She didn't care. She had forgotten how good she was at this. That's what happened when you spent a childhood playing pool at the Kettle.

The moment transported her back in time—to the many nights spent in this exact spot, a quarter burning in her palm as she and Zach battled it out at this very table.

The Kettle had always been the local gathering spot—pool tables in the back, exposed brick walls, and the scent of wood-fired pizza wafting through the air. The adults would sit at their usual booths, nursing beers and laughing loudly. Meanwhile, the kids—Madison, Zach, Emily, Liam, Jackson—had lived at the pool tables, fueled by soda and quarters their parents handed out as long as they stayed out of trouble.

Liam leaned in. "Come on now, Maddie, aren't you at least gonna give us a shot?"

She tapped her cue against the floor, pretending to consider it. "Hmm. I suppose I can do best two out of three. It is your birthday, after all."

"That's very generous of you," Liam said dryly.

Madison was already lining up the final shot when she felt him move behind her.

Zach.

She had just drawn her cue back when he bent down low, his breath grazing the side of her neck.

"Don't overshoot it," he murmured, voice low, just for her.

The heat of him at her back, the warmth of his breath against her skin, the scent of cedar and whiskey lingering from his flannel.

Her grip faltered.

The cue slipped at the last second, and she struck too hard and too high.

She watched in horror as the cue ball smacked into the eight ball, sending it rolling toward the corner pocket.

"No, no, no—" she whispered.

The eight ball dropped with a loud clack.

Madison whipped around, practically nose-to-nose with Zach.

"You did that on purpose!"

Zach smirked. "Damn straight."

Madison glared.

"You said best two out of three?" Zach reached for the triangle to re-rack the balls.

Kit elbowed Madison. "You want me to deck him?"

"Not worth it," Madison said, narrowing her eyes at Zach. "He wants to play with fire?" She grabbed her cue. "He'll get fire."

"Alright, alright," Liam cut in. "Seeing as we're making this interesting, let's have a wager, shall we? If the ladies win, Zach has to... go out with Madison?" He looked around the room, eyebrows raised.

"I'll throw ten on that!" Mrs. Bishop shouted from across the bar.

Zach nearly choked on his beer. It was clear from his expression that he couldn't imagine anything worse.

Nice. Madison tried to play off his reaction by taking a drink, but it stung. The feeling was sharp and deep, and hurt more than she would have expected. She didn't *want* to date Zach. That was the last thing she wanted. But seeing him look so horrified, like the idea of being with her was the worst thing imaginable, hit a nerve she didn't realize was still raw.

Maybe it was because, deep down, she wanted him to want her. To at least *see* her. To acknowledge that whatever had been between them hadn't just disappeared.

"And if the boys win?" Kit pressed.

Liam nudged Zach. "Yeah, Zach. What do you want?" Liam was clearly enjoying this.

Zach locked eyes with Madison.

That wasn't just anger, was it? There was something else there. It was hot and deep, primal. Madison's breath hitched, and her pulse fluttered. He felt it too; she was sure of it.

Then he looked away, letting the moment die between them. "Losers buy drinks," he said with a shrug, his voice flat, like it meant nothing.

Madison shook her head and looked away. He wanted to ignore whatever this was?

Fine.

Two could play that game.

Maybe it was the Old Fashioned flowing through her veins, or maybe it was the slow burn of Zach's gaze following her every move, but suddenly, Madison didn't feel cautious or careful anymore.

She felt dangerous. Vengeful. She wanted him to feel the way she felt when she walked into this bar all those years ago and saw him with that other woman—ignored, replaced, insignificant.

Madison picked up the chalk, rolling it between her fingers before dragging it across the tip of her cue with slow, deliberate strokes. Her gaze locked onto Zach the entire time, daring him to look away. "You're going down."

Zach raised an eyebrow. "Is that a threat or a promise?"

Madison tilted her head, "Wouldn't you like to know?"

Before he could respond, she reached for the hem of her sweater and slowly pulled it over her head, revealing a ribbed tank top that hugged her in all the right places, leaving very little to the imagination.

Gram cheered from across the bar. "That's right, honey. You show him who's boss!"

Zach visibly swallowed. His fingers flexed around the cue stick so tight she thought it might snap.

Madison smirked. "Just a little warm in here, don't you think?" she mused, tossing her tangle of curls over her shoulder.

Zach grunted, lining up his shot, determined not to reply. But Madison saw the way his broad shoulders tensed, the way his focus wavered before he exhaled sharply and took his turn.

"Please don't," Emily said with a laugh, seeing the way her brother reacted.

"Sorry," Madison mouthed to Emily, but didn't back down. It was way too much fun tormenting Zach.

Madison quickly regained control of the game, sinking shot after shot. They hit the pockets with a satisfying thud.

They were quick to the last shot of the game.

She felt Zach step closer, just like before, close enough that she could feel the heat of him against her back, drink in the scent of whiskey that clung to him.

"Is that the only trick you know?" she said over her shoulder, tossing the words casually—until she turned her head fully and realized how close he really was.

Zach's lips parted as if he had been about to say something, something most likely dry or sarcastic. The air simmered between them. It was dizzying, being this close to him.

For a split second, Madison thought he might close the gap. Capture her lips in a searing kiss in front of everyone. It would be madness. But she felt it. Their desires mingling together, the air a dance of pheromones.

Her heartbeat pounded in her ears. It throbbed through her fingertips, her throat, the very tips of her toes. The world shrank to just Zach.

To the roughness of his stubble, the tensed muscles in his jaw, the way his gaze dipped for the barest second to her lips.

Then Zach took a slow step back as if he was physically forcing himself to pull away.

Madison smiled, masking how shaken she was, how she had to tamp down her frustration into a ball deep in her stomach.

She turned back around, rolling her shoulders, forcing herself to refocus.

This time, when she took the shot, she didn't miss.

Kit cheered, throwing her hands in the air while Liam groaned, and Zach shook his head despite himself.

"Now that's how you do it!" Kit exclaimed as if she'd dominated the game herself.

Madison smiled, but the feeling of victory was weak compared to the thrum of emotions Zach stirred in her.

As the night wound down, the crowd at the Kettle thinned, leaving just a handful of locals lingering about. Waitresses wiped down tables and flipped up chairs. The lights would be coming back on soon.

Madison looked at her glass, planning on tossing the whiskey back and heading home, when Zach slid onto the stool beside her.

Her heart gave a little traitorous skip.

"You here to ask me out on that date?" Madison asked matter-of-factly. The alcohol buzzed in her brain, making her feel braver, bolder.

Zach braced the bar top. Knuckles white. She'd caught him off guard. Good.

"You didn't have to react that way, you know." Her voice was soft. "You could've played along; it was just a joke."

Zach gave her a level stare. "Nothing with us is ever a joke."

Whatever insult she was about to sling back died on her lips.

"I'll cheers to that," she said finally. Madison lifted her glass and clinked it with his before tipping the rest of it back.

The whiskey should've burned her throat, but she felt nothing but the ghosts of her past circling around, of what they were, and everything they had left unsaid and unfinished.

They sat in silence for a couple of minutes until Madison looked over and saw Zach smile. She was about to ask him what was so funny when he said, "You remember that time Liam challenged you in the hot wing eating competition?"

Madison laughed at the memory. They were the hottest wings she'd ever eaten in her entire life. An entire platter of them. "And I won!" she said proudly.

"He claimed it was because he'd just had a burger..." Zach started to say.

"But we all know he can't handle much spice," Madison finished with a grin. She always did like her wings with an extra kick.

"Hey! It was because of the burger," Liam called out from across the bar.

"Sure, sure," Madison replied. "Anytime you want a rematch, just let me know!"

Liam laughed and Madison could hear him retelling the

story to Emily and Zoe. Not that they hadn't been there that night.

"Do you still like your hot wings with a side of fire?" Zach asked.

"You know me, the hotter the better," Madison replied with a smile.

"Did someone say fire whiskey?" Liam asked, coming back.

He motioned to the bartender. "Sir, five shots of your best fire whiskey," he said in a highbrow voice.

Madison thought it was a very bad idea, but she couldn't very well back down now.

"To Liam," Emily toasted, raising her glass. The rest of the group followed suit. "And to Jackson," she added. There was a collective nod. "Hope you have the best of birthdays. Cheers!"

"Cheers!" Madison clinked her glass and downed the drink, letting the slow burn fill her senses.

Liam, Zoe, and Emily walked back to their table, talking about getting in one more round of darts, leaving Zach and Madison at the bar.

Zach leaned in slightly, close enough that she could smell the warm spice of his cologne and feel the heat of him in the small space between them. The air was charged and her mind betrayed her.

She imagined leaning toward him, closing that small gap, feeling his hand find her waist, his mouth slant over hers like he used to. Deep, possessive.

She wondered if he would still kiss her the same way. If his hands would still slide into her hair, fisting just enough to tilt her head the way he liked. If he would still murmur her name against her skin as he explored lower, lower, until she was gasping beneath him.

Could he still make her come undone with his mouth as he laid her back and watched? The things that man could do...

Stop. Madison gripped the edge of the bar. She wasn't running anymore.

She cleared her throat. "You know, the last time I saw you in this place, there was another girl hanging all over you. While we were still dating."

Zach's head snapped up, eyes narrowing. "What?"

"Yeah. I'd flown home to surprise you. For our anniversary," she said, bitterness edging her voice. "And I saw you. There you were, drinking with her, letting her touch you like—"

"I—Madison, I had no idea. Why didn't you tell me? I didn't know you were coming home. And that girl, that was nothing. Nothing happened." His voice was sharp but shaking. "She tried to kiss me, but I wouldn't let her."

Madison's eyes were narrowed, incredulous.

"I was drunk, Mads, because I thought you'd forgotten about us. You had barely been in touch with me for weeks. Then on our anniversary you didn't pick up, you didn't call—"

"My phone was on airplane mode," she shot back, "because I wanted to surprise you. I wanted to ask you to come to New York with me."

They stared at each other, the air heavy with all the years and words they hadn't said.

"Did you really not do anything with her? What would have happened if I'd seen you push her away?" Madison whispered after a long pause. "If I'd stayed, if we'd just talked?"

Zach swallowed, voice raw. "I don't know. Maybe I would have come with you. Or maybe we would have found another way. But I sure would have fought for us, Madison, if I'd known you wanted me to."

The silence between them ached with the realization that their reality didn't have to be this way.

Neither of them moved, both afraid that if they spoke, it would break whatever fragile thing was holding them in this moment of honesty.

Zach's fingers tapped once against the side of his glass, almost absently. Then he set it down with a soft clink, cleared his throat, and said, voice low and rough, "Come on. I'll walk you home."

Madison blinked, her brain short-circuiting for a half-second.

He shifted slightly, almost like he regretted the offer, but he didn't take it back.

"I'm heading that way anyway."

For one breathless second, she almost said no, almost let fear of what might happen win out.

But then she caught the flicker of something raw in his eyes. It was as uncertain as it was protective, and heaven help her, she wanted to know what it meant.

"Sure," she said, keeping her voice light as she slid off her stool, grabbing her sweater. "Lead the way."

They stepped out into the cool night air. The stars were hidden under a thick layer of clouds, but Madison knew they were up there, shining down on them, waiting, watching to see what would happen.

And all she could think was that the distance between her and Zach had never felt so small, or so dangerous. Like the atoms between them were about to explode.

SIXTEEN

ZACH

The town was dead quiet at 2 a.m., and the air was unseasonably warm. Zach inhaled the sharp mineral scent of wet pavement and damp leaves.

It must've rained when they'd been in the Kettle. He hadn't even noticed. A few area shops had nightlights on, bathing their display windows in a soft glow. The night was silent except for the sound of Zach's and Madison's footsteps as they walked down Oak Way.

Zach kept his hands jammed deep in his pockets, his shoulders hunched against the cold, and against the temptation walking beside him.

Zach was fighting with himself to make sense of the past. He was reeling, stunned. Nothing was how he thought it had been, not really. Madison hadn't just left him without a look back all those years ago. It was all a damn misunderstanding that had kept them apart all these years. Zach didn't know what to make of that. Or where to go from here.

So instead he thought about Madison.

The way she had smiled as she'd lined up her shots, the way she'd toyed with him, pulling her sweater off like she didn't know exactly what it did to him, flashing him that ribbed tank top, the hem riding just a little too high over those hips he used to grip when he—

Zach growled under his breath and shoved the thought away.

She walked a little ahead now, her body still tucked into that tank top, her sweater off her shoulder, and jeans that hugged every curve.

And when her fingers accidentally brushed his, Zach nearly lost his footing.

Madison didn't seem to notice. But Zach did. Every nerve ending lit up, his body attuned to her like it always had been.

He was about to say something, anything, just to kill the silence between them when Madison caught her foot on the uneven curb.

She stumbled with a soft gasp.

Zach reacted without thinking, reaching out and grabbing her waist, pulling her tight against him before she could fall. It wasn't lost on him how many times Fate had placed her in his arms.

"Careful." His voice came out rough. "You keep falling into me like that, and I'm going to start thinking it's on purpose."

Madison's palms were on his chest. She looked up, her eyes locked with his. "Third time's the charm?"

Zach froze. He could feel the quick stutter of her heartbeat against his ribs.

Jesus. He should have let her go. He knew he should have let her go.

But he didn't move. Neither did she.

His hands flexed against her hips, drawing her a fraction closer without meaning to. Her scent hit him, something faint and sweet like apples and ginger, and it undid whatever strength he had left.

Zach swore under his breath and dipped his head, sealing his mouth over hers before he could talk himself out of it.

The kiss was soft at first. Tentative. Like he expected her to push off his chest and cuss him out any second. But she didn't. She kissed him back, cradling his face and pulling him down, as if she'd been waiting for this.

She wanted more.

How could he resist? He could be that man. He could give her what she wanted. What she needed.

His hands slid up her back, pulling her scarlet hair as he deepened the kiss, hunger for her overtaking him.

Madison gasped against him, and he swallowed the sound.

Zach slanted his mouth over hers again and again, taking everything she gave him and giving it back twice as hard. She moaned softly and desire surged through him. It was frantic, all-consuming. As if the world would end soon and this was the last moment they had.

They stumbled backward together, Zach's boots scraping the sidewalk, until Madison's back hit the cool brick of a nearby building—an alley tucked between two shops. Shadowed, private.

He pressed her into the wall with the weight of his body, his hands roaming on her hips, waist, ribs, everywhere he'd missed for far too long.

Her body pressed against his was driving him wild. It short-circuited his brain.

He kissed down the line of her jaw, along her throat, desperate to taste every inch of her, to hear those soft, breathless sounds that used to drive him crazy.

"Zach," she whispered, her voice cracking with need.

It shredded him. He slipped one hand into her hair, fisting it just enough to tilt her head, and took her mouth again—deeper, rougher. His hips ground into hers without thought, his body begging for more.

God, he wanted her. Right there. Right now. He couldn't wait.

And judging by the way Madison clutched at him, the way she moaned quietly against his mouth, she wanted him just as badly.

Then—

Laughter. Loud, stumbling footsteps.

Zach stilled, his chest heaving.

Down the sidewalk, a group spilled out of the Kettle. He recognized Liam's voice, loud and teasing, and Emily's laughter as Kit sang off-key.

Zach's heart pounded against Madison's chest as they froze together, barely breathing, pressed against the brick wall like fugitives.

For a moment, Zach was half-crazed, still poised to kiss her again—to take this all the way together, the hell with consequences. But he forced himself to step back a fraction, his hands falling away, his breathing ragged.

They stood there, pressed into the shadows, silent, while their friends' laughter and footsteps echoed past them down the street.

Madison's lips were kiss-swollen, her cheeks flushed, her scarlet curls wild from where he'd gripped them. He could see the golden flecks in her eyes, the freckles over her nose. She was the most beautiful woman he'd ever seen, and it wrecked him. What was he doing? She'd moved on, moved away. She was here for a heartbeat, until she'd rescued the inn. Then she'd be gone. He couldn't handle the pain of losing her all over again.

For a beat, neither of them said a word.

Then Zach raked a shaky hand through his hair, cursing under his breath.

"This was a bad idea," he rasped, voice low and crumbling.

Madison's brows drew together, hurt flickering across her face.

Zach forced the words out, hating himself even as he said them. "I've had too much to drink. Let's not pretend we're who we used to be."

Madison flinched, her mouth opening like she wanted to say something, but nothing came out. She just stared at him, her eyes darkening, pulling her arms tightly around herself like she was trying to hold something in.

Zach took another step back. "Come on," he muttered roughly, jerking his head toward the sidewalk. "I'll walk you the rest of the way."

Neither of them said another word. But Zach could still taste her on his lips, feel her in his blood.

And God help him, he already knew he would never get enough.

SEVENTEEN
MADISON

October 13th

After a sleepless night, Madison hit the trail behind the inn just as the first hints of dawn broke across the lake. She tilted her chin up to the pink- and gold-streaked sky, hoping it would warm her face. The air was sharp with the bite of coming rain and cold wind. Nothing serious. No storms, thank God, but it was chilly. She pulled her sweatshirt sleeves over her hands and picked up her pace, her sneakers crunching over the winding, leaf-strewn path.

Running always helped clear her mind. At least, it used to. She didn't run as much as she'd like in New York because she preferred running outside rather than on a treadmill. In the city you couldn't just step outside and start running. Well, you could, but she didn't like it. There were people everywhere, so you had to take a ride to the park and even there, you couldn't mentally check out. Not like here.

And this morning, Madison definitely needed the run. Last night kept replaying on an endless loop—the heat of Zach's body, the rough drag of his hands around her waist, the fierce, desperate kiss they'd shared like neither of them had any choice.

She still felt it, in her chest. In her blood.

And God, she wanted more.

Madison pushed herself harder, arms pumping, heart hammering in time with her feet.

She had no business wanting more. What was she playing at? She was leaving soon. She had a life back in New York—a career she loved, a future she'd fought for. She'd interviewed for *Plated* for God's sake. The top culinary magazine in the country had wanted her for an editorial job, and the position might still be hers.

Zach had never left Maple Falls and he never would.

Besides, what was last night really? A kiss stolen in the dark? Two people caught up in the past? It didn't mean anything.

She ran faster, as if she was trying to chase the memory out of her body. But it was branded onto her, that kiss that had knocked the air out of her lungs, the bones from her legs. The best she had ever had, intoxicating, electric.

Until Zach had said it was a "bad idea" and stepped away from her like she was poison.

He certainly didn't want more. He clearly didn't want her. In fact, Madison couldn't help but think that if Zach had his way, Madison would just disappear. Because she was a *bad idea*.

That kiss, and its abrupt ending, haunted her more than she'd like to admit. All night, in fact. Which was why Madison had tugged an orange knit beanie over her messy curls, zipped up her sweatshirt, and slipped quietly out the back door of the inn.

The last thing she had wanted was to get sidetracked by conversation or, worse, run into Gram before she'd had coffee. Madison was pretty sure Gram had left early with her date last night, and Madison definitely didn't want to hear about that.

So, Madison ran until her legs screamed and her lungs fought for breath. If you could win a medal for running away from your problems, Madison would come in first.

When she couldn't run any longer, she slowed near the edge of Bear Lake, bending low, hands on her knees, sucking in air as the sun burned off the fog across the water. As she stood, catching her breath, she watched the waves lapping along the shore, the falling amber leaves, and the ducks that paddled near the shoreline, dipping their beaks underwater.

Maybe I'll come back later and bring them something to eat, she mused.

Then the memory settled over her, how when she was a little girl, she and her mom would come down to feed the ducks. Her mom had kept a bag of cracked corn under the kitchen sink. Madison would fill her pockets with it, and they'd head down to the lake hand-in-hand to feed the ducks. She used to name them, making up elaborate stories about their duck families and adventures before they flew south for the winter.

There were a million memories to be found in this town, and each one was precious. It was funny how she'd forgotten about feeding the ducks with Mom. How could she have? It was like realizing part of her childhood had slipped through her fingers without her even noticing. Had she really been gone that long?

By the time she finished her lap around the lake, Madison had waved to a handful of early risers—joggers, dog walkers, and a fisherman unloading his boat at the dock.

Memories of her mom had nudged her thoughts back to her purpose here: Save the inn. So, as she'd run, she'd forced herself to focus, banishing the kiss from her mind. And she'd come up with a brilliant plan. Well, brilliant in her mind.

The inn was in dire need of a refresh. Halloween was at the end of the month.

What if they closed down for a couple of weeks and

relaunched the inn on the thirty-first? They could have a big Halloween-themed party.

Her mind raced with ideas. Not just pumpkins on the porch, but the works—cider stations, caramel apple bars, pumpkin carving contests on the lawn. They could raffle off a free night's stay, maybe a dinner-for-two certificate. They'd partner with local businesses—Liam's fledgling farm shop for gourmet jams and cider, the outdoor outfitter for cozy knit mittens, Emily's bakery for fall-themed pastries. Visitors could stay at the inn and sample everything Maple Falls had to offer at a discount.

Maybe the tree crashing through the roof had been a good thing, in an odd way. It was an excuse to shut down and start fresh.

She was just rounding the final curve, coming back upon the inn, mentally ticking through the list of businesses they could partner with for the Halloween launch, when she stopped dead in her tracks.

Zach was standing outside the honeymoon cabin wearing nothing but a pair of low-slung jersey shorts. Barefoot. Barechested. Despite the bite of chill in the air.

The golden morning light caught on his bare shoulders, highlighting the taut muscles in his arms, the way his chest rose and fell with each deep breath. His hair was damp, like he'd just finished showering, and he looked completely unbothered by the cold.

Madison wished she had even a fraction of the calm he exuded.

She dragged her gaze up—past his carved stomach, past his broad chest—to his face. His jaw was rough with stubble, his mouth slightly parted. His eyes grabbed hold of hers as if they'd never let go again.

Her brain screamed at her to look away, but her body didn't

get the memo. Heat flooded her cheeks, her chest, rushing straight through her core.

EIGHTEEN
ZACH

Zach woke up this morning feeling like he had spent the night wrestling an alligator—and lost. His body ached, not from doing anything physical but from the sheer effort of trying to keep himself in check.

Last night had been brutal. He hadn't been able to sleep, not with the taste of Madison still on his lips, not with the memory of her pressed up against him like she belonged there. He had lain awake for hours, staring at the wooden ceiling of the honeymoon cabin, his mind refusing to stop replaying every glorious second.

The way she smiled with those dimples of hers, the fierce expression in her eyes, the way she had teased and taunted him. It was all a test—the pool game, the bet, everything—and Zach couldn't believe how badly he'd failed.

Now he knew that in a parallel universe, if he'd never gone to the tavern and got drunk that night, or if Madison had just waited a little longer and seen him push that girl away, things might have worked out differently. Maybe they'd even still be together now. But what happened happened; there was no point digging it all up again. That way would only lead to heartbreak for both of them. They weren't the same people they used to be. Six years had passed since they were a couple. She was a New Yorker. His life was here. Where he wanted it to be. And she was only passing through town.

If he let himself believe, even for a second, that she would stay or that there was a chance they could somehow make it work this time, there was a very good chance he'd be setting himself up for a world of pain, all over again. This time, Zach wasn't sure he could survive.

Plus, she had someone back in New York, didn't she?

"And how is your lovely Jo?" Edith had asked.

"Misses me," Madison had replied—or something like that.

Zach didn't know the details, obviously, but there was something there between the two.

Maybe he was being a coward. Maybe he should fight for her. Tell her how badly he still wanted her, needed her. But when it came to Madison, Zach knew better than to trust what he wanted over what he knew was true: She didn't stay, and she wasn't built for small-town life. She was made for bigger things —for bright lights and city streets.

Zach was just a slow-living kind of guy with rough hands and a pickup truck who could fix a roof and run a mile without stopping. He couldn't give her the life she deserved.

Still, here he was, standing shirtless in the cold morning air, hoping some fresh air would shock her out of his system.

It wasn't working. Not when she had been in his head all night. The feel of her against the brick wall, the taste of her mouth, the way she fit into his arms like a piece of him he hadn't realized was missing until she slid back into place.

Zach exhaled sharply, rubbing a hand over his stubbled jaw. He needed to get her out of his head.

Today was opening weekend at Liam's pumpkin patch. It wasn't Zach's normal scene, every family in town would be there, but Zach knew Liam couldn't do it on his own. Even with his family and the extra farmhands, he needed help. Liam's twin, Jackson, would be home soon, but he wasn't here yet. Helping Liam would keep Zach busy too, and he needed to keep his mind occupied.

It was a solid plan until he looked up and saw Madison jogging through the trees toward him, looking down at the leaves crunching under her sneakers.

Then she looked up and stopped frozen just a few feet away, her chest rising and falling as she regulated her breath. Her cheeks were flushed and some stray wild curls had slipped out from under that ridiculous orange beanie. Her black leggings hugged her thighs and he swallowed, already hard for her.

He should've said nothing. But the invitation that fell onto his tongue seemed like the most natural thing in the world, like the script had already been written. His voice came rough and low. "Got a fresh pot of strong coffee on, if you want. Freshly ground."

Madison's dragon-green eyes blinked, startled. Zach hated himself for how badly he wanted her to say yes.

"Raw sugar. Fresh cream," he added, hoping she remembered the special way he used to make it for her. Would she still want it that way? How much had she changed?

For half a heartbeat, she hesitated. He saw the way her fingers curled into her sleeves, the way her body tilted almost imperceptibly toward him.

God, he could already see it. Her standing near his bed in the cabin, cradling a mug in both hands, leaning against the counter like she used to lean against his truck. She was warm, familiar, his.

He remembered the times they had spent in this cabin all too well. Remembered holding her on the couch, her head resting against his bare chest. Or the way she'd unbutton her shirt, daring him with nothing more than a glance. And he would go to her. He'd slide his hands up her thighs, tug that flannel higher until it was bunched around her waist. And lift her onto the counter with a low growl against her throat, tasting her skin, feeling her breath catch as she squeezed her legs around him and he slid into her, slow and deep.

Zach swore under his breath and shoved his hands into his pockets.

None of that mattered now. Their relationship was in the past. He could want her all he wanted. She was no longer his.

Madison shifted her weight from foot to foot. For a second, Zach thought maybe she'd say yes. Maybe she'd step closer, cross the distance. Then everything would fall apart, or maybe finally fall into place.

Instead, she gave him a tight smile. "Thanks," she said, breathless. "But I should get going. Lots to do at the inn."

Zach swallowed the disappointment like a shot of whiskey.

He watched her turn and head toward the Cinnamon Spice Inn. He had to force his feet to stay rooted to the spot. But even as she ran away, Zach swore he could still feel her there. As if in another dimension, she'd stayed.

NINETEEN
MADISON

Coffee.

It was just coffee.

But Madison couldn't shake the way her heart had melted at his words.

It was like an olive branch after all the friction between them. Because coffee, especially in that cabin, was their thing. And he remembered, like he always had. Just how strong she needed it, with raw sugar and fresh cream for an extra treat. He knew she couldn't start a day without at least two cups, usually three. But Zach's was always the best. She used to steal sips from his travel mug just because it tasted better when it came from him.

For one stupid, reckless second, she'd almost said yes. Almost walked toward him, toward the warmth she could already smell drifting from the open cabin door.

But Madison had caught herself just in time.

Let's not pretend we're who we used to be; Zach's words from last night replayed through her head.

So she'd turned him down politely, mumbled some excuse about things to do, and forced herself to walk away—because if she hadn't, she wasn't sure she would have stopped at coffee. The chemistry between them didn't care that her mind was in knots, and she didn't want them to make just another "mistake."

But something had flickered in Zach's eyes when she'd said no. He'd covered it quickly, giving a short nod. It was that easy, casual way he used when he was hiding something bigger. He'd always been good at masking his emotions, unlike her.

Madison's chest ached at the thought of that flicker in his eyes. She had just stepped into the inn, and almost said *screw it* and turned around, when she saw Emily inside the lobby.

"Hey, just dropping off a couple pastries for you," Emily said, standing next to the registration desk in a caramel-colored knit sweater and dark jeans. Her blonde hair was tied back into a messy bun that framed her heart-shaped face. "Your dad said you didn't need them for guests, but I figured you could still use a little sweetness to kick-start your day."

"Thanks so much, we really appreciate it," Madison said, pulling off her beanie.

"We really do!" Gram added from behind the counter, already licking icing off her fingers. A half-eaten pumpkin cheesecake muffin sat on a napkin beside her coffee. "Consider this my official taste test, and these are divine!"

Emily beamed and then looked at Madison. "I know things are crazy right now, but when they slow down, we really need to catch up. We can get some coffee, walk around the lake or something?"

"I'd love that," Madison said. The words felt both too small and too big all at once. "Definitely."

"Perfect," Emily said with a smile. "I'll text you, okay?"

"Sounds good." Madison waved her old friend out the door.

"Take care, love," Gram called, washing down a bit of her muffin with a sip of coffee.

Madison eyed the pastries Emily had dropped off. They looked sinfully good. She poured herself an oversized mug of coffee and spotted a leaf-shaped sugar cookie nestled in the box. She plucked it out, then walked over to meet Gram at the counter.

"Do you know where Dad is?" Madison asked, breaking off a corner of the cookie. "I wanted to talk to you both about the inn, make sure we're on the same page."

Gram hummed, considering. "Well, I imagine he's feeding Aspen his breakfast."

Madison nodded, taking a sip of her coffee.

It tasted like heaven.

Okay, maybe not heaven.

Heaven would've been the coffee Zach had offered her this morning. Fresh, hot, and handed over with those rough hands that used to know every inch of her body.

She wrapped her fingers tighter around the cup.

Why did she say no? Madison had already admitted to herself that she was still wildly, stupidly attracted to him. That wasn't even a question anymore. Not after finding out the truth about what had happened in the tavern all those years ago. Not after the kiss last night. And especially not after the way he had looked at her this morning, bare chest, damp hair, standing outside the honeymoon cabin like something straight out of her filthiest dreams. He didn't just think she was a big mistake. He didn't just want her gone. He'd offered her coffee. He'd invited her in.

But to what end? Last night, Zach had been clear their kiss was a mistake. And he was right. She knew they could never work long-term, not with her future away from Maple Falls. But part of her, the reckless, aching part, was seriously trying to remember why they couldn't have a little fun for old times' sake.

Nothing serious. Just for fun. Like a summer fling, only in the fall. That could be a thing, right? Why not? They were grown adults.

Or maybe it was a chance for closure. They could spend

some time together, remember what they had, and then move on. It could be therapeutic.

Before she could think about it any further, the front door swung open, and George stepped inside with Cocoa close at his heels, barking and tugging on his pant leg.

"Ho, ho! Good morning, you two," he greeted Madison and Edith cheerfully.

"Hang on, you'll get your biscuit," George said down to Cocoa, ducking behind the registration desk and pulling a dog treat from the cookie jar he kept stashed there. "Sit, come on now, you can do it." Cocoa plopped down, tail wagging wildly. "There's a good girl."

Madison took a breath, shifting gears. Time to focus. She was here for the inn, and they had work to do. "Dad," she began. "I wanted to talk to you about Halloween. What if we shut down, use the next couple of weeks to fix up the inn, and have a themed grand reopening?"

"Oh?" Gram asked, clearly intrigued.

"It could be amazing," she continued, feeling the excitement build, her ideas taking shape. "We could have pumpkin-lined, candlelit walkways, spooky cider tastings, maybe even a costume contest or trick-or-treat trail for the kids. Oh, a bonfire by the lake, too!"

George looked lost for words and Madison pressed on. "We could start promoting it during the Pumpkinfest and partner with local businesses. Discounted rates if you buy a basket of local goodies from Liam's farm shop, or donuts from the bakery, or hand-knit scarves from the outfitter. That kind of thing. We could even raffle off a full weekend getaway for the holidays."

She glanced between Gram and her dad.

Gram lifted her coffee. "Sounds great to me, Honey Pie."

George looked between Madison and Edith, reading their expressions. "Are you sure you can get it all done in time?"

"Positive. We've got this, especially with Zach helping. It'll be ready."

"Even the honeymoon cabin?" Gram asked.

"Even that," Madison said tightly, not dwelling on the space that held so many memories for her and Zach.

"Which reminds me," Gram said, turning a finger toward George. "There's a Pumpkinfest committee meeting this morning at the café."

"I already told Mrs. Bishop and Mrs. C. that I'd be there," Madison said, speaking up. "I'll find out what they still need, volunteer us for it, and start putting feelers out for promotional partnerships."

In past years, the inn had hosted an open house for the annual Pumpkinfest, with carnival games and prizes on the front lawn. They'd be closed this year, but they could at least have a stall outside and serve her mom's famous cinnamon rolls —with Kit's apple butter center twist—and start promoting the reopening.

"It'd have to all be outside, but we could fix up just the front porch, go all out with decorations, and set up a refreshment stand," she mused. "Something cozy and inviting. That could work, right?"

"I'm sure they'll need a sponsor for an event or two, as well," Gram said.

At that, George fell silent. He stared off toward the window, lips pressed together, and Madison recognized that look instantly. It was the same one he always got when her college tuition was due.

Money. She knew he was worried.

"I'll talk to the committee," Madison assured him gently. "Hopefully, they just need manpower from us, not funding. I'm sure they'll understand."

George nodded, but he said nothing. Instead, he crouched

down to give Cocoa another treat, scratching behind the pup's ears.

Madison sighed. "Alright, I'll fill you in when I'm back from the meeting."

"Perfect," Gram said with a broad smile.

George's smile was less than convincing, but it would have to do.

One step at a time.

They could still save this place.

She just had to believe it, and it would be true.

TWENTY
MADISON

The bell jingled overhead as she stepped inside, and warmth wrapped around Madison instantly.

Anita's Maple Leaf Café was everything she remembered. Small, cozy, and overflowing with charm. Exposed brick walls framed a collection of shelves filled with old cookbooks, Mason jars of preserves, and vintage teapots. The glass bakery case near the register was filled with a selection of homemade cakes, pies, and perfectly golden biscuits. All the chairs had thick, comfy cushions, and the oversized menu was three pages long. They were tucked into plastic trifolds and handed out to each customer. There wasn't any QR code to scan here.

The Maple Leaf Café served up the most iconic hometown eats—grilled cheese and homemade tomato soup, local pasties stuffed with beef, potatoes, and bacon, ladled with rich brown gravy. Hearty breakfasts with omelets and sausage that could keep you full until dinner. You never left the café hungry, that was for sure. More importantly, you never left feeling alone. Whether you wanted them to or not, someone was always going to sit down and talk to you—either to share town gossip or to try and get a little out of you.

The murmur of conversation blended with the low hum of an old record player spinning Ella Fitzgerald. The entire café smelled like buttery pastry, bacon, and dark-roast coffee.

And at the center of it all, bright like the sunrise, was Anita Whitaker, Zach's mom.

"Well, well, well! Look who's finally come to visit." Her hands were dusted with flour, with a smudge on her cheek, and yet her grin was completely unstoppable.

Madison barely had time to process the sheer joy on Anita's face before she wrapped her in a tight embrace. "I didn't get to hug you last night."

Madison hadn't known what to expect, but there she was, feeling the closest thing to a mother's hug that she'd had in the past three years.

Anita placed both hands on Madison's shoulders and took a step back to get a good look at her. "Well, you look as beautiful as ever," she said with a wide smile.

"So do you. It's so good to see you," Madison said, feeling a lump rise in her throat at Anita's warmth.

"You're here for the Pumpkinfest meeting, is that right?" Anita asked.

"Yep," Madison confirmed, glancing toward the back of the café, where the unofficial committee had gathered in the corner, already deep in discussion.

"What can I get you?" Anita asked, pulling her notepad from the pocket of her apron.

Madison glanced down the table, where the committee members were already tucking into their lunches.

"I've got a maple bacon BLT on the menu today," Anita offered. "Goes good with a cup of soup. It'll fill you right up and keep you warm. That wind's supposed to pick up this afternoon, and I'd hate to have it blow you away." She chuckled.

"That sounds great. Thank you."

"With a Coke?"

"Yes, please."

Anita smiled and disappeared behind the counter, and Madison turned her attention to the conversation happening at the table. She could've sworn she'd just heard her name.

"Now, as I was saying, just because Madison's back in town doesn't mean the inn's suddenly going to do a complete one-eighty," Mrs. C. was saying, her tone clipped.

Madison frowned. What exactly was going on here? She walked forward to join them.

"The Cinnamon Spice Inn has been in that family for generations. You can't expect them to want to sell it," Mr. Alders countered.

"It doesn't matter if they want to or not. We need an inn that's fully functioning and bringing in tourists. If not, we're all in trouble. You know I'm not wrong," Mrs. C. pressed.

The mayor pursed his lips.

Madison stood up straighter, her heart thudding. "What exactly are you talking about? The inn isn't for sale," she said, jumping right in.

Mrs. Bishop jumped in her seat and turned around. "Oh, Madison, didn't see you there," she started to say, but Mrs. C. just kept right on going.

"Have you considered that maybe it should be?" Mrs. C. asked, folding her arms. "Now, don't get me wrong, your father is a lovely man, but he's in over his head. Every time I turn around, he's rescuing another animal. Maybe he should buy some land and start a farm instead—leave running a business to someone else."

"Now, Betsy, that's not fair," Mrs. Bishop interjected, coming to Madison's defense.

It was probably a good thing Mrs. Bishop had spoken up, because the words forming in Madison's head were not going to be as kind. Her pulse pounded; her face heated.

Madison leveled a look at Mrs. C. "Listen here. The inn

might've had a rough patch, but I'm here now. And I'm going to set things straight. I'll make sure we get things running exactly the way they need to be."

Mrs. C's sharp expression softened slightly. "But for how long?" she asked. "You're not staying forever, are you?"

Madison hesitated, her throat suddenly dry.

"That's what I thought," Mrs. C. said knowingly. "Listen, sweetheart, I love that you're here, wanting to help your family. I do. But we have to think about this entire town. When people don't have a good place to stay, it hurts all of us. Sales are down across the board, and that directly ties back to the inn. We need visitors to come to Maple Falls. More importantly, we need them to want to stay a while."

Madison shook her head to stop Mrs. C. "You misunderstood me."

Mrs. C's eyebrows rose.

"I'm staying," Madison said confidently. She had no idea where those words had come from. She wasn't staying. She couldn't. She had a whole life waiting for her in New York.

"You are?" Mrs. Bishop's face lit up like a moonbeam.

Mrs. C. looked shocked. Mayor Bloomfield clapped. Mr. Alders even stood up and gave her a congratulatory pat on the back.

Madison knew she couldn't backtrack now. Not right this second. She shouldn't have said it, but she just wanted Mrs. C. to quit listing all the reasons her family should sell the inn.

Thankfully, Mrs. C. let the conversation drop just then as Mayor Bloomfield redirected it. "Right, then, where do we stand with the festival, Mrs. Bishop? Do we have enough pumpkins ordered for the square?"

"Yes, sir. I talked with Liam myself last night. He'll be sure to deliver them bright and early Friday morning in the town center."

While the conversation continued around her, Madison's

insides swirled with anger and frustration. She still felt blindsided by Mrs. C's comments.

Clearly, she hadn't sent the letter. She'd probably contact a realtor before reaching out to Madison. But that didn't mean someone else around this table hadn't sent it. Someone who knew the town was plotting to persuade her dad to sell.

Madison knew that the inn had been struggling since her mother had passed. She could see that with her own eyes, but she'd had no idea that people were actively discussing whether her family should sell the inn. The idea stung. It was not only an attack on her father but on her mother's legacy. And that wasn't something she would stand for.

The conversation switched to the hay bale maze in front of the Kettle, and how the setup was going, but Madison still wasn't really listening. Instead, she sat there, trying not to glare at Mrs. C. She felt hell-bent on proving her wrong.

Madison wasn't going to let anyone talk about her family like they couldn't handle their own business. The inn might have fallen into disrepair, but that didn't mean it was lost. She was here now, and she was going to fix this.

Kit came out just then, running food to their table. "Hey there!" Kit said, putting the plate before her. The BLT was served warm on toasted sourdough, and the loaded baked potato soup looked rich and cheesy, with bacon bits and scallions on top.

"Hey, I didn't expect to see you here," Madison said, accepting the dish.

"Today is my last day. I told Anita about the inn. I hope that was okay."

"Of course. I hope she doesn't mind that I'm stealing you away?"

Kit shook her head. "I was just helping out here temporarily; Anita knew that when she took me on. Trust me, she's loads happy that I'll be managing my own kitchen. I don't think she likes me under her feet so much," Kit added with a whisper. "Speaking of which, are you free in a little bit? I'm stocking Liam's pumpkin patch with fresh scones and a couple of new recipes and I thought maybe you'd like to try them."

"Yeah, I'd love that."

"Okay, I'll meet you at the inn around two and we can go to the pumpkin patch together?"

Madison smiled and nodded, just as Mrs. C. cleared her throat to get her attention.

"Definitely. See you then," Madison said before turning her attention back to the table.

"So, Madison, do you think your family is up for running the carnival games on Saturday?"

"Of course," Madison declared. *In for a penny, in for a pound*, she thought. "But just as a heads up, we're going to be closing for the next couple of weeks. Just to refurbish a few things," she added before Mrs. C. could suggest selling the place again. "With the tree crashing through the roof and all, we thought it would be a good time to freshen up the place. We're going to relaunch at Halloween with an amazing new chef, new décor, the works. I promise you it's going to be just what the town needs. And we're planning on using the Pumpkinfest to promote the relaunch."

"That settles it then. With any luck, this will be our best fall ever." Mayor Bloomfield pounded the table enthusiastically.

TWENTY-ONE
MADISON

A few hours later, Kit pulled up in front of the inn. She waved from the driver's side. Madison noticed how perfect and seasonal her bright orange beret looked against her dark hair.

Madison was dressed in the same clothes she'd worn to lunch. Time had gotten away from her. She had meant to spend a few moments hunting for the carnival games in the basement, but ended up spending hours cleaning up the front porch instead. She used her mom's wicker broom, the same one that had been in the front closet since she was a kid, to brush off all the dried leaves. Then she used one of her dad's rags from the shed to dust off the rocking chairs. What they really needed was a fresh coat of paint. Maybe she'd find time to tackle that, too.

It wasn't perfect yet, but it was a start.

As Kit and Madison pulled into Liam's family farm, Madison had to admit that she was nervous. It had been years since she'd been out here. She had heard that Liam had taken it over from his father, but she had yet to see it.

When they were in high school, Liam used to have the

wildest parties with the biggest bonfires. Everyone wanted to come to Liam's house on Friday nights, which always ended up with a game of hide-and-go-seek in the corn stalks at midnight—and Liam and Zach scaring everyone to death when they jumped out at them.

Madison smiled at the memory, but what had once been a quaint little farm now looked to be the destination for fall family fun. A wrought-iron archway swooped over the drive with the words "Winding Creek Farm" etched out in big, blocky script. The entire archway had been decorated with artificial sunflowers and brightly colored leaves. A parking area was off to the side, with workers directing traffic down the lane. The pumpkin patch and market would be open every weekend from now through November, and it was packed.

"Wow, this is a production," Madison said, taking it all in.

"It wasn't like this when you lived here?"

"Not at all. We always got our pumpkins from Liam's dad, but he didn't sell them to the public, not like this."

In the distance, Madison could see a tractor pulling guests around for hayrides. Bouncy houses and a petting zoo were also set up, and the barn looked like it had been turned into a retail shop with various décor for sale. A food truck serving spiced cider and donuts set off the space.

Visitors could pick a pumpkin from the stands out front or take a wagon out to the fields to choose their own. A photo station had been set up with a charming wooden bench framed by potted mums and pumpkins, and families were lining up to take pictures. Nearby, oversized wooden cutouts of smiling scarecrows, pumpkins, and ears of corn invited visitors to poke their heads through for a fun photo op.

"Help me carry these in?" Kit asked, popping the back end of her SUV. She had it stacked with goodies.

"Do you want me to grab one of the carts?" Madison asked.

Metal carts with oversized wheels were all lined up in front of the barn.

"Yeah, that would be perfect."

Madison quickly fetched a cart and returned to load up the boxes. Together, they made their way toward the barn.

Even though it wasn't yet three o'clock in the afternoon, a bonfire was already crackling out back, sending up wisps of fragrant smoke. Families sat around it, wrapped in flannel blankets, sipping on steaming cups of cider while kids ran around, their laughter filling the air.

And if Madison wasn't mistaken, the same musician from the Kettle last night was strumming a guitar in the background.

"Hey, you made it. And look who you brought with you," Liam greeted them inside the barn.

"This is amazing," Madison said, taking the barn in. The place smelled so cozy, like a candle factory in the fall—nutmeg, cinnamon, and cloves blended together, wrapping around Madison like a warm blanket. Shelves overflowed with hand-stitched towels, handmade soaps, artisan candles, decorative wreaths, baked goods, and plenty of sweatshirts with the farm's logo. Kids were eating sticky caramel apples and handfuls of kettle corn while their parents browsed the selection of gourmet jams, local honey, and handcrafted gifts.

"Here, let me take that from you." Liam took the handle of the cart and maneuvered it behind the counter.

"I'm going to have to keep a few of those, though," Kit said, turning back to Liam. "I promised Madison she could sample them before we finalize what we serve at the inn."

"Works for me. I'll set you up with a plate."

But before Liam could even grab a dish, a shout rang out across the farm. "Hey! The tractor's stuck! We need some help over here!" a farmhand hollered.

"Again?" Liam shook his head. "Always something."

Madison followed him out. She wasn't wearing muck-around boots like Liam, but she'd help if she could. It was just her way.

But when she got to where the tractor was stuck, she stopped short.

There was Zach. He stood behind the trailer, his sleeves pushed up to his elbows, revealing strong, tanned forearms corded with muscle. His jaw was clenched in concentration, his brows furrowed as he braced his stance, boots digging into the dirt as the farmhand revved the engine.

The mid-afternoon sun hit just right, highlighting his blonde hair, the sharp angles of his face and the sheen of sweat at his temple as he exhaled hard and pushed with everything he had.

God, he was something. Brutal, stubborn, beautiful.

Madison found herself staring, heat pooling low in her belly before she could even try to stop it.

For a brief moment, nothing happened. The wheels spun, stuck in the soft earth, but Zach didn't let up. He adjusted his grip, bending slightly, his broad shoulders flexing beneath his shirt.

Madison felt her breath hitch, her entire body hot and under pressure, like a volcano waiting to blow. Memories of his strength, the way he'd once held her up against the side of his truck, making love to her under a starlit sky, came rushing back with dizzying force.

Then, with one final powerful shove, the tractor lurched forward, breaking free of the rut.

The crowd erupted into cheers, clapping and whistling. Even Liam gave an impressed nod.

Zach, meanwhile, just rolled his shoulders, brushing it off as if he rescued hayrides on a regular basis.

Madison, however, could barely breathe. She swallowed hard, her heart hammering against her ribs.

Because, hell.

Zach Whitaker had always been strong, but there was something about seeing him like this. He looked solid, capable, completely in control, and it sent a shiver racing down her spine.

There was a primal, magnetic pull to him now. Not just the way his muscles flexed, but the way he threw himself into the work without hesitation. The stubbornness. The grit. The heat. He was grounded in a way that made something inside her twist and ache. The feeling was deep and secret and hungry. All Madison could think about was how it had felt to have that body pressed flush against hers the night before. The alley. His hands. His mouth.

She was feeling way, way more than she should. The need, sharp and electric, hummed under her skin. The memories, bittersweet and aching, pressed against the edges of her heart.

Because no matter how much time had passed, no matter how many walls she'd tried to build, one look at Zach, and she was right back to where it had all started.

Now the question was, what was she going to do about it?

TWENTY-TWO
ZACH

Zach hadn't expected to see Madison there. He'd thought she'd be busy at the inn.

One second, he was focused on the tractor, digging his boots into the dirt and using every ounce of strength to push it free. The next, he glanced up and there she was—standing at the edge of the crowd, her green eyes wide, lips parted just slightly.

His stomach did that stupid twisting thing it always did at the sight of her.

She stood there in her oversized sweater, hands on her hips, hair tumbling in messy waves down her back, and he had to remind himself to breathe.

Zach rolled his shoulders, wiped his hands on his jeans, and pretended he didn't feel her gaze burning into him. He caught Liam's eye, gave a nod, and planned to get back to work. But as he turned, he caught sight of Madison again, just for a second.

She was standing a few feet away, arms crossed over her chest now, eyebrows raised, a smile playing around her mouth.

He wiped a hand over his jaw then took a few slow steps toward her. He kept his voice low, so only she could hear. "Like the look of farm work, city girl?" His lips turned up in the corner just enough to be teasing.

Madison blinked. "I—" She huffed a breath. "I'm just surprised you didn't demand a trophy or something. That was quite the show."

Zach smiled fully. "Didn't need one. The look on your face was enough."

Her eyes narrowed and she stepped closer, tilting her chin up at him. "You really think that highly of yourself, huh?"

He shrugged. "I might not know much, but I know when someone's impressed."

Madison exhaled a laugh, shaking her head, but he caught the way she glanced at his arms before she could stop herself.

It had stung when she'd turned down his offer of coffee that morning. But that spark between them, the one he'd tried to ignore for years, was still there. Still crackling. Light a match, and they'd go up in flames.

He should walk away, like she had. Be smart. Keep things easy between them.

His brain knew that, but his body had other ideas. Zach knew she still noticed him, still wanted him, even if she wasn't ready to admit it.

And he liked it. Liked that he still had that effect on her, even though he knew they could never work.

He leaned in just slightly, his voice dipping low. "Careful, Mads. Keep looking at me like that, and I might start thinking you missed me."

Then, before she could fire back, he winked and turned, strolling off toward Liam like he wasn't entirely aware of the way she was still staring after him.

"That was some show," Liam said when Zach walked over to him.

"Shut up, man," Zach replied with a shake of his head.

"I don't know, it looked like Madison was into it. What are you gonna do about that?" Liam asked.

"What do you mean, what am I going to do about that? Nothing. She'll be out of here in a minute, just like every other time she's dropped into town since our early twenties." Zach tried to keep the bitterness from his voice but failed.

"Rumor has it she might be staying this time," Liam said casually.

Zach's head snapped up. "What? Where'd you hear that?"

"Your mom told my mom. Something about a festival meeting at the café? That's all I know." Liam shrugged, tossing a small white pumpkin from hand to hand.

Zach tried to act like that information didn't change anything. Like the Earth hadn't just shifted on its axis.

"Look, man, if you're looking for a green flag, here's your chance," continued Liam. "Every time you look at each other, fireworks go off in your eyes—both of you. Hell, seeing the two of you together, all hot and flustered, makes me wanna have a cigarette, and I haven't smoked a day in my life." Liam laughed.

Zach cracked a smile despite himself, but his gut was a mess.

He bent down and started stacking pumpkins onto a wagon, needing something to do with his hands.

Madison Kelly wasn't just any girl. She was the only one who had ever wrecked him—and the only one he hadn't been able to forget.

Zach shoved the last pumpkin into place and stalked off toward the barn.

If Madison was really staying, that could change everything.

But could he risk opening his heart again?

TWENTY-THREE

MADISON

That evening, Madison pulled her mom's handwritten recipe for cinnamon rolls out of her beloved family recipe book for Kit to review. The index card was yellowed from age, but her mom's scripted writing was as elegant as Madison remembered it. She didn't need to look at the card for the recipe. Madison knew it by heart.

But still, she stared at it, her fingers tracing over the indentation of the ink as she pictured her mom writing out the recipe all those years ago.

"Mind if I take a picture of it?" Kit asked, taking out her phone.

"No, go for it. That's probably the best way to do it." There was no way Madison was lending the card out.

Kit skimmed over the recipe. "Buttermilk? No wonder they tasted so good."

"Mmm-hmm, that and lots of butter."

And before long, Madison was biting into her mom's cinnamon roll for the first time in three years. The soft, yeasty roll, the layers of cinnamon sugar, the sweet, creamy icing. Tears instantly came to her eyes.

"I take it I nailed it?" Kit asked hopefully.

"This is heavenly. I honestly can't thank you enough." Madison grabbed a napkin and wiped away her tears before she completely lost it. Having her mom's cinnamon rolls there, in her kitchen, made it feel like part of her was still alive with them.

"Should we try it with the apple butter, or no?" Kit held up a jar of Zach's apple butter.

Madison nodded, wiping away her tears once more. "Sure," she said, clearing her throat and trying to pull herself together.

Kit slathered on a thick slab of the butter right on top of the icing.

"Cheers," Kit said, breaking the roll in two and handing half to Madison. The roll pulled apart easily, soft and pillowy, still warm from the oven.

Madison didn't think they could've improved her mom's recipe, but here she was, officially in pastry heaven. "This is so good," she said, licking her fingers. It shouldn't have worked—but it did. Just like the inn. Just like her and Zach.

"I think we have a winner," Kit agreed.

In high spirits, Madison and Kit cleaned up the kitchen and took a bottle of red wine and some glasses down to the waterfront. The sweet, buttery scent of cinnamon still clung to their clothes, mixing with the brisk autumn breeze that rolled off the water.

The shoreline shimmered under the moonlight, silver ripples rolling in. Madison pulled her cardigan tighter around her shoulders as they crossed the worn path leading to the firepit area. Her boots crunched over stray acorns along the way. Her dad had built up a fire, even though there weren't any guests tonight. Normally, she'd expect to see him and Gram out here, but the chairs sat empty, their usual mugs of tea nowhere in sight.

Madison's gaze drifted past the fire toward the honeymoon

cabin at the edge of the property. The windows were dark. Empty.

She exhaled, turning her focus back to Kit as she sat beside her.

"This is the life." Kit sighed, taking a deep breath. "I mean, I thought I wanted to be in the city, but nothing beats this fresh air. Am I right?"

"It is nice," Madison admitted, stretching her legs out toward the fire.

Kit squinted at her. "But?"

Madison exhaled, swirling the wine in her glass. "I don't know anymore. Things in New York were fun and exciting, and I absolutely loved it."

"Loved?" Kit pounced on the past tense.

Madison smirked. "Are you always this inquisitive?"

Kit beamed. "Always."

"Jo is there," Madison added as a matter of fact, as if that answered anything.

"Who's Jo? Do we like him? Do we hate him? What's the story there?"

Madison laughed. "Jo is my best friend. And he is a she."

"Ooooh," Kit said, dragging the sound out with interest.

"She basically took me under her wing when I moved there. I knew I wanted to be a food writer, but I didn't have any connections. Jo had already made it—she'd opened her own restaurant. We met at a wine tasting, hit it off, and she put me in touch with the right people. I wrote a few articles, and my career just... took off."

Kit studied her. "You feel like you owe her?"

Madison shook her head. She knew that she and Jo would always be close, no matter where she lived. "Not exactly. I felt like I belonged in New York with her. I love my job. But coming back home, seeing everything that needs to be done and remembering what it feels like to be here? It makes me feel... unsettled. Unsure. Life in New York can be a lot..."

Madison involuntarily looked back toward the cabin. She was instantly annoyed with herself. She hated how much space Zach took up in her mind—even when he wasn't here. How just the memory of him leaning in close, voice low and teasing, could make her heart stutter.

It was ridiculous. She wasn't some lovesick teenager anymore.

Kit took a sip of her wine, watching her over the rim of her glass. "Is there a special someone in New York you're thinking about?"

"New York? No. Is there a special someone in Maple Falls you're thinking about?"

Kit grinned. "The only thing that holds my heart is cheesecake."

Madison laughed, but Kit wasn't letting her off the hook.

"So, no one serious?" Kit pressed.

Madison hesitated, then shrugged. "I've dated a few men in the city, but nothing's ever lasted. I mean, they were... fine."

Kit gave her a knowing look. "But something was always missing?"

Madison sighed, swirling her wine again. "Yeah, exactly. They were polished, successful. They had their careers together, knew who they were... but none of them ever made me feel the way—"

She stopped herself, staring across the lake. The moonlight shimmered on the water's glassy surface, too still, too revealing.

"... the way Zach made me feel." The words slipped out before she could stop them. The first time she'd ever admitted it —to herself or anyone else.

Kit grinned. "Honey, you've been comparing every man to Zach this whole time, haven't you?"

Madison groaned, tipping her head back. "Apparently."

Kit bumped her shoulder gently. "Hey, you're talking to the queen of impossible standards. Try finding a woman who's smart, can bake, likes horror movies, and understands the difference between a Cabernet and a Syrah in a town of fifteen hundred."

Madison blinked, surprised—and then smiled, the pieces clicking into place. "You ever think about looking outside Maple Falls?"

Kit shrugged, playful but a little wistful. "Maybe someday. For now, I'm holding out hope that my soulmate is hiding in a corn maze somewhere, waiting for me to rescue her."

Madison laughed, the sound bubbling up more easily this time. "Well, if anyone can find her, it's you."

Kit raised her glass. "To soulmates, wherever the hell they are."

Madison looked back at the cabin once more. It was still dark. Still empty.

She told herself it was just nostalgia. Just the season. Just the magic of Maple Falls playing tricks on her.

But deep down, she knew better. Because no matter how much she tried to deny it, to stuff it down or pretend it didn't exist, the truth was terrifying in its simplicity:

She still wanted him. And he still wanted her too.

She wanted her career. But she also wanted the only man who'd ever really had her heart.

Madison tipped her head back, watching a thin trail of smoke from the fire disappear into the vast, star-strewn sky.

"To impossible standards," she whispered under her breath.

It would have been far too easy to finish off the bottle of Merlot by the fireside with Kit, letting the night and the wine take her thoughts away. The air had turned cold, the kind of chill that hinted winter wasn't far behind, and the lake glistened under a blanket of stars. The fire crackled and popped beside them, keeping them warm as long as they stayed close.

Still, Madison knew there was too much work waiting for her at the inn the next day—too many lists, too many repairs, too much riding on getting everything right. So, instead, they called it an early night, and she headed inside.

Gram was in the great room, curled up in the recliner. Another fire crackled in the hearth, complementing the soft glow of the Tiffany lamps on the end tables. A plate of her famous shortbread cookies sat on the coffee table next to a pot of tea.

"Back early," Gram said as Madison came in through the back door.

"Figured I should call it a night, especially with everything that needs to be done around here."

"I hear you there. But if anyone can do it, it's you. Shortbread?" Gram motioned toward the plate.

"Why not?" Madison reached for one and settled onto the couch. Gram's shortbread was *almost* as famous as Madison's mom's cinnamon rolls. The only reason why it wasn't was because Gram didn't bake it for just anyone. The woman was rather particular with who she shared it with.

Madison munched on the buttery cookie and looked about the room. She stopped, taking in the patchwork quilt draped over the couch, and a wave of nostalgia hit her.

Her mother had made that quilt when Madison was a child. She still remembered helping to pin out the squares, lining them up just so. Madison hadn't quite mastered it yet, but her mom had been patient—unlike Madison.

Madison reached for the quilt and curled up with it on the couch. She continued to look about the room. Her mother's presence was everywhere—the old recipe books stacked on the shelf, the tea lights arranged on the fireplace mantel, even the rug beneath the coffee table.

"You look tired, Honey Pie," Gram said softly.

Madison leaned her head back on the couch. "Maybe I am, just a bit."

"You know, your mom loved this place," Gram continued. "But she loved you more. You don't have to fix everything on your own."

Madison tried not to feel defensive, but she couldn't help it.

"I want to do this, and I know I can." Emotion built up in her chest. "You remember how great this place used to be, Gram. We had reservations booked months out, the dining room was always packed. It might've been small, but it was respected." She swallowed, her fingers gripping the quilt a little tighter. "Now it feels like a ghost house. I want to see it thrive again."

"Well, just don't try to do too much on your own. Let us help you more, or we'll find someone who can," Gram gently urged.

Madison barely heard her. Her eyes had wandered out the back window, where she could see the cabin down by the lake. A light flicked on inside.

Zach was home.

Noticing a sparkle in Gram's eye, Madison fought to change the subject.

She took a steadying breath and then said, "I got a letter."

Gram looked up, her brow lifting. "A letter?"

Madison nodded. "Someone sent me a typed letter. It said the inn was in trouble. Asked me to come home. But there was no signature; I don't know who sent it."

Gram set her tea down carefully. "A typed letter? Well, you know that didn't come from me. I hate computers. I'd have just picked up the phone and told you like it is."

Madison let out a small laugh. "I know you would. So why didn't you?"

Gram thought for a moment, then sighed. "I guess it's one of those things... You don't realize how bad something's gotten when it changes little by little each day." She took another sip of tea. "Whoever sent that letter did us all a favor. When you find out who it was, let me know—I'd like to send them a thank-you note."

"Don't say anything to Dad, though, okay? About the letter. I don't want to hurt his feelings."

Gram pursed her lips. Then, instead of answering, she asked, "Do you know how he rescued Cocoa?"

Madison frowned. "I assumed from a shelter?" Madison had stopped paying attention to where her dad picked up the animals from.

"That dog showed up in a crate on our porch," Gram said with a nod. "And if I'm not mistaken, there was an anonymous letter with her too."

Madison straightened, her mind running with the new information. "Wait—you think it's connected? Could it have been Anita? Or Mayor Bloomfield? What about Mrs. Bishop? She seems to be in everyone's business."

Gram shook her head. "Now that, I don't know. But it looks like this family has got itself a guardian angel." She leaned back in her chair. "And we'd better do right by them and get this inn back in tip-top shape."

TWENTY-FOUR

ZACH

October 16th

Ever a creature of habit, Zach stood barefoot on the front porch of the honeymoon cabin. He was holding a mug of black coffee in one hand, the other on his hip, as he stared across the lake. He'd grown accustomed to starting his mornings this way. There was no better view, except for when Madison stopped by on her daily run.

This cabin had seen better days with its missing window screens, loose porch rails, and dated fixtures, but it still had charm and he liked it out here. Liked the quiet, the space to breathe, especially when he was preparing for a busy day ahead. Three days ago, he'd overheard Madison's grand plan to revamp the inn in time for Halloween. She had fire in her eyes when she spoke about it, and whether or not he wanted to admit it, that fire still got to him. What she cared about, he cared about.

He'd already repaired the ceiling in the dining room and fixed up the exterior, and now, he wanted to talk to her about adding pine overlay to tie everything together. Make it feel cozy, warm. Something that felt like her mother's touch still lingered here. Meredith would have liked that.

Zach missed Meredith. He had never talked to Madison about it. Couldn't share his condolences because she'd avoided him at the funeral. He'd longed to go to her, to give her a hug, but she'd kept her distance and he'd respected that.

Her mom had been the kindest, warmest soul. She'd brought out the softer side of Madison, and she'd welcomed Zach into the family. It couldn't have been easy, your only daughter getting serious with her first boyfriend. But Meredith and George hadn't made life hard for them. If anything, they'd made it easy—inviting Zach over for the holidays, buying him a present for his birthday, treating Madison and Zach's relationship with respect.

The inn felt like his second home. And now he could build, fix, patch, shape things back into something worth loving again.

He took a last sip of lukewarm coffee, and soon he was headed toward the inn to look for his tools. He swore he'd left them in the kitchen. Or maybe it was the office. After coming up empty-handed in both spots, he stood in the middle of the lobby.

The space was mostly empty except for Cocoa, who immediately bounded over, barking like Zach was public enemy number one. The tiny pup pranced on the worn floral carpet, begging for attention. Zach bent low and scratched her between her ears.

"You seen my tools, girl?" he muttered.

"Back pantry," Edith's voice said as she joined them. "I saw them last night when I was making shortbread."

Sure. Why not? The pantry makes perfect sense.

Zach managed an "Alright, thanks," and headed that way.

It wasn't Edith's fault he was such poor company.

No, the problem was Madison. He'd been working hard on the inn each day, and yet Zach hadn't slept a full night since he'd kissed her behind the Kettle. And now he knew she might be staying, but he didn't know if he could believe it. Not yet.

He'd lain awake hour after hour, staring at the cabin ceiling, one arm slung over his face like it could somehow block out the memories. The way her body had curved into his. The way she used to brush sleepy kisses over the side of his neck before sliding on top of him, warm and so eager, it made him crazy just remembering.

He swore he could still smell her some nights—coffee and ginger, like autumn leaves clinging to his sheets.

He hadn't even touched her since that kiss in the alley, but it didn't matter. Every nerve ending he had was already attuned to her again.

Every time he heard her voice across the lobby, or caught a glimpse of her laugh crinkling the corners of her eyes, something inside him went hot and restless and furious all at once.

Zach strode toward the small pantry in the corner of the kitchen. Why the hell someone had stored his tools here was beyond him. He should've just kept them at the cabin.

As soon as he stepped inside, he smelled her.

Apples and ginger. A sweet and spicy scent that made his pulse race and his blood rush.

Zach shook his head and focused on finding his tools.

A light would've been good; the pantry was original, built in the home in the late 1940s. It was more like a broom cupboard than anything else.

He had half a second to reach for his phone, to flick on the flashlight, when—

Someone walked right into him. It was Maddie. He could tell by the little surprised sound she made when the door clicked shut.

His hands instinctively caught her arms, steadying her. "Mads," Zach said, voice low, rough, already betraying everything he was trying to hold back.

She sucked in a breath, her hands bracing against his chest. "What are you doing in here?"

"Looking for my tools. You?"

"Cast-iron skillet. Kit's coming over... we're making cornbread." Her voice wavered. Just enough for him to hear it.

Just enough to make every cell in his body tighten with need. Zach hadn't thought it was possible to want the woman any more than he already did. But here they were, mere inches apart, and his body was aching to hold her.

The pantry was tiny, barely big enough for one person let alone two. They stood together in the darkness, her hands on his chest. He could feel her pulse syncing with his.

And he knew with absolute certainty that if she let him in, it would change everything.

In the darkness, trapped there together, it felt like they were suspended in time. The air was different. Thicker. Charged.

Zach feared moving. Feared breaking the moment. But he couldn't stand there forever. Not when the woman he wanted more than breathing was mere inches away.

Zach took a step closer, reaching for her waist, pulling her against him.

And when she didn't pull away, when her fingers curled slightly into his shirt, hesitant but inviting, it was all the permission he needed.

His hand found her cheek, tilting her face toward him. He didn't need to see her. He knew her—the curve of her lips, the slope of her nose.

He could feel the way her breath hitched, the way her body leaned into his without hesitation.

Her hands slid to his hips, gripping, anchoring. He bent forward, achingly slow, and captured her mouth in a kiss.

It was soft at first; his lips grazed hers, once, twice, three times before she pulled him deeper, taking charge and not letting him go.

It was everything he wanted and not enough at the same time.

He shouldn't want Madison anymore, not after all these years. He shouldn't even dream of wanting her.

But by God, all he could think about was her. The fire in her eyes, the sharp wit of her tongue.

He didn't know when raw animal instinct had taken over. But suddenly, his hands were gripping her waist roughly, desperately, sliding beneath the hem of her soft sweater, fingers finding the bare skin at the small of her back. Her voice whispering his name.

TWENTY-FIVE

MADISON

The first brush of his mouth was maddeningly slow, barely a tease. But the second was deeper. Hotter. Demanding.

Madison let out a small whimper against his lips. She couldn't think. Could barely breathe. It was really going to happen this time.

All she could do was feel.

The years fell away in a heartbeat.

There was no past or future, no hurt, no fear, no promises broken.

Only this. Only them.

She fisted his shirt, dragging him closer, opening to him. He groaned low in his throat, sliding his hands beneath her sweater —rough palms on bare skin, searing a trail up her ribs.

Her body pressed instinctively into his, desperate for more.

His tongue swept into her mouth, tasting of caramel and chocolate, like he'd stolen one of Gram's cookies before finding her. She wanted to steal him.

In the small dark space they shared, surrounded by shelves of flour and spices, they could've been transported into another world.

Madison was hyperaware of Zach's breath, of the need building through her body, of the desire pulsing in his veins.

One alleyway kiss would never be enough. She wanted more.

She wanted everything.

She wanted to forget that the last six years had ever happened and just stay here, in this secret world with him, forever.

Madison sighed against his lips as the searing heat of his touch lit her nerves on fire.

A low, guttural sound rumbled from Zach's throat—a sound she felt more than heard, one that sent a thrill through her.

He wanted this just as badly as she did.

She smiled against his lips and her hands skimmed beneath his shirt, fingertips tracing the firm ridges of his stomach. His muscles twitched. God, it felt good to make him react this way.

There was no denying it. Madison wanted him. Bad. And Madison had never been one to hesitate. It was how she had taken the leap to New York in the first place, how she had built a career from nothing.

And right now, she wanted to take this all the way.

She knew all too well just how short life was, how the moments that defined it—the risks, the chance encounters, the reckless, passionate leaps—were what mattered.

This was it, right here. A moment to leap into the unknown. She wasn't looking beyond the horizon. She only wanted what was in front of her right now.

She felt him everywhere—his thigh pressing between hers, his arm around her back, his breath ragged against her cheek as he lifted her against the wall.

Her legs locked around his hips and he pushed into her once, twice, grinding against her in a way that made her whimper and clutch at his shoulders.

Then his mouth left hers to trail down her neck, pressing

hot, open-mouthed kisses against the hollow of her throat, the line of her collarbone. Every scrape of stubble, every exhale of his breath against her skin sent lightning bolts through her blood.

"Madison," he growled. "Tell me to stop. If you don't want this, you have to tell me now."

"Never." Madison cupped his face between her hands, dragging his mouth back to hers.

Zach shook his head, breaking the kiss. "I don't have a condom," he said, "but I can—"

Madison didn't let him finish the sentence. "I'm on the pill."

"Good."

Zach lifted her higher, pressing his hips against her again until she was clutching him tighter, feeling the heat spiral out of control.

"God, Mads," he muttered against her mouth. "I missed you. I missed this."

He leaned back just enough to reach the waistband of her jeans.

Madison tilted her hips, desperate for more.

He didn't hesitate. With a roughness that sent another shiver down her spine, Zach popped the button on her jeans and slipped his hand inside, fingers sliding beneath the thin cotton of her panties.

Madison let out a sharp exhale. It was part shock, part pure pleasure when his fingers found her already wet and wanting.

God, she was already so ready for him. There was no hiding that now.

Zach swore softly against her neck, like he was wrecked too, like he was barely hanging on.

"You're killing me," he rasped.

Then he kissed her again, hard, while his fingers moved against her with maddening skill—stroking, teasing, circling just right.

She gasped into his mouth, one hand braced against the shelves behind her, the other clutching his shoulder so tightly her knuckles ached.

The world narrowed to the slow, devastating drag of his fingers, the slick heat of her need. He knew exactly how to touch her. It was like he remembered every inch of her, every secret, responding to every sound she made when she was about to fall apart.

And she was falling apart.

Right here, right now, in his arms.

She was about to shatter for him when—

Bzzz. Bzzz. Bzzz.

The vibration rattled through the tiny pantry.

Madison barely registered it. She could hardly hear anything beyond the blood rushing in her ears and the pleasure building in her body.

She wasn't even sure what it was. Her cell phone? His cell phone? Did it even matter?

But it did.

For some god-awful reason it did.

Because one second she was about to come undone on Zach's hand and the next he was pulling away.

"What?" Madison whispered, dazed, still breathless, still trembling from the edge he'd driven her to. How could this be happening?

Cut short again, just like in her dream. Like the gods of sex, if there were any, were just having a great big laugh at her expense.

Zach exhaled sharply, dropping his forehead against hers for a heartbeat before stepping back so fast she nearly stumbled without him.

His expression shut down. "I shouldn't have—" His voice was rough, controlled, but she could hear the regret creeping in. "That shouldn't have happened."

Madison blinked, reality crashing into her.

"What?" she repeated, her mind still scrambling to process the shift—how only seconds ago, he had touched her like he needed her, like he couldn't breathe without her, and now...

Now, he was moving away like he'd made a terrible mistake. Again.

"That was wrong," he muttered, running a hand through his hair as he switched on the light on his phone, pointing it at the door and then trying to push it open.

Wrong. She felt the loss like a slap.

Her body still ached with the imprint of his hands, her lips still tingled from the way he'd taken her, like he'd wanted her so badly it physically hurt—and now he was going to act like it hadn't happened? Like something this good could just be wrong?

Hell no.

Madison squared her shoulders, her heartbeat hammering faster, anger rushing to the surface. "Wrong?"

Zach didn't meet her eyes, still shining his light and pushing at the door as if he couldn't get out quickly enough. "Yeah."

Madison laughed bitterly. "Funny. You didn't seem to think it was *wrong* when you had your hand down my pants." She pointed down to her unzipped jeans.

Zach clenched his jaw. "Mads."

"No. Go ahead. Say it," she snapped, arms crossed so tightly she couldn't breathe. "Tell me you didn't want it. Tell me you haven't been thinking about this, about me, about what we had. Tell me it was just the heat of the moment, a mistake. Say it, Zach."

His silence was answer enough.

"That's what I thought." Madison looked away.

She couldn't believe this man.

Even worse, she hated how much she still wanted him, even

as she wanted to shake him, scream at him, make him admit the truth.

But instead, he did what Zach always did. He shut down.

He turned, banging his fist against the pantry door. "Edith!" His voice sounded gruff, impatient. "Door's stuck."

Footsteps echoed on the other side of the door, and a second later, it opened.

Gram stood there, eyes twinkling with amusement. "Well, well. What do we have here?"

Madison barely heard her.

Zach was already grabbing his tools and brushing past, mumbling a "thanks" before disappearing through the kitchen.

Madison looked past her grandma and watched him go, unable to process all that had just happened.

"What did I miss?" Gram asked innocently.

TWENTY-SIX
ZACH

Zach stalked across the lobby, tools in hand, jaw clenched so tight he thought his molars might crack. He would've walked right off the inn's property and never looked back if he hadn't already agreed to the job. A job he planned to finish, no matter how much it killed him.

The air smelled like cinnamon rolls and fresh paint, and Zach wanted to escape it more than he'd ever wanted to escape anything in his life.

What the hell were you thinking? he bit out silently.

From the moment he'd laid eyes on Madison again, he should have known better. It didn't matter how many years had passed—she was still the same spark to his dry timber, and he was still the fool ready to burn for her.

He was a goddamn idiot.

"Zach, there you are, my boy." George's voice rang out as he stepped into the dining room, a half-eaten cinnamon roll in his hand. "How's the work coming along?"

Zach clenched his jaw, forcing his expression into something neutral.

"Dining room's fine," he said, his voice gruffer than

intended. "Structurally, everything's set. Just need to know if you want another coat of paint or if you'd rather finish it with knotty pine to match the rest of the place."

George chewed thoughtfully, then grinned. "Well, now, that's a Madison question." He turned toward the kitchen. "Why don't we ask her ourselves? I saw her headed this way just now."

Zach felt like he was in his own personal hell. His planned escape hadn't gotten him very far.

"Morning, Maddie," her father said with jolly good cheer. "Did you hear? Zach's just about done with the dining room. He said something about pine or paint. What was it again there?"

Zach didn't meet Madison's eyes; instead, he answered her dad directly.

"Knotty pine. They sell it in planks in town. Thought it would be nice to tie in with the place."

George raised his eyebrows at Madison. "What do you think?"

Zach risked a glance.

And—yeah. If looks could kill, he'd be six feet under.

She stood stiffly, arms crossed over her chest, her expression tight. Those green eyes, usually sparkling with humor or mischief, were guarded now. Angry.

Good.

Let her be angry.

It couldn't come close to whatever the hell he was feeling.

Because one look at her, and his body remembered every desperate kiss, every panting moan, every inch of skin he had tasted before reality had sucker-punched him.

It was her phone. A message he hadn't meant to see but couldn't unsee.

He hadn't caught all of it, just enough to shatter him.

An image. Personal, private. Clearly sent to her by Jo. The guy from New York.

He hadn't meant to look—but it didn't matter. It was burned into his brain now.

And it ripped through him like a blade.

Because no matter how badly he wanted her, no matter how perfect she still felt in his arms, she wasn't his. And he wasn't the kind of man who stole another man's girl, no matter how much it killed him.

Zach shoved the ache down. Buried it deep.

Hell, he hadn't even meant to touch her, but all it took was five seconds in a dark space, their bodies pressed against each other, and all self-control in him snapped.

It was years of passion and longing, of remembering what it was like to be with her, to have her in his arms.

Being with Madison was a thirst he couldn't quench. He'd drown before ever being satisfied, and it scared the hell out of him.

That alone should've been enough for him to step back, but it hadn't been. He'd been seconds away from making her come and then burying himself inside of her. It would've been fast and hard, and just a taste of what he could give her.

If that text message had never come across, he would've had her come undone not once but twice in that pantry before carrying her off to the cabin to do it all over again. Slower this time. Painstakingly so until she melted beneath him.

That fucking text message.

And yet—she had let him touch her. She had kissed him back, like she felt it too.

Had she just been using him?

Madison had always been too bright, too big, and too much for this town. She had dreams, ambitions, and a life waiting for her in New York, and Zach knew exactly where that left him—in the rearview mirror, just like before.

"Sounds good," Madison said shortly, bringing him back to the present. She looked around the dining room, not meeting his gaze. She was professional, distant.

Fine. Two could play that game.

"Great," George said, clapping Zach on the back. "You two can sort out the details."

Zach nodded once and turned to walk out of the room before Madison could say another word.

He needed air. He needed to remember who the hell he was. He was a professional, a man who kept his promises. He had a job to do—and he was going to do it. Even if it killed him.

Even if every single day spent working on this inn, with Madison right here, so close yet so far away, drove him completely out of his mind.

He was staying and finishing what he started.

But Jesus Christ...

How was he supposed to keep his hands off her now?

TWENTY-SEVEN

MADISON

October 18th

Madison had never been more furious in her life.

Well. That was probably an exaggeration. But Zachariah James Whitaker was doing his best to climb the ranks of men she wanted to strangle.

Two days ago, he hadn't just touched her. No, he had destroyed her. They'd been seconds away from having hot animal sex in the pantry.

And then he'd just walked away. Like it was nothing, like she was nothing.

Now, he had the nerve to act like everything was normal.

Madison caught sight of him through the front window, loading a few last pieces of lumber from his truck. His body was relaxed, his movements easy and under control. Clearly, she wasn't even on his radar. The nerve of him.

Madison practically growled as she yanked the final bundle of autumn garlands from the storage bin. She would not let him ruin this day.

She hadn't come back to Maple Falls for him. She had more

important things to focus on. Her family. The inn. So if Zach wanted to act like their kiss never happened?

Fine. Two could play that game. She stomped toward the front porch, where a delivery truck was backing in with a fresh shipment of pumpkins, hay bales, and cornstalks—her grand vision for a fall harvest display that would make her mother proud.

Gram was already waiting by the curb, supervising with all the authority of an army general.

"Oh, good, Maddie," Gram said, glancing up as Madison approached. "I was just about to send someone to find you. We need all this set up before sundown."

Madison looked at the size of the delivery truck. It was going to be a lot, but she could handle it. "Don't worry. I've got it."

"Good." Gram nodded approvingly. "Are there any extra fall leaves upstairs? We've got our craft circle at Dolores's next week. I need a few."

Madison thought back to the totes upstairs. "There's probably enough."

"Could use an extra pair of hands there, too. Or at least some fresh eyes on the glitter choices."

Madison grinned. "I'll think about it."

"Thinking about it means you're already halfway there," Gram replied with a wink. Then, like the devil himself had sent her, Gram waved Zach over.

Madison froze. "You have got to be kidding me," she muttered under her breath.

"Zach, sweetheart," Gram called, smiling sweetly as he wiped his hands on his jeans and made his way over. "Be a dear and help Maddie with this, will you?"

Zach's expression didn't change, but Madison saw the tension in his shoulders.

"Gram, I can do it," Madison said quickly.

"Nonsense." Gram waved her off. "Zach's got those strong arms, and you've got..." She trailed off, eyeing Madison up and down before sighing. "Enthusiasm."

Zach smirked. The first real flicker of amusement she'd seen from him all day.

It infuriated her. She didn't care how strong his arms looked hefting hay bales like they weighed nothing. She didn't care how the sleeves of his worn flannel shirt clung to his biceps in all the right places. She definitely didn't care how the low afternoon sun caught the lighter strands in his hair.

"Fine," Madison bit out, hefting a half-bale of hay into her arms. "Let's get this over with."

Madison went a little overboard decorating the front porch. She attached bunches of cornstalks to each and every white column, stacked over two dozen pumpkins along the front steps, arranged the front planter boxes full of sunflowers and chrysanthemums, and added hay bales as extra seating along the way.

Lifting pumpkins and hay bales should not have been intimate work. And yet somehow, it was.

Maybe it was because every time Madison turned around, Zach was right there.

Maybe it was because the first time their hands brushed over the same pumpkin, a jolt of electricity shot up her arm so fast she nearly dropped it. Maybe it was because he was avoiding her eyes so much that she wanted to grab his stupid, handsome face and force him to look at her.

But mostly, it was because every time she took a step, he seemed to be in her way.

She was starting to think he was doing it on purpose.

Madison spun around, a half-bale in her arms—only to slam straight into a solid wall of muscle.

Zach caught her shoulders on instinct, his fingers warm and firm—but he let go too quickly, like touching her burned him.

"Jesus, Mads," he muttered, stepping back.

"Oh, excuse me, am I in your way?" Madison snapped, eyes flashing. "Because I don't recall you being the one carrying half a bale of hay—"

"I told you, I'm helping," Zach said, gruff, avoiding her gaze. "That's what I do."

Oh, that does it.

Madison dropped the hay bale, planting her hands on her hips. "What is wrong with you?"

"Nothing," Zach snapped.

"Bullshit," she shot back.

His jaw ticked. "I'm just trying to be professional."

Oh, hell no.

Before Madison could verbally cut into him, Gram showed up.

"I've been thinking about that letter you got," Gram said.

What?! Where did that come from and why now? Madison stiffened. She hadn't planned on mentioning a word of it to Zach.

Zach, standing beside her, frowned. "Letter?"

Gram just kept right on going. "Oh, haven't you heard?" she said, her tone far too casual. "Madison got a mysterious letter saying the inn was in trouble. Asked her to come home."

Honestly, what with all her work on the inn, Madison still hadn't had much time to think about the writer's identity.

Zach straightened, turning to her fully now, his expression sharpening.

"You got a letter?"

Madison cleared her throat. "Fine. Just before I got here, someone sent me a letter. No signature. No return address. It just said that the inn was in trouble—and that I needed to come home."

Zach's frown deepened. She could practically see his brain kicking in, trying to solve it. That was Zach. He solved problems. It's what he did. It was one of the things they had in common, their love of solving things.

But the way they went about it was completely opposite. Zach was calm, calculated. He took his time to figure things out. Like when they were younger and did summer scavenger hunts down at the library. Zach would take time to analyze the clues and look for the hidden meanings, while Madison took off, guns blazing.

They made a good team really, but she didn't want his help with this. It was personal, and anyway, he clearly didn't want anything to do with her. He'd made that abundantly clear.

"Why didn't you say something?" he asked.

"Say something? To you?" She laughed without humor. "Oh, I don't know, maybe because I've been a little busy?" She gestured around them, where deliveries were still being unpacked, flowers waiting to be potted, and pumpkins placed just so. "And, you know, maybe because every time I turn around, you're pretending like I don't exist?"

Gram suddenly became very interested in adjusting the pumpkin display on the steps.

Zach's jaw tightened. Madison swore he was going to say something just as biting, but then he said, "And you have no idea who sent it?"

"Nope," Madison said. She didn't mean to pop the P, but she couldn't help it when she was around him. She felt explosive. "But I do know one thing: It worked. I'm here." She held her hands out at her sides, palms out.

The truth was, Madison hated not knowing.

She hated that someone had reached across time and distance, poked right into the softest, most protected part of her heart, and dragged her back here without even signing their name.

Gram clapped her hands, jolting Madison out of her spiraling thoughts.

"As I was saying," Gram chirped, "I was thinking about that letter, and I realized I know someone who might help. Anita. Everyone talks at the café. I figure if anyone's heard anything, it'd be her."

Zach spoke up. "Yeah. In fact... she got a letter too."

"What?" Madison's head whipped toward him.

"It was about the inn as well," Zach said, casual as anything —like it wasn't the biggest bombshell of the day.

"She did?" Madison looked between Zach and Gram.

Gram shrugged her shoulders.

"What did it say?" Madison pressed.

"I have no idea. I didn't actually see it. Mom just told me about it. She asked if I would come help out at the inn, just after the tree fell down in the storm. It wasn't a hard sell, since I already planned on it. But we knew George wouldn't accept charity, which is why I agreed to fix up the cabin in exchange for a place to stay. Anyway, I guess it's possible she knows more about who might have sent it."

So, Zach hadn't been staying on the property just to torment her. He'd been doing something kind.

But who had started this? Who had written those letters? They weren't just pulling strings. They were pulling at the very heart of what, and who, Madison cared about most.

"Well, I know where you two kids are headed off to." Gram clapped her hands together, effectively sealing their fate. "Do you want me to call Anita and tell her you're on your way?"

Zach glanced at his watch. "The lunch rush should be over. She should have a minute."

Madison hesitated, glancing at the crates of pumpkins and decorations still waiting to be sorted. She hated leaving Gram with all of it, hated feeling like she was letting anyone down.

But this mattered too. She had to find out what was going on, she just had to.

"Go on, get out of here. I'll get started on this and give Hank a call, see if he can lend me a hand."

Zach took a step closer, so close she could catch a hint of soap and sawdust clinging to his skin. "Come on," he said, his voice low, his eyes catching hers, and holding. "Let's go."

His fingers brushed lightly against her back as he guided her toward the steps. It was barely a touch, but it lit up her skin like a live wire.

Madison knew she should pull away. Tell him she didn't need his help. Not when she still tasted him in every breath she took.

But instead, she followed after him. Almost as hungry for the truth as she was for his touch.

TWENTY-EIGHT

MADISON

The afternoon air had turned chilly and Madison shivered, wishing she'd worn more than just her thin knit sweater and faded jeans. Her hands were already cold and her cheeks tingled from the wind. A cozy jacket, a scarf, anything more would've been smart.

Zach, on the other hand, seemed as comfortable as could be in his thermal shirt, sleeves pulled up, hands casually in his pockets. Absolutely maddening.

The downtown streets had already been closed off in preparation for tomorrow's festival, with wooden barricades marking each end of Oak Way, effectively turning the area into one big street party. Vendors were in the midst of setting up their festival booths, featuring handmade crafts and other goods like local jars of honey, artisanal soaps, and jewelry.

The Pumpkinfest wasn't just about a celebration of fall with pumpkin spiced lattes and scarecrow contests, although there were plenty of those. No, it was a celebration of Maple Falls itself, where people from far and wide came together to shop, eat, and take in the magic of the town.

The street corners were lit with gas fireplaces, each

surrounded by decorative concrete and clusters of Adirondack chairs. People were already gathering, pulling up seats with steaming cups of mulled cider and hot buttered rum, chatting around the warmth of the fire. There was a relaxed warmth to it all, a sense of belonging so natural it almost made Madison ache. No rushing, no jostling crowds, no clipped conversations over takeaway coffees. Just neighbors lingering, swapping stories, savoring the change of season together like even the gap between every moment mattered.

Madison let herself absorb it all, just for a moment. The leaves swirling in the air, the twinkle lights strung between lampposts, the sound of laughter, and the occasional strum of an acoustic guitar from a street musician. This life was what she had missed. And she hadn't even realized it.

Despite Zach's insistence that they walk down to the café together, he didn't say a word. And she was hardly going to break the silence.

Madison didn't know if she could handle talking to him without snapping. One wrong word out of his mouth, and she might just lose it right here in the middle of downtown.

She bit the inside of her cheek, stuffed her hands into her sweater sleeves, and kept walking.

"Twice in one week—well, isn't this a surprise!" Anita greeted them with a warm smile as they stepped into the Maple Leaf Café. "And with my son, no less."

"Mom," Zach said flatly.

Before he could say more, Madison spoke up. "We actually have something we need to talk to you about," she said.

Anita's brows lifted slightly, curiosity in her eyes. "Given the looks on your faces, I'd say this calls for some tea. Why don't you two pop over to that corner booth? I'll join you in a minute."

Zach and Madison did as they were told. Madison tried to ignore the curious glances from the other patrons, like Mr.

Alders from the hardware store, and Mrs. Humphrey, having a late lunch with her schnauzer.

Madison read the chalkboard menu hung up by the register. The daily special was a melt with roasted turkey, sharp cheddar, and thinly sliced apples on grilled multigrain bread. And the soup of the day was roasted butternut. The smoky scent of the roasted squash soup lingered in the air, mingling with the sharp, fragrant bite of freshly ground coffee beans.

The soft hum of conversation filled the space, broken only by the occasional clatter of dishes. Regulars lingered at their favorite tables, tucking in to hearty meals or oversized cups of coffee. Everyone was all friendly smiles, trying to be subtle about their interest but failing miserably.

Zach shifted uncomfortably in his seat.

A moment later, Anita appeared, setting down three steaming mugs of ginger lemon tea. Madison leaned forward and inhaled the spicy citrusy aroma. It instantly helped calm the nerves dancing in her belly.

"Alright, now. What's this about?" Anita slid into the booth. "I hope everything's okay at the inn." Concern creased her forehead.

"It is, we're all just busy getting it ready for the relaunch," Madison assured her. "Speaking of the inn, though... Zach told me someone sent you a letter about it. I was wondering if you could tell me anything more about what it said?"

Anita hesitated.

"It's alright. Mads got one, too. That's why I told her," Zach said, encouraging his mom.

"It's true. I've been trying to find out who sent it," Madison added.

Anita exhaled before wrapping her hands around her tea. "It's just... the letter said to keep it a secret."

Madison's pulse kicked up a notch. "A secret? What else did it say?"

"Well... I don't have it on me, but it said that the inn could use some help, in any way I saw fit." Anita took a sip of her tea then set it down with a thoughtful frown. "Truth be told, I have been wondering if you sent it," she admitted, looking at Madison.

"Me?" Madison's brows shot up. "No. I didn't even know how bad things were."

Anita gave her a pitying look, one that made Madison's stomach drop. She hadn't realized just how out of touch she'd been with her family.

"Well, be that as it may," Anita continued, "there wasn't much I could do except encourage Zach here to lend a hand. I knew that honeymoon cabin was empty and needed fixing up. Your mom used to say it fetched a pretty penny back in the day. Figured that would help your family out, along with any other work he could do on the inn."

Madison's gaze flicked between Anita and Zach.

Zach was staring into his tea, still untouched.

"Other than that"—Anita shrugged—"I wasn't sure how else I could help. Maybe just being a listening ear for George, checking in on things."

"Do you know if anyone else got a letter?"

Anita shook her head. "No, but I didn't mention it to anyone except Zach. If you didn't send it, I'm not sure who did. Heaven knows Edith would just come right out and tell me if she needed something."

Madison laughed. "That's true."

Anita's voice softened. "So, how are things going at the inn, really?"

"Better." She smiled. "Zach finished the dining room, the roof's all repaired from the tree caving in. And Kit's ready to start testing out a few dishes. We're giving them a trial run tomorrow at the Pumpkinfest ahead of our Halloween relaunch."

"The cabin's about done, too," Zach added.

Madison looked over at him in surprise. She'd yet to step inside that space. She wasn't sure she could.

Because the cabin wasn't just a place; it was their place. She would never forget the two of them sneaking away as they often did, desperate for a few moments alone together. He'd grasp his hand in hers and they'd run through the woods, laughing as they slipped away into the night. She could still feel it all as if it was imprinted on her DNA, how Zach would press kisses along her throat, hands fumbling at her jeans, her fingers gripping his shirt, tugging him closer.

The heat of him, the way his hands knew exactly where to touch, how to unravel her completely. The way nothing had ever felt more right than the two of them, tangled up together, hearts racing, skin burning.

And now, sitting here with Zach only inches away, an older, rougher, even more beautiful version of him, Madison felt it all again.

"I heard about your relaunch. I think it's brilliant." Anita smiled, drawing Madison from her memories. She reached over and gave Madison's hand a gentle squeeze. "You're doing good, sweetheart. I hope you know that."

Madison swallowed hard and managed a smile. "Thanks."

Zach stood, brushing a hand across the back of his neck. "We should probably get going. Still lots to do before tomorrow."

Anita gave them both a look that hovered somewhere between maternal pride and amusement. "Well, don't let me keep you. But if you find out who sent those letters, you better let me know."

Madison smiled. "Trust me, I will. I hate a mystery I can't solve."

TWENTY-NINE
MADISON

Madison dropped another sandbag onto the corner of the pumpkin slingshot, dust puffing into the evening air. Across from her, Zach tightened a knot on the festival game posts, sleeves shoved up, forearms flexing with every tug of the rope.

They still hadn't said much since leaving the café but the air between them crackled louder than any conversation.

Every time she turned, she caught the rough brush of his shoulder. Every time she knelt to adjust a weight, she felt his gaze flick toward her, and then away.

Mayor Bloomfield, or Hank as Gram called him, shuffled by, arms loaded with pumpkins for the slingshot. "Almost there, folks," he said, whistling a little tune.

Madison gave a tight smile but she couldn't relax. Because even with Mayor Bloomfield's easy chatter filling the air, she could still feel the tension humming under her skin. She couldn't shake the memory of Zach's mouth on hers, the way he'd touched her like she was the only thing that could possibly matter, and the way he'd pulled away like it had meant nothing.

And still... here he was. Helping. Staying. Fighting for this town, for her family's inn—even if he wouldn't fight for their relationship.

She told herself she was grateful. She told herself she didn't need anything more from him. And she nearly believed it. That was until he caught her eye over the edge of a hay bale, and for half a heartbeat, the whole world narrowed to just the two of them again.

It was a couple of hours later, after everyone had left, that Madison had a moment to herself. Gram and Hank had stepped out for a nightcap, while Zach headed home, and Madison went downstairs and found her dad in the great room. A fire was crackling in the fireplace, casting dancing shadows onto the carpet below.

George was sitting comfortably in his recliner, newspaper open, with Cocoa sleeping peacefully at his feet. It had been a moment since Madison had even seen her dad. He had taken revamping the fence to a whole new level, even installing new posts, which he had been busy painting the last few days.

"You're not going out tonight?" George peered over the top of his paper.

"No, not tonight. I figure tomorrow will be busy enough. Best to call it an early night."

George chuckled. "Tell that to your grandmother."

Madison curled up on the couch, tucking her mother's quilt around her legs, and reached for a mystery novel. It was a new book. Something Gram had picked up thinking Madison would like it. She'd bring it up to bed with her later. "Have Gram and Mayor Bloomfield been dating long?" Madison asked casually, running her fingers along the front cover.

George folded the newspaper. "Here and there. He's a fine fellow, and I know he makes her happy. That's all one can ask for, is it not?" George looked down at Cocoa and a smile tugged at the corner of his mouth. Cocoa lifted her head and her tail thumped lazily before she got up and put her paws on George's leg, begging to be lifted. George obliged, and Cocoa tried to lick his chin before settling into his lap.

"I suppose tomorrow will be a big day. Things are going good, right?" George asked.

"I think they are. That is, if I can rein Kit in. She's baked so many cinnamon rolls that we might be eating them for the rest of the week."

That earned a chuckle from her dad.

"It's odd, though, seeing the inn so quiet," Madison added, taking in the empty space. Even when she was a child, and they'd hang out in the great room, there were always people coming and going. She would hear people walking down the halls, showers starting, muffled voices through the drywall. That's just what it was like growing up in an inn.

She had groups of friends that would come and go, people who would stay for a day or two, and then there were the regulars who came back year after year. It was a different way of growing up, but Madison wouldn't have changed it for the world.

"I don't think I've ever seen you sit down for longer than ten minutes," Madison joked.

George smiled softly. "Your mother always said I couldn't sit still if my life depended on it."

"That she did. I'd say you're still that way." Madison thought back to how her dad would have a cup of coffee with Mr. Alders at the hardware store in the morning before moseying on down to the café or popping into the bakery. Come to think of it, he knew just as much of what was going on in this town as Mrs. C. and Mrs. Bishop combined. The only difference was her dad didn't feel the need to share it all.

George looked down at Cocoa and patted her head absentmindedly.

"I've been meaning to ask, how did you rescue Cocoa?" Madison had heard Gram's side of the story about the letter, but she was interested to hear how her father would tell it.

"You know, it was the darndest thing. One day, I went out to fetch the paper, and there she was, tucked up in a basket with a letter."

Madison still didn't want to tell her dad about her own letter saying the inn needed help. She didn't want him to think it was the only reason she had come home—even if it was true. And she knew its message would hurt his pride. Instead, she said, "A letter? Like an anonymous one?"

"It was typed up and everything." George nodded, rocking back in the recliner a bit. "It asked me to take care of the pup. Said we both needed each other," George said, looking down lovingly at Cocoa.

Madison frowned. "And it wasn't signed?"

"'Fraid not," George replied, continuing to rub Cocoa behind the ears. "Whoever sent it was right. This pup here has been a blessing. Helps fill the quiet a bit." George looked out the window at the vast expanse of the lake that was lost in the darkness. "She's made this place feel less empty since your mother passed." George's voice was low, soft.

Madison's throat tightened. Even though her dad was always socializing, always moseying about town, she realized for the first time how lonely he must be.

"Dad, have you ever thought about selling the inn?"

"Oh now, where is this coming from?" George seemed taken aback.

"Mrs. C. I told her we weren't selling and that I was here to fix the inn up." Madison left off the part about saying she would stay.

George gave her a long look, the kind only a father could give. It was a look that saw more than she said aloud. "Honey Pie, this inn is a part of our family. It's more than a business."

Her father smiled. "It's where you learned to ride a bike in the lobby, where we celebrated every birthday, every holiday. This is our home. *Your* home." He made sure she heard the emphasis.

Madison sniffed, trying to stop the tears from flowing down her cheeks. "I think about Mom all the time," she said thickly. "I'm sorry it took me so long to come home, after."

"Hush, dry up those tears," George said gently. "You shouldn't have had to come home and bail me out. I should've been able to handle it on my own. But now that you're here," George said, clearing his throat, "I realize I needed more than just help running the place. I needed you, Honey Pie. I'm so glad you've come back, for however long. And I'm so, so proud of you."

Madison couldn't stop the tears this time. "Thanks, Dad."

THIRTY
ZACH

Zach's family farmhouse was on the outskirts of town. It was set back from the road, down a winding dirt driveway. Right now, it was flanked by sugar maples that were dropping their fiery red leaves. Not that Zach could really see that in the dark. Not without electricity.

The house still smelled the same, though—like the cinnamon apples his grandmother used to bake and his grandfather's pipe smoke. It smelled like Sunday dinners when the whole Whitaker family would still get together and birthday parties with the cousins.

He missed his grandparents every day. They had been there when his father had left and Anita had come back to Maple Falls. They had welcomed them all, making the town their home, and wrapping them in love. He felt that in the farmhouse, even though both of his grandparents had since passed on. The emotions remained, ingrained in the walls.

Zach turned on a flashlight and looked around the kitchen—or what would be the kitchen. He currently had it stripped down to the studs, planning a complete overhaul. The only things he had were the fridge and a stove.

Madison would like the space, he thought. An oversized farmhouse sink in the center island. Marble countertops, gold accents. Zach could see her in the kitchen. They'd spend lazy Sundays cooking together, maybe making apple butter or something fancy she'd picked up in New York.

Zach shook his head. He was a fool. Isn't that why he was here? To get Madison out of his head?

It was too much—the way the townspeople stared at them. Too much—the way his mom looked at him, as if she couldn't be happier to see him and Madison together again.

It was too much because Zach wanted all of that. He wanted the impossible. He wanted this farmhouse to be their home. He wanted to tuck Madison into bed next to him every night and wake up to her every morning.

He swore if the universe gave him that, he would never ask for anything ever again.

Zach stared off, eyes unfocused, as that future played out before him. If only that were all possible.

He had to force himself back to the present. To stay grounded. This evening, his goal was simple: rewire the kitchen and maybe the hot water heater. If that was done, he could move back. The idea of staying another night at the inn's cabin, with Madison so close, drove him insane. He needed space.

Zach plugged in an orange power cord to the old gas-powered generator out in the shed. It barely supplied enough power to keep a single work light glowing, but it was enough. It had to be.

"Listen, I'm more than happy to make a beer run out here," Liam said when he showed up about an hour later. He twisted the cap off a bottle and tossed it back into the box. "But I thought you were staying at the inn."

"Had work to do here," Zach muttered, examining the

wiring in the exposed wall. Zach reached for a wire. A sharp zap jolted his fingers, and he hissed in pain, shaking out his hand.

Liam arched a brow. "Man, you might want to take a step back before you end up killing yourself. How many times have you told me you need a clear head when you're working with electricity?"

Zach gritted his teeth and looked down at his hand. A faint black streak ran beneath his nail, evidence of the electrical current that had bitten him. "It's fine."

"Yeah, tell that to the next live wire you grab."

Zach ignored him and turned back to the breaker box, muttering under his breath as he adjusted the wiring. He'd already rewired the main line from the box, but something still wasn't connecting right, and Liam had a point. It was time to call it a night. He'd just have to go back to the cabin for now and try to deal with his closeness to Madison.

Liam leaned against a half-finished section of wall, taking a slow drink of his beer. "So, you gonna tell me what's got you all tied up in knots, or do I have to guess?"

Zach just exhaled hard through his nose, jaw tightening.

Liam smirked. "Ah. Got it. Madison."

Zach scowled.

"Man, I get it," Liam continued. "I mean, it's gotta be hard seeing her again after all these years. But you could've just, I don't know, told her how you felt instead of trying to electrocute yourself into an early grave."

Zach shot him a look. "That's real helpful. Thanks."

Liam shrugged. "Hey, just calling it like I see it."

Zach ran a hand through his hair, already regretting the entire conversation. But Liam wasn't wrong. The last few days had wrecked him. Madison was everything: passionate, determined, headstrong. He couldn't get the way she laughed out of his head, the way she fit so effortlessly back into town after all these years. The way she kissed and touched him like she was making up for all their lost time.

And then, the gut punch.

The damn text message he'd seen.

"She's got someone in New York," Zach finally said, still not meeting Liam's eyes.

Liam, who had just twisted off another beer cap, paused. "What?"

Zach exhaled hard through his nose and took the bottle Liam handed him, knocking back half of it before speaking again.

"She's seeing someone," he said flatly. "Guy called Jo."

Liam's brow furrowed. "And you know this how?"

"Saw a text message when we were together." Zach leveled his look.

Liam's grip tightened around his beer. He knew Zach wasn't talking about just hanging out, painting a fence.

Silence stretched between them. The only sound was the generator humming outside.

Liam broke the tension. "Look, man. I don't blame you for needing space. But maybe—just maybe—you should ask her about it before jumping to conclusions?"

"Ha. Not necessary. The dick pic didn't leave much to the imagination."

Liam visibly winced.

"And let's not forget the hearts popping up whenever the guy calls," Zach added bitterly.

Liam took a slow pull of his beer, watching him. "I'm sorry, man. That does sound bad."

Zach scoffed. Understatement of the goddamn year.

He let out a sharp breath and ran a hand over his face. "I made an ass out of myself enough already. Can we just drop it?"

Liam nodded. "Yeah, alright. I won't push. Can't promise anything about the rest of the town."

Zach snorted but didn't respond.

Liam had a point, though. The whole town seemed hellbent on shoving him and Madison together, like they hadn't already been a spectacular failure. Like she hadn't left him behind once before.

He'd been a fool to think—just for a second—that anything had changed.

Because nothing had. She wasn't his. She never would be.

And yet he knew that tonight, back in the cabin, his dreams would be full of her.

THIRTY-ONE

MADISON

Madison hadn't gone up to bed yet. She'd just been sitting there, reading her book, trying to focus on the pages while her eyes kept drifting up to the window. Then the honeymoon cabin light flicked on. She headed out the back door, into the cold night, without a second thought. Adrenaline pulsing through her veins, she let her legs march her all the way to the cabin, and she knocked on the door, hard.

She was so tired of the emotional back and forth. Tired of the games they were playing with each other. Tired of him kissing her one minute and giving her the cold shoulder the next.

It was ridiculous. It was infuriating. It was madness. And one way or another, tonight, she was getting answers.

All Zach needed to do was open the blasted door.

Nothing. Silence. She forced herself to slow her breathing and look around, calm her nervous system before she knocked again. The air was crisp and full of fall; she could see her breath in front of her. The lake stretched out, black and endless under the moonlight, the surface rippling in the chilly breeze.

She was just about to knock again when Zach finally

opened the door. He looked tired, and somehow vulnerable, his hair messed through.

"We need to talk," Madison said, voice sharp, anger flaring.

Zach frowned but stepped outside onto the porch, letting the door swing shut behind him. So, he wasn't going to invite her in, then.

They stood there for a beat, the cold biting at Madison's skin, the firelight from inside casting a soft glow around them.

It didn't take long for the fight to start.

"I shouldn't have kissed you," Zach muttered, voice low. "It was wrong. And if I had known—"

Madison's frustration boiled over. "Why do you keep saying it was a mistake? Why do you keep apologizing?"

Zach's gaze locked on hers, his hazel eyes so calm and steady it infuriated her.

"Don't you get it?" she continued, the words tumbling out. "Being with you… it's what I've wanted all along. Do you have any idea what it felt like to finally have that happen, us kissing, being together—to finally have you again only for you to throw it in my face and call it a mistake?"

The words were messy, raw, and unfiltered, and hot tears spilled from her eyes.

Zach's jaw clenched. "But you're seeing someone back in New York," he said softly.

Madison blinked. "I—Whaaaaat?"

His calm demeanor finally broken, Zach threw his hands up in frustration. "Jo, Madison! Jo."

Madison's brow furrowed. "Jo?"

Zach let out a sharp, humorless laugh. "Yeah, Jo. The guy blowing up your phone with…" He made a wild gesture. "Dick pics. Eggplants. Squirting emojis. God knows what else."

Madison stared at him like he was from another planet. "Jo? Are you freaking kidding me?"

Zach narrowed his eyes. "Yeah, Jo. What the hell is so funny?"

Madison glared. "Jo is a woman. She's my best friend. Her name is Jolene." Madison shook her head. She couldn't believe this was happening. "And, for the record, when she sent those flirtatious eggplants, she was teasing me about *you*."

"And the..."

"Dick pic? Mr. October from her Hot Hunks calendar. She likes to send me the good ones." Madison continued to stare at Zach. He just stood there, processing.

"She's a woman?" he repeated.

"Yes. And very much into men." Madison was pissed. All this angst because of an ill-timed text message.

"You're serious?"

"One hundred percent."

Zach stood there, silent, stunned.

Madison crossed her arms. "So let me get this straight. You pushed me away because you thought I had a boyfriend? And you didn't think to ask me about it?"

"What was I supposed to think? You and I don't talk. And I sure as hell wasn't about to share you with another man." Zach lifted his gaze to hers. And she saw it—the wrecked look in his eyes. The regret. The yearning. All there, a deep ocean beneath the calm surface he usually showed.

A coyote howled nearby, its call echoing in the trees.

Madison could see the tension in Zach's shoulders, his jaw.

Her throat went dry. She swallowed, trying to find her voice. "Zach..."

She shifted her weight toward him slightly.

Zach's eyes darkened. Madison swallowed. He wasn't touching her, but she felt him everywhere.

She longed to reach out and close the distance. To wrap her arms around his waist, and feel the warmth of his body.

Zach's fingers flexed at his side like he was fighting himself. Like he wanted all of that, too.

She knew exactly how he'd feel against her. How hard he would be.

She knew how his hands would fit on her waist. How his mouth would feel as it claimed hers.

Heat pooled low in her stomach, a slow, aching burn.

If he touched her, she knew she'd fall.

If she reached for him, she knew he'd let her.

"Mads," Zach rasped, voice wrecked. "Do you want to come in?"

She nodded once, unable to speak.

The cabin smelled like pine and warm leather. The fireplace was lit, flickering its soft light along the honeyed wood walls. Madison's eyes swept the space, taking in all the changes Zach had made. The four-poster bed looked newer, the sheets fresh and inviting. But the essence of what this place had been for them was still here.

Her gaze caught on the window ledge. The carvings. Their initials.

A log turned, and she looked at the fireplace, sparks flying.

"Is this new?" she asked, running her fingers along the wooden mantel.

Zach shrugged. "It's from the old maple tree. Thought it was important to keep it."

Madison swallowed as tears swam in her eyes. "I love that," she said, clearing her throat.

She tried to focus on something else, anything else, to keep from getting all emotional. She took in the rest of the room. "You kept a lot of it the same."

A shadow flickered across Zach's expression. "Some things shouldn't change. This place... it means something to me."

Their eyes locked.

The air between them shifted, memories rushing in fast and unfiltered.

The late-night laughter when they were barely adults, lying out under the stars, talking about everything they wanted from life.

Bodies tangled on that old worn leather couch, sharing whispered dreams about the future—about a home with a porch and a view of the lake. A place full of laughter, dogs underfoot, coffee cups left half-finished because life was too good to rush through.

Zach moved over to the kitchen area and pulled out some mugs while she moved around the cabin, running her hands along the couch, along the window ledge and the mantel.

"Are you alright?" Zach asked as he came over with a mug.

Madison readily accepted it, grateful for something to do with her hands, something to keep her lips from betraying her thoughts. The cup was warm in her hands, and she brought it to her lips, expecting a calming sip of tea—only to nearly choke.

She sputtered, coughing as her eyes widened. "Bourbon?"

"Just a splash," Zach admitted, the corner of his mouth twitching into an unapologetic grin.

Madison shot him a mock glare but took a second sip, this time prepared for the fiery warmth that followed. The bourbon wasn't overpowering—it was just enough to loosen the tension that had gripped her chest since she'd walked through the door. It made her feel warm and relaxed, and was just what she needed.

Zach gestured toward the couch; his expression betrayed his emotions before he could mask it. "Make yourself comfortable."

She sank into the cushions, her fingers brushing against the fleece blanket beside her. She looked down at her hands, unsure of what to say. Did they have to talk? Could she not just follow what her body longed to do?

Zach sat beside her, their knees brushing. The fireplace

crackled, and she shivered despite the heat. He was staring at her, his gaze so intense, so unflinching, it pinned her right there, breathless. She swallowed hard, but it did nothing to steady the frantic rhythm of her heart.

This wasn't just old chemistry sparking to life.

This was something different. Something bigger.

Madison could feel it deep down, deeper than all the scars and years apart. She was falling in love with him all over again. No walls. No running away. No excuses.

Just that terrifying, beautiful feeling of being cracked wide open.

And she could see it in his eyes, too.

The way he looked at her now, like she was something he needed to be alive, like she was his life force, more vital than the blood pumping through his veins.

There was no turning back from this. Tonight, they weren't going to hold back.

Tonight, they were going to remember exactly what it felt like to belong to each other.

Their eyes met again, and she knew.

This was the moment before the fall.

THIRTY-TWO
ZACH

Zach couldn't explain the pull Madison had on him. It defied logic. It always had.

Even after all these years, after all the hurt and distance, he wanted her more fiercely than ever before. Because Madison wasn't just a memory or a pretty face. She was home. She always had been.

It wasn't just the way her wild hair fell in messy, beautiful waves over her shoulders, or the way her green eyes sparked when she laughed—though God knew that undid him, too.

It was her fire. Her stubbornness. The way she threw herself heart-first into everything she cared about. The way she stood up for the people she loved without hesitation. The way she filled every room she walked into—not with noise but with life. No one else ever matched that.

Time stopped as he held her gaze. The only thing Zach could hear was the crackling of the fireplace and the beating of his heart. Then, as if drawn by an invisible force, he leaned forward. Madison did the same.

Their lips met in a kiss that was slow and achingly familiar. Zach took his time, brushing his lips against hers, purposely keeping the kiss soft. Waiting to see where Madison wanted this to go. One ounce of hesitation, and he'd stop. He needed her to know she was in control. He wanted this to be her choice.

Her mouth opened, inviting him in. His tongue slid against hers, tasting her. So sweet. So soft. Her hands sank into his damp hair, pulling him closer.

Zach shifted his weight, pressing her back against the couch.

All he could think about was wanting more. More of her.

His rough hand trailed underneath the softness of her sweater, moving along her side, feeling the dip of her waist. So soft. So warm.

His hand moved higher, his thumb tracing the lace of her bra. The feeling caused her to shiver under his touch.

God, he wanted her. He wanted to devour her. He wanted to claim her.

He wanted to cage her between his arms and let her feel the weight of his body pressing down on hers.

He wanted to kiss her until she saw reason. Until she stopped trying to leave and realized this was where she belonged. Underneath him. Beside him.

Just here.

He couldn't think. He just wanted.

Which was why he pulled back. Because as much as he wanted her, as much as he wanted this, he wanted Madison to want it even more. He wanted—no, needed—for her to say yes.

"Do you want me to kiss you again?" Zach asked, easing his weight off of her, giving her space.

Madison looked down, tracing the seam of his jeans with her thumb, gathering her thoughts. "You should know, Zach, that I'm not sure if I'm staying," she admitted, her voice softer now.

"I know," Zach replied simply.

"But I do know I want this right now. I want you. That's why I'm here. And I think..."

"What do you think?"

"I think you should take off your shirt."

Zach had never done anything faster. He reached behind his neck and tugged the shirt over his head in one swift motion, tossing it aside.

"Better?" Zach asked, his grin softening as his hands found her waist, his thumbs grazing the fabric of her sweater.

"You're still unfairly hot," she said, leaning forward and trailing a line of kisses from his stomach to his chest and then his neck.

Zach sucked in his breath. Trying to hold still, wanting to stop her, but not wanting her to stop at the same time. "And you're still maddening in every way," he managed to grind out.

"Charming," she teased, her fingers tracing the lines of his chest. She was on her knees now; they both were.

Zach kissed her deeply, meeting her on the same level, taking everything that she gave him. This time, there was no hesitation, no holding back. He was tired of being afraid of tomorrow. Of being afraid of her leaving.

He didn't want to think of anything past this.

He kissed her neck and Madison arched further, offering herself to him, her head falling back as a broken whimper escaped her lips. "Zach," she murmured, her voice barely audible.

Zach lifted his head. Her cheeks were flushed, her eyes dark with desire, and her chest rose and fell with every shallow breath.

"You want more," he said, his voice a low rumble.

She nodded, biting her lip as her hands gripped his shoulders. "Please," she whispered.

That was all he needed.

THIRTY-THREE

MADISON

Madison felt the heat of his hands through the thin fabric, but it wasn't close enough. There were benefits to being with a man who worked with his hands all day. And in that moment, Madison wanted to feel those callused hands all over her soft skin.

She lifted her arms for him to tug the sweater off over her head. And then her lips were back on his. She cupped the back of his head, holding him steady so she could kiss him.

"How... are you... so perfect?" he asked between kisses. "So... beautiful."

Madison reached behind her back, her fingers fumbling slightly before she unclasped her bra and slid it off, tossing it aside without hesitation. The cool air brushed against her skin, causing her nipples to tighten, or maybe it was because Zach's eyes darkened as he took her in.

"Perfection," he said.

His hands were slow, deliberate as they traveled down her stomach, his fingers brushing her skin in a way that sent sparks dancing along her nerves.

He paused at the curve of her waist before sliding back up,

his touch leaving a trail of warmth in its wake. When his hand cupped her breast, Madison's breath hitched, and her body instinctively leaned into his touch.

Zach lowered his head, his lips brushing a featherlight kiss across her chest before he took her nipple into his mouth. The sensation was electric, his tongue swirling in deliberate, torturous strokes that made Madison's back lift off the couch.

She moaned softly, her hands tangling in his hair, holding him close. Suddenly Zach scooped her up as if she weighed nothing. Madison let out a startled laugh, the sound bubbling up before she could stop it.

He didn't have to travel far, laying her back on the ottoman, the sheepskin throw beneath her. Madison's hair spilled over the back of the low bench, her arms stretching above her head.

Zach slowly peeled her jeans off and she looked up at him. There was no shyness, no uncertainty. Only desire. She wanted this. She wanted him.

Zach dragged the ottoman closer, his movements slow and deliberate. He sank onto the couch, his hands resting on her thighs, spreading her open before him. Madison shivered in anticipation.

He bent forward, his lips brushing over her inner thigh before dipping between her legs. Her head fell back, a gasp tearing from her lips.

Every nerve ending lit up, every coherent thought obliterated, as Zach's mouth worked its wicked magic.

She fisted the soft sheepskin throw beneath her, her knuckles aching from the strain as wave after relentless wave of pleasure rolled through her body.

Zach was thorough, always had been. He knew exactly how to draw every ounce of pleasure from her, and he remembered all the ways she loved to be kissed and touched, as if no time had passed at all.

"Zach..." she whimpered, her voice trembling as the pressure built higher and higher. She didn't want to let go yet, didn't want to give in so soon. But Zach was persistent, his tongue and fingers working in perfect harmony, pushing her closer to the edge with every deliberate stroke.

Her body tensed.

And then she shattered.

Finally. And my God, it was worth it.

Beyond anything she could have dreamed of, bigger than anything she had ever experienced.

Her climax ripped through her with a force that left her gasping for air, a broken cry of his name spilling from her lips.

Pleasure consumed her. For a moment, she literally couldn't even remember where she was—only that she was in his hands, his arms, his orbit, and she never wanted to leave.

Zach chuckled, his lips pressing two soft kisses on either thigh before pulling back. The sound of his laughter– low and rough, filled with satisfaction—sent a fresh wave of heat through her. And she knew there was more.

"Come here," he murmured, scooping her up in his arms.

Zach carried her over to the four-poster bed, setting her back gently against the pillows like she could break.

Madison was still breathless, her heart slamming wildly against her ribs.

"Why are you still dressed?" Madison asked, her tone playful as she moved to sit up.

"Trust me, I'm about to fix that," Zach replied, his voice thick with want.

He unbuttoned his jeans and stepped out of them, taking his boxers along with them.

Madison sucked in a breath because, good God, he was beautiful. All lean muscle, bronzed skin, and hungry eyes locked on her like she was the only thing he needed in the whole world.

She came up onto her knees, meeting him halfway.

"There," she whispered, pulling him in for a kiss. "That's better."

Zach groaned low in his throat, letting her guide him down onto the bed with her.

Madison loved the weight of Zach on top of her. The feel of him pressing her back into the mattress. She parted her legs and reached down to guide him.

Zach stilled, his forehead resting against hers.

"You sure?" he asked, voice hoarse, strained with restraint.

"I'm sure," she breathed.

Still, he paused, giving her that look—the one that said he would stop if she even hesitated.

"Please," she whispered, body full of need.

That was all the permission he needed.

Madison gasped as he slid into her, slow and thick and deep, filling every inch of her until there was no space between them anymore.

Her body stretched to take him, welcoming him like he belonged there.

He did belong there. He always had.

Zach cursed low under his breath, his forehead pressed against hers as he stilled inside her, giving them both a moment to feel it, to feel everything.

"I knew you'd feel good," he said, his voice filled with wonder. "You always felt so good."

"You feel even better than I remember," Madison confessed, her body melting into his.

"Is that so?" Zach replied, rolling his hips just right, drawing a moan from her lips.

He leaned down, kissing her slow and deep, his fingers threading through her hair.

Every stroke of his hips, every grind of his body against hers, sent her spiraling higher and higher.

She was going to fall again—she could feel it building, wild and inevitable.

"Come for me, Madison," Zach murmured, his voice rough and commanding. "Let me feel you."

He leaned back just enough to slip a hand between them, his thumb tracing deliberate circles over the sensitive nub between her thighs. His other hand found her breast, pinching and rolling her nipple in rhythm with the growing tension inside her.

Madison came apart, her body convulsing around him, clenching so tightly that Zach lost control too.

He groaned her name like a prayer, thrusting once, twice, and then he was spilling inside her, his body shuddering with release.

They stayed like that for a long moment, tangled together, their breathing rushed.

And for the first time in a long, long time, Madison felt whole again.

She didn't know what tomorrow would bring.

But tonight, Zach Whitaker was hers.

THIRTY-FOUR
MADISON

October 19th

The next morning, Madison woke, her senses slowly coming back to her. She felt safe and warm, cocooned against Zach's chest. His arm rested across her, caging her in. Protecting her. Madison lay there, feeling the weight of him and listening to the steady rise and fall of his chest as he continued to sleep soundly.

For a second, Madison could almost pretend it was years ago—that nothing had changed. That they were still that young couple who could barely keep their hands off each other, wrapped up in the small world they'd created in this very cabin.

But they weren't. And everything had changed.

She blinked the room into focus. Sunlight streamed through the cottage's lace curtains. Dust motes danced in the air. The air smelled faintly of cedar and smoke from the small wood-burning stove. Outside songbirds chirped in the cold October air, but inside, the room was nice and toasty. She'd forgotten how hot Zach slept. He was like her own personal furnace.

Madison carefully turned in Zach's arms so that she was now facing him. Here, he was just Zach. Tousled hair, stubbled jaw, and those lashes that should have been illegal on a man. Seeing him so relaxed stirred something deep in her chest. It hit her hard, knowing just how much she missed him. How much she missed this. How no one else could ever come close to him. Here, she felt safe. Here, she felt like she was home. She hadn't felt this grounded in years, not in New York, not with anyone else.

God, how many nights had she lain awake wishing for exactly this?

Last night had been magic. But now the morning sun felt like a harsh wake-up call. Her heart wanted nothing more than to linger, to lie in bed and have a lazy morning as if that were possible. But Madison's brain was already running in overdrive.

Today was the Pumpkinfest.

Today the entire population of Maple Falls would be out in full force, buzzing around town, snapping pictures with the pumpkins, gossiping over cider donuts and spiced lattes.

If anyone found out what had happened between her and Zach—if anyone even suspected—the news would spread faster than frosting on Kit's cinnamon rolls.

She could already imagine Gram's sly winks, Mrs. Bishop whispering behind napkins at the Maple Leaf Café while Anita proudly looked on. It would be a lot of pressure, especially when she still wasn't sure what their future could look like. Madison in New York, Zach in Maple Falls. How could it possibly work?

Madison frowned. Now was not the time to worry about the future or about what other people thought. Let them talk, let them watch. She wasn't going to hide away anymore.

Zach came to with a sleepy smile on his face and pulled her closer, wrapping her in a hug.

"Morning. You sleep okay?"

"Better than okay," Madison confessed. "But I should get back to the inn, we have a big day ahead."

"Five more minutes," he mumbled into her hair.

Madison melted, momentarily giving in and burrowing deeper into his chest. "I wish," she murmured. Because five more minutes sounded dangerously good. Five more minutes could turn into forever, and they could have every morning like this. They wouldn't be borrowed. Or secrets. Just theirs.

He kissed the top of her head before rolling onto his back, stretching his arms above his head. The blanket fell to his waist.

Madison couldn't help but like what she saw, and Zach noticed.

"Sure you can't stay?" His voice was groggy but amused.

"Not that it's a bad plan," Madison said, propping herself up on one elbow so she could look at Zach, sprawled out bare-chested.

She remembered everything that had happened between them the night before, and it took every ounce of strength to stop herself from going back for more.

"I really should get going," Madison groaned, but she couldn't resist leaning back and planting a trail of kisses up his arm to his shoulder and to the side of his neck.

Zach's breath hitched, and she could practically feel the tension crackling between them. She saw the hunger in his eyes, and she knew it mirrored her own.

"Later, Pumpkinfest time, inn," she mumbled, getting up reluctantly. She grabbed her jeans and yanked her sweater over her head backward before realizing and quickly fixing it.

After one last slow kiss, Madison slipped outside into the fresh morning air. The ground was muddy, the grass wet with dew. She tugged her sweater straight and picked up the trail curving around the lake.

It would be fine. She'd go back to the inn all innocently, pretending she'd been out for a casual early stroll. All she had to do was channel Zach's calm energy. She could pull that off, right?

Then, even though she knew everyone would find out soon enough, they could at least keep their steamy night in the cabin to themselves a little while longer.

All was good until she rounded the corner of the inn and spotted Kit standing at the kitchen window, grinning like a fox.

Madison's face instantly flamed.

Kit stood on her tiptoes and pushed open the window with her wrists. "Late night at the cabin?" she teased.

Madison shot her a look. "Keep it quiet," she whisper-yelled.

"Sure, but it'll cost ya." Kit winked.

Madison slipped into the kitchen, her heart still racing. The kitchen smelled of roasted apples, biscuits, and sausage gravy.

Kit leaned against the counter, arms crossed, wearing an amused expression.

"Not now, Kit! I swear if you say one word..." Madison warned, pushing up her sleeves and heading to the coffee pot.

"Oh, I don't have to say anything. Your hair is doing all the talking." Kit pointed to Madison's tangled mess. "That's a rode-hard-and-put-away-wet look if I've ever seen one."

Madison stood up straight and ran a hand through her curls, trying to brush them out with her fingers. "Please. I just... overslept."

Kit plated a piece of apple tart and slid it in front of Madison. "Oh sure, overslept. In the honeymoon cabin with Zach. Dudes have never done it for me, but a man like Zach? He might make me change my mind!"

Madison tossed a damp kitchen towel at her new friend. "Kit!"

Kit just laughed and caught it. "What? I said with a man *like* Zach. It's a good thing you scooped him up when you did—he wasn't going to stay single forever."

Madison reached for her coffee. "I'll tell him you think he's such a catch *after* Pumpkinfest today, or it might have to wait until after the reopening. There's so much to do."

Kit softened. "Don't worry about the inn. It's coming along."

"I know. It's just..." Madison sighed. "I don't know what's going to happen."

Kit knew they were no longer talking about the inn. "You love him."

Madison stared down into her coffee "I guess I always have."

Kit leaned in, dropping her voice. "So... are you two, like, officially...?"

"We haven't talked about it yet." Madison absently picked at the tart. "I've got a lot of thinking to do. But I need to focus on the inn now."

Kit lowered her voice as if she was imparting a secret. "You're allowed to have something for yourself, Madison. This inn will still be here tomorrow." She gave her a knowing look before standing. "Okay, now that I've delivered my daily dose of wisdom, I need to peel some more apples. And you"—she pointed at Madison—"are going to take ten deep breaths and remember you're allowed to be happy."

Madison watched Kit tackle a fresh bushel of apples, leaving her alone with her coffee, her thoughts, and a restless heart.

THIRTY-FIVE
MADISON

Madison couldn't sit for long. Out front, the inn's yard had been completely transformed into a fun fair with colorful booths, carnival games, hay bales stacked for seating, and a big wooden sign that read: "PUMPKINFEST FUN FAIR—WELCOME!"

It looked incredible.

Madison should have been proud. Instead, she was trying very hard not to look like someone who had just spent the night tangled up in the sheets with her first love. And what a night it had been. Madison shook her head lest she start replaying it scene by scene, leaving her face as crimson as her sweater.

Act normal. Smile. Don't be weird.

She adjusted a stack of cider cups at the drink table, sneaking a glance across the lawn.

There he was.

Zach stood near the new fence, talking with her dad, looking disgustingly good in a worn flannel and scuffed work boots. His sleeves were rolled up, his arms crossed loosely over his broad chest, every inch of him relaxed and easy.

Meanwhile, Madison felt like she might spontaneously combust.

It wasn't just how good he looked; it was the way he stood there. Solid. Confident. Like you could depend on him. Madison had once. Maybe she still could.

Get it together. She tore her gaze away and busied herself setting out caramel apples.

Madison wondered how the whole town didn't yet know they were together again. Because to her, nothing felt normal. It felt monumental. Like the world had shifted overnight and no one else had noticed. How could Zach be so chilled out?

Within two hours, the inn's front lawn was packed. Kids skipped from game to game, screaming and clapping with joy every time they won a prize. Plastic bags filled with kazoos, yo-yos, and candy dangled from their wrists. Parents stood around in clusters, watching their kids have fun while drinking steaming cups of cider and catching up with friends.

Madison smiled and soaked it all in. Why had she avoided all of this for so long? She regretted it, she could see that now—letting the distance grow further and further between her and all those she loved.

That was changing now, though. Wasn't it?

Every time she caught herself glancing Zach's way—or worse, every time she caught him looking back—her heart kicked into a wild rhythm.

Maybe they could sneak away to her bedroom...

"Madison, hello?" Kit called out, snapping her out of her dirty thoughts. She'd ditched the beret for a red bandana, tying her hair back. She wore a navy chef's coat and white apron around her waist.

"What? Huh?" Madison asked, turning and giving Kit her full attention.

Kit went up on her tiptoes and spotted Zach over Madison's shoulder. She tsked and shook her head. "Girl, you need to focus. We've got a festival to run here and an inn to promote!"

"I am! I'm focused. What do you need?"

"What I need is more cinnamon rolls, but I don't think that's going to happen."

"You already sold out?" Madison looked incredulous.

"All five hundred." Kit beamed, hands on her hips.

Wow. Madison mouthed the word.

"I know. I was just trying to tell you that I think we'll be sold out of everything within the hour." Kit had set out tasting trays of sweet potato fries with marshmallow dip, maple-glazed sausage bites, and mini butternut squash soup cups.

"That's incredible," Madison murmured, watching Kit scribble down feedback on a notepad, already adjusting ingredients in her head.

"Thanks." Kit shot her a grin. "Consider this my audition for best chef in town."

"Pretty sure you've already won that title," Madison answered honestly.

"Zoe is also looking for you," Kit added, organizing the remaining tasting trays.

"Flower shop Zoe?"

"Mmm-hmm. Heard you were partnering up with local businesses for the relaunch. Wanted to see if you'd be interested in fresh flowers around the inn, like in the guest rooms. She said something about discounted pricing. I told her that was all you."

"Okay, I'll have to find her because that's a great idea."

"And," Kit said dramatically, "Mayor Bloomfield mentioned his great-niece was coming into town. She's going to start working for him, handling social media. Elsie's her name, I think. Anyway, he wanted to chat with you. Thought it might help with the relaunch."

"He's right. That would help. I'll look for him too." Kit was right; Madison's head had been too filled with Zach. She needed to focus on the inn, on the community, and making their Halloween relaunch the best it could be.

Madison didn't find Zoe, but she did find her dad.

George was in his element, giving kids pony rides on Aspen and handing out pellets to feed the goats. He'd also set up a tiny petting zoo, where Honey and Biscuit had become the main attraction.

Madison relaxed a little bit. Maybe she could get through today without obsessing over Zach. Maybe she could enjoy the festival. Maybe she could even broker a few partnership deals for the reopening.

Except, as always, Zach looked ridiculously good. Flannel sleeves rolled up. Jeans that had seen better days, hugging his thighs. That stupid, knee-weakening smirk.

Focus, she reminded herself fiercely. *Smile. Act normal. Do not, under any circumstances, climb him like a tree.*

Zach was standing near the pumpkin slingshot, of all places. The slingshot and runway had been set up in front of the inn at the end of the street with a plywood backstop, and it had drawn quite a crowd.

Mrs. C., who had somehow appointed herself the official game referee, spotted Madison eyeing Zach and couldn't help herself.

"Alright, alright," Mrs. C. called out, beckoning her over. "Who's up for a little friendly competition?"

"I—What?" Madison said quickly, holding up her hands once she realized the older lady was talking about her.

Zach's brows lifted, joining them. "You volunteering, Mads?"

"No," Madison insisted quickly. Absolutely not. She could barely remember how to breathe around him, let alone operate a slingshot.

"What? That's not the Madison Kelly I know!" Mrs. C. declared.

Mrs. Bishop leaned in. "You scared, sweetheart?"

Madison scowled. *Oh, these meddling old ladies are good.*

"Yeah, what's the matter, Mads? Afraid you'll lose?" Zach's lips twitched into a smile.

Madison narrowed her eyes. "Lose? To you?"

Zach nodded.

"Ha, please! Lead the way." If there was one thing Madison never did, it was back down from a challenge.

The surrounding crowd cheered.

The game was simple—three pumpkins, three shots, and whoever knocked down the most targets won.

Zach went first. He pulled back the slingshot, took a calculated aim, and launched a pumpkin straight into a spread of bowling pins. The pumpkin exploded, knocking down the majority of the pins. The crowd whooped and clapped.

He lined up his second shot, eyes narrowed in concentration. This time, the pumpkin hit lower, knocking down the remaining pins on the left side of the lane. A few pins wobbled but stayed standing.

"Finish them off, Zach!" someone in the crowd yelled.

Zach didn't even acknowledge it, just picked up his third pumpkin, took a breath, and launched it. The pumpkin hit its target; the last pins finally fell with a satisfying clatter.

The crowd roared their approval, high-fiving him as he stepped back with a small, smug grin.

Madison took her turn next. She planted her feet, adjusted her aim, and let her pumpkin fly.

STRIKE!

All the pins went down. The crowd roared.

But it was like the sound was muted, far away. Because Zach was right there and his gaze had caught on hers. It was a charged, knowing look, and for a second, the world shrank to just the two of them.

Normal, she told herself. *Normal, normal, normal.*

"Alright, tiebreaker!" Mrs. C. interrupted, shoving a ridiculously large pumpkin into Madison's arms.

Madison struggled with it, adjusting her grip until Zach came to help.

"Here," he said, stepping behind her.

He was close. Too close.

Madison held her breath as his chest brushed her back. His arms came around her, steadying the slingshot as she fumbled to get the massive pumpkin in place. Once in the pocket, Zach's fingers curled around hers, and it all came flooding back. The weight of him beside her. The sound of his laugh in the dark.

The thought of asking for more.

Of asking for everything, even if she didn't know how it would all work out.

"On the count of three," Zach said. His breath felt hot compared to the cool autumn air.

Madison forced herself to nod.

"One."

His fingers tightened over hers.

"Two."

His chin brushed her shoulder, just the faintest touch, but enough to steal the air from her lungs.

"Three."

They released together.

The pumpkin was so large it stayed in the pocket, shooting forward and then back, falling out and smashing into the cement with tremendous force. It exploded on impact, sending a burst of orange guts and pulp flying in all directions. Including directly onto Madison.

The crowd roared. The kids absolutely loved it.

Madison looked down at her boots, her jeans, and her hair; it was everywhere.

Then she looked over at Zach. He was clean as could be. How was that possible?

A slow, wicked smile curled her lips.

Zach's smirk faltered.

"Uh-oh. I know that look," he started to say.

Before he could react, Madison bent down, scooped up a handful of pumpkin guts, and flung them straight at his chest.

SMACK.

The crowd hollered, some cheering her on while others gasped in delight.

Zach stared down at his now pumpkin-covered flannel, blinking like he couldn't quite believe what had just happened.

Slowly, his gaze lifted to hers, Zach took a step closer, eyes dark with challenge.

The tension crackled like an autumn bonfire.

"Yeah?" he said, his voice deceptively calm. "I guess that means I get a turn."

Madison's eyes widened. "Oh, no you don't—"

But it was too late.

Madison turned and tried to run.

Zach lunged, grabbing a handful of pumpkin and smearing it across her arm before she could get away.

"Zach!" she yelled, laughing despite herself.

He grinned. "What? I was just evening the score."

"Oh, that's how we're playing?"

"You tell me. I thought that's how you liked it." Zach's voice held a playful edge.

Madison bent down to grab another handful of pumpkin, but Zach was faster.

In one swift move, he grabbed her wrist, spinning her around as if he were twirling her on a dance floor.

Madison yelped, but she was laughing, as her back was now flush with his chest.

"Nuh-uh," he murmured in her ear. "I think you've done enough damage."

Madison tilted her head back to look up at him.

His hands were still wrapped around her wrist, his grip warm, strong, but gentle.

The laughter lingered on her lips, but her breath caught.

Zach's thumb grazed her skin, slow and deliberate. Her pulse pounded.

The sounds of the festival faded away.

For a long, stretched-out second, it was just them.

A woman could get lost in moments like this. Madison didn't care that they were in the middle of the street with dozens of people around them. She only cared about the man looking down at her with eyes so deep she could fall into them forever.

She turned around so that she was facing him, arms around his neck, and kissed him softly, slowly, like it was their first time.

"Alright, alright!" Mrs. C. clapped loudly. "Get a room, you two!"

The moment broke.

"Hey now!" Madison said, stepping back. "You started it!" she said to Mrs. C.

"Don't you dare throw any of those pumpkin guts on me!" The older woman rested her clenched fists on her hips.

"Don't worry, I'll keep her in line," Zach replied with all bravado and no bite.

"You will, will you?" Madison got that playful look in her eyes again.

"On second thought, Mrs. C., you're on your own!" Zach laughed and ran toward a group of kids, knowing Madison wouldn't dare follow him.

"Chicken!" she yelled out after him, turning around and running back toward the inn to quickly get changed.

If Maple Falls hadn't known they were back together before that, well, they definitely did now.

THIRTY-SIX
ZACH

"There you are! Where have you been?" Anita called out, her voice cutting through the music and laughter.

Zach had stripped off his flannel, leaving him in a black fitted tee, and he was standing with Madison again. He hadn't meant to walk directly over to her when she came back out, but he hadn't been able to stop his feet from moving in her direction.

She'd changed her sweater, going for a fall dress. It was striped in navy blues and mustard yellows with a swooping neckline. If he didn't know any better, he'd swear she was trying to drive him wild with that peek of cleavage and all that leg.

"What do you mean, where have I been? I've been working."

Anita waved off his protest. "That's fine and dandy, sweetheart, but I signed you up for the auction, and you're up!"

Zach dug his heels in. "Auction? What auction?"

Too late.

His mother was stronger than she looked, and before Zach could protest further, he found himself shoved up onto a makeshift stage where Mayor Bloomfield was already speaking into the mic.

Madison followed, unable to hide her amusement.

"Here he is, folks! Have no fear, friends—Zach Whitaker has arrived, and not a moment too soon!" the mayor announced.

The crowd burst into cheers and applause.

Zach stood dead center onstage, face hot, arms crossed, glaring at his mother, Madison, the entire town—really, his whole universe.

Madison, of course, was front and center in the crowd, grinning like this was the greatest thing she'd ever witnessed.

"You all know him as your favorite handyman," the mayor continued, "the man who can fix just about anything. Let's give a round of applause for Zach Whitaker! Bidding starts at twenty dollars!"

"Twenty!" Rita, the chocolate shop owner, hollered from the back.

"Thirty!" Edith shouted. Madison looked over her shoulder at her grandma and laughed.

"Fifty!" Mrs. Humphrey threw in.

"Seventy-five!" came the woman Mrs. Bishop had tried to set him up with at the bar last Friday night.

Zach's stomach dropped.

From the crowd, Tanya Lockwood waved her cash in the air, giving him a slow, pointed smile.

Zach's eyes went wide.

He knew for a fact that Tanya had at least five minor household projects that needed tending to. He also knew that she had zero interest in getting them fixed.

The last time he'd been at her house, she had "accidentally" spilled lemonade on his shirt and then insisted he strip off so she could wash it.

Hell no. That was not happening again.

Zach caught Madison's eyes. She was still standing there,

arms folded, laughing at the scene. He held her gaze, silently begging her to save him.

Madison's brows lifted, like she was enjoying this way too much.

The bidding war escalated.

"One hundred!" Rita shouted.

"One twenty!" countered the girl from the bar.

"One fifty!" Tanya screamed.

Zach was two seconds away from throwing himself off the damn stage when—

"Two hundred and fifty dollars!"

The crowd gasped.

Zach's head snapped toward Madison.

She was standing tall, arm raised, with a determined expression.

Mayor Bloomfield clapped his hands together. "Well, well! Sold to Madison Kelly for two hundred and fifty dollars!" He turned toward Madison. "Come on up here and claim your prize, young lady."

The crowd groaned, or maybe it was just Tanya complaining loudly enough for everyone to hear her.

Madison took her time climbing onto the stage. She stopped in front of him, tilting her head in mock innocence. "You're welcome, by the way."

Zach exhaled in relief. "You have no idea."

"Oh, I do."

The second they were offstage, Zach draped his arm over her shoulders. It was instinct, really. Muscle memory from years of doing it without thinking. She fit under his arm like she always had, and today, Zach didn't let go.

After watching the rest of the auction they spent the rest of the day together, building a scarecrow for the front porch of the inn, sharing bites of pumpkin pie from the tasting table—Edith won, no contest—and strolling among the vendors hand in hand, like it was the most natural thing in the world.

Zach stood by her side while she struck a deal with Zoe for fresh flowers for the inn's reopening and listened while she chatted with the mayor about his great-niece.

"When it comes to the internet, I don't know what I'm doing. I'd rather avoid it if I could," Mayor Bloomfield confessed. "But Elsie's got all these plans. Thought she could start with you."

"Sounds good. Just let me know when she's in town and we'll set something up," Madison said before they headed toward the street fair.

"I'm surprised you're not here selling your apple butter," Madison said, eyeing the jam stand from another farm.

Zach shrugged. "Been a bit busy, but I need to do that soon enough. I keep it stocked at the hardware store."

Maybe that was something he could find time to do in the next few days, now that his kitchen had power again. All he needed was a stovetop and a counter to slice up the apples. It was easy enough.

"You know Kit's using it for the inn's cinnamon rolls, right? It's delicious."

Zach looked down at Madison. "Coming from you, that's quite a compliment."

"It's the truth."

Madison's cheeks were flushed from the wind and the cider, and she had that easy smile again—the one he hadn't seen in too long.

For the first time in weeks, the tight knot in his chest loosened just a little.

They wandered past a long line of booths, hand in hand, the tents thinning toward the end of the street where the vendors grew sparse.

A pop-up art stall blocked half the alleyway between two brick buildings.

Zach glanced around, catching sight of a narrow path behind one of the booths. He couldn't let the opportunity pass by. Not when he'd been thinking about Madison all day since she'd left his bed.

"Come on," he muttered under his breath.

"Where are we going?" She laughed but followed him anyway, trying to keep up with his longer strides.

They slipped behind the tent, half hidden by hanging quilts and painted wooden signs.

The second they were alone, Zach's hand was at her waist, pulling her into the shadowed nook, walking her back until she was hidden completely from view.

"Zach," she gasped, but he was already there, his tongue dipping into her mouth.

The kiss was slow and sensual. He wanted to drink every ounce of her in.

Madison kissed him back just as deeply, as if they were melting into each other.

Somewhere in the distance, the fair music played, a guitar and a folk singer, but it sounded far away, muffled by the blood rushing through his body.

When they finally broke apart, both breathing hard, Zach pressed his forehead to hers.

"I've wanted to do that all day," he said, voice rough.

Madison closed her eyes, savoring the moment. "Me too," she confessed.

He pulled back just enough to look at her, his thumb brushing her cheekbone.

"You remember the first Pumpkinfest we snuck out here?" he murmured.

Madison laughed softly. "Yeah. You won me that stupid stuffed pumpkin from the ring toss."

"And you kissed me behind the church, under the oak tree."

"You tasted like caramel apples and trouble," she whispered.

Zach smiled. Madison looked utterly bewitching. He tucked a strand of hair behind her ear.

"We should get back," he said, as if it killed him to say so.

Madison gave him a look. One that showed how much she really, really wished that wasn't so.

Zach chuckled. "Keep looking at me like that, Mads," he said, his voice dangerously low, "and we won't make it out of this alley."

THIRTY-SEVEN
MADISON

The fire crackled softly, flicking pops of orange and yellow against the inky nighttime sky. The lake stretched out beyond them, glassy and still. The moon was hidden, making the night seem quieter, hushed.

The festival had moved further down from the inn to the lakefront park, where live music, food vendors, and a beer tent would keep locals entertained through the night.

Here, it was just them.

Madison eyed the cabin, just down the hill, wondering if she should have this conversation out here in the open, or inside, in private. Because there was something she needed to say. Something she should've said a long time ago but had never been brave enough.

Zach sat back in the Adirondack chair, legs sprawled, a half-finished cider forgotten beside him.

Madison lingered near the firepit, arms crossed loosely, her dress fluttering in the breeze. She decided, *Screw it, best to have the conversation and get it over with.*

She took a deep breath and crossed the few steps toward him.

"Zach," she said quietly.

He looked up, seemingly surprised to hear the seriousness in her voice. "What, what is it?" Zach immediately went on alert.

"I just want to apologize," she started to say before stopping, taking a moment to control her emotions. She cleared her throat. "For what happened when I left. For how it all fell apart. For never properly talking to you about it all."

Zach's silence gave her the space to continue.

"I didn't mean for it to happen that way." She closed her eyes, remembering the anxiety and the excitement of those early days. How much she loved the big city, immersing herself in the culinary world, and that world opening to her.

"Partly I was hurt. I wanted you to come with me, or at least to fight for me to stay. I guess we could have made it work long-distance and I should have made more effort. But I just got so caught up in my new life; it was a whirlwind, and I was so young.

"And then I saw you that night at the Kettle and I... I jumped to conclusions. I let it hurt me, and I let it push me away. I never asked you what really happened. I just... assumed." Her voice cracked, tears threatening. "The point is, I never looked back, and it was wrong."

Madison braced herself for Zach to cut in. To tell her how much she had hurt him, how badly she'd messed up.

But he didn't say anything. He just watched her, that guarded, quiet intensity in his eyes. She could see the pain lingering there, and it bit into her heart.

She took a steadying breath, forcing herself to meet his gaze head-on. "I thought... at first I thought if I worked hard enough, if I chased it all, I could somehow have everything—" She broke off, forcing the tears to stay away. "But somewhere along the way, I lost sight of what mattered most."

Zach shook his head. "You mattered most to me," he said simply.

"You did to me too," she whispered. "Even when I tried to convince myself you didn't."

Zach stood and closed the distance between them. "You're here now," he said.

Madison's breath caught as he reached for her. Not roughly, not urgently—just a slow, deliberate pull, like he'd been waiting years to do it right.

His hand found her waist, sliding over the soft fabric of her dress, pulling her close to him.

Her heart hammered against her ribs. She could feel the strength in his touch, the quiet desperation he'd kept bottled up for far too long.

She tilted her chin up, eyes pouring into his.

There was no hesitation in Zach now. No distance. Only them.

When his mouth finally met hers, it was both fierce and aching, like a dam breaking wide open. Madison's fingers fisted the front of his shirt, dragging him closer.

Zach deepened the kiss immediately, his mouth demanding, his body pressing her back toward the Adirondack chair by the firepit.

Zach dropped heavily into the chair, pulling her with him, settling her astride his lap.

Her dress bunched around her thighs as she straddled him, her knees bracketing his hips, her breath coming in ragged gasps. His hands slid up her sides, palms hot through the thin material.

Her own hands found the back of his neck, tracing the warm, strong line of him as he crushed her mouth against his again.

Everything else, the fire crackling beside them, the cool

night air, the entire town only a few hundred yards away, faded to nothing.

It was just Madison and Zach, laid bare, rediscovering everything they'd thought they'd lost.

His fingers slipped under the hem of her dress, teasing along the curve of her thigh. She tugged at the button of his jeans until she freed him, her hands stroking him with a tenderness that made him shudder.

"Jesus, Mads," he whispered.

"I want you," she replied, sliding her panties aside.

Zach groaned low in his throat as he guided her down onto him. He kissed her throat, her collarbone, and she moaned with every roll of her hips.

"You drive me crazy," he fought to get out.

"You love it," she teased, breathless.

"I do," he growled.

The rhythm built between them, their breaths syncing. She felt the pleasure coiling tighter and tighter inside until she thought she might come apart in his arms.

Zach's hands slipped beneath her dress, palming her ass, and she bit her lip hard, wanting it to last for longer.

Zach caught her chin, forcing her to look at him. "Don't hold back," he said. "Let me see you."

That was her undoing.

Madison came, her body tightening around him, her cry muffled against his neck.

Zach was right there with her.

The air felt cooler despite the heat at her back. Madison leaned against his chest and he wrapped his arms around her. One hand slid up into her hair, cradling the back of her head, while the other splayed across her lower back, keeping her anchored. Her body still trembled with the last waves of pleasure.

Neither spoke, leaning into the moment. The memories. The realization of how good it still felt to be together after so many years apart.

Madison finally pulled back, tipping her face up. "I don't think I could ever get tired of this, of you."

"I know," Zach said, his voice rough. "I'd want this in any lifetime, in any world. Always you. I love you, Madison."

His eyes met hers and her breath caught in her throat as she saw it all. The universe of love that had never left. The ripping pain of falling apart. The wonder of being back in each other's arms.

There were words forming on her tongue, but she couldn't get them out. Her chest ached from how badly she wanted this to last. With how badly she wished they hadn't spent all these years apart.

But what would happen to them now?

Zach exhaled and kissed her forehead.

She blinked back sudden tears. "What are we doing, Zach?"

He hesitated, and for a moment she thought he might deflect, crack a joke, pull away. But then his brow furrowed like he was trying to form a truth he hadn't let himself speak aloud.

"I don't know what's going to happen when you go back," he admitted. "And it scares the hell out of me."

Madison's throat tightened.

"But I do know this," he continued. "I'm not going to pretend I don't love you anymore. I'm not going to act like this doesn't matter."

She pressed a hand to his chest. "It matters. You matter," she said, stumbling over the words as if she'd forgotten how to talk.

His arms squeezed around her.

Madison looked up at the stars overhead—so many, scattered across the sky.

She leaned in and kissed him, slow and deep, sinking into it with every part of her. She hoped that in that kiss, he could feel what was carved onto her soul.

And when she pulled back, her voice was barely a whisper. "I don't want this to end."

Zach pressed his forehead to hers. "Then don't let it."

THIRTY-EIGHT
MADISON

October 21st

"So, have you hooked up with the sexy carpenter yet?" Jo asked on a call two days later as Madison was getting ready.

"Funny you should ask," Madison said, tugging on a pair of jeans and tossing an oatmeal knit sweater over her white tank top.

"Ha! I knew it!"

Madison glanced at herself in the mirror and saw the blush creeping up her cheeks. Jeez Louise, she couldn't even reference Zach without turning red. Flashes of the cabin, of the late night around the campfire, of the way their bodies fit together. How her mind had gone from trying to forget their history to daring to hope about their future.

And yet, when she had some distance from Zach, she had to question what she was doing.

He'd forgiven her for the way she'd left years ago, and that meant the world to her.

He'd said he loved her, words she'd never thought she'd hear again.

But it was too late. She wasn't staying in Maple Falls, was she? She'd just told Mrs. C. that to get the woman to shut up. She and Zach both knew her life was in New York.

Even if it felt more and more that her life was here. Or at least it could be.

The only thing Madison knew for sure was that she wanted Zach.

One thing at a time, she told herself. *Focus on the inn.*

"Hello?" Jo interrupted her spiral. "Are you fantasizing about Mr. Tool Belt over there?"

"Maybe just a bit," Madison replied with a grin. She twisted her hair into a messy bun and pocketed her Chapstick.

Her plan was to head to the bakery and grab a coffee. It was quickly becoming her morning routine: caffeine, catching up with Emily, and maybe casually running into Zach outside the cabin. Seeing him shirtless taking in the view was the best way to start the day. Those broad shoulders, tight pecs, solid abs...

Madison changed her train of thought before she decided to skip the caffeine and head right down to the cabin. Coffee was too important. A woman had to have priorities.

"I actually have you and your creative texts to thank for interrupting us the first time," Madison added, shaking her head as she wrapped an orange wool scarf around her neck.

"Excuse me? Moi? I thought you'd appreciate the artful placement of Mr. October's gourds," Jo said with zero shame.

Madison laughed. "Oh, I appreciated it. Except Zach saw it and thought it was from some guy named Jo—thought it was your gourds on display."

"Shut up. He did not." Jo cracked up.

"Oh, he did. He definitely did."

"Oops, sorry. My bad."

"It's not your fault. Mr. October was rather... impressive."

Jo's grin was practically audible.

Madison snickered. "And for the record, Zach and I did talk, I told him you were a she, and everything's good now."

"Oh yeah? How good?" Jo asked playfully.

"Like I've had more orgasms in the past two days than the past two years good."

"Love it. That's what I want to hear. Go get 'em, tiger!"

Madison shook her head. "I'll keep you posted."

"You better. Catch up later, alright?"

"Promise. Take care, you."

When Madison reached the front desk, she found Gram chatting on the phone with a potential guest and Zach walking through the front door all flannel-shirted and beard-y like a scene straight out of a fall romance.

"Good morning," he greeted, his voice lower and huskier than she remembered. Or maybe she was just imagining it.

Their eyes locked.

She had to fight the urge to shiver.

"I'm going to the bakery," Madison blurted, desperate to put some distance between them before they combusted in front of her grandmother.

Zach opened his mouth, but Gram cut in, hand over the receiver. "Zach, why don't you go with her? Bring me back one of Emily's apple spice lattes, and grab something for yourself while you're at it." She gave them both a knowing wink.

Madison swallowed hard.

"Mind?" Zach asked Madison, eyes searching.

"Mind? No, not at all." She was already halfway to the door.

They walked side by side down the sidewalk. Shop owners were sweeping their sidewalks, rearranging their potted chrysanthemums and adding extra pumpkins here and there. Madison tried to look anywhere but at Zach.

She was hyperaware of him, of the heat radiating from him, the faint scent of his cedarwood cologne, the way she fell in step with him, like no time had passed. When his hand brushed against hers, she curled her fingers around his.

She stole a look at him and didn't bother hiding the smile that tugged at her lips.

Mrs. C. and Mrs. Bishop eyed them the moment they walked through the door. The bakery's delicious aroma made Madison's mouth water. She could really use an extra-large coffee right now, and one of Emily's cookies.

"Hey, you two," Emily said while restocking the sugar cookies. "Your usual?" she asked, standing.

"That would be great, thanks, Em," Zach replied.

Madison caught the look that passed between the siblings and knew Emily was just itching to ask them questions.

Zach shook his head ever so slightly, his eyes shooting his sister a knowing look.

Emily just paused, smiled, and then said, "Coming right up."

"Thanks." Madison turned away before Emily could change her mind.

"You two made quite the pair on Friday," Mrs. C. said, calling out from her table, angling for gossip.

"Always knew you'd find your way back together," Mrs. Bishop added.

"No, you didn't. You just tried fixing him up with that Alyssa girl. I'm the one who said they'd get back together," Mrs. C. insisted.

"I'm the one who lost fifty bucks when she left town. Maybe I can get it back now," Mrs. Bishop added.

"Maybe you will," Zach replied with easy charm.

"Oh, say, Madison, you're coming Tuesday afternoon, aren't you?" Mrs. C. asked while stirring her coffee.

Madison wasn't sure what the older woman was talking about, and that must have been clear on her face.

"Crafting club. Your grandma said you volunteered to bring the leaves," Mrs. Bishop supplied.

Madison narrowed her eyes. "She did, did she?"

"Course I wouldn't blame you if you had a hot date." Mrs. Bishop lowered her chin in Zach's direction.

"I'll be there," Madison replied before the exchange could get any more awkward.

"Perfect. See you then," Mrs. Bishop said with a knowing smile.

Madison turned to scan the menu board, trying to ignore the heat blooming across her cheeks, when Mrs. C.'s voice floated behind her.

"And that mystery letter writer thought we needed to intervene," she was saying with a huff. "Shows what they know."

Madison's ears perked up. She turned to Zach. "Did she say 'mystery letter writer'?"

Zach raised a brow, just as intrigued.

Madison spun back around. "What's this about mystery letters?"

Mrs. C. and Mrs. Bishop exchanged glances and then Mrs. C. finally spoke, setting her coffee cup down. "Well, if you must know, I received an anonymous letter. Told me to help out at the inn. Said you'd be in town, and I should encourage you in any way I saw fit."

"And when did you get this letter?"

"Let me think... I guess it was this past Tuesday," Mrs. C. replied. "So, a few days ago."

Madison's mind raced. She'd returned to town ten days ago, so the letters were still going out.

Whoever the mystery writer was, they were still at it. But why?

"Do you still have the letter?" Madison pressed.

"Not on me," Mrs. C. replied, taken back.

"Was it handwritten? Typed? Was there postage?"

The older woman chuckled. "Typed. Not sure about the postage. And don't you worry, it sounds like you have everything under control."

Madison replied with a tight smile. That might be true, but she still wanted to find out who had so effectively pulled the strings in her life, and was still pulling them. "Will you bring it with you Tuesday? To the crafting club?"

Mrs. C. looked unsure.

"I know it might have said to keep it a secret. But it's important," Madison pleaded. She stared at the woman, heart in her eyes.

"Alright, dear. I'll put it in my purse tonight." Mrs. C. nodded.

"Thanks, I appreciate it," Madison said before looking back at Zach.

Big mistake. The man was trying to look innocent but failing miserably. She could swear he was undressing her with his eyes. Piece by piece until she felt completely exposed.

The electricity simmered between them, alive and reckless.

"Here you go," Emily said, interrupting their silent fireworks. She glanced between them, eyebrows lifting slightly, but —bless her—she said nothing. Just gave them their coffees.

"Come on. Let's go before you get us both into even more trouble," Madison said, handing Zach his coffee.

"Not my fault. You keep looking at me like that," Zach said under his breath as he fell into step beside her. His hand closed around hers again, and something switched on inside her.

She hadn't said it to him yet, but Madison knew. She couldn't run away from it anymore.

It was as unstoppable and as inevitable as the seasons turning.

She was in love with Zach.

THIRTY-NINE
ZACH

That evening as the sun dipped into the flaming horizon, Zach was back at his farmhouse. He told himself it was to get work done, but that was a lie. After putting in a solid ten hours at the inn, sanding and repainting window trim, his body was still restless. It was like he couldn't burn off enough energy even if he tried.

He was trying to play it cool around Madison and not talk about the future, but every time he got too close, he felt like a schoolboy. Zach had spent so many years convincing himself he was over her. That she'd moved on, and he had too. But every minute he spent with her now, he knew the truth.

Madison was it for him. She always had been. All he wanted, all he had ever wanted, was her. He wanted all his mornings with her curled up against him in his bed. Coffee brewed while she sat on his counter, looking at him like he hung the moon.

He wanted the life they'd once dreamed up together, lying on a blanket under the stars when they were too young to know how rare their love was.

Back then, they used to talk about it all the time, building their house, their lives.

Madison wanted a big wraparound porch. And a fireplace, of course. Something to keep the chill away on those frigid Midwestern winter nights when they'd cuddle up inside. And a backyard for cookouts when it was warmer. The kitchen would be at the heart of it. A space where she could cook anything she could dream up. He could still hear her voice, clear as day, laughing as she mapped it all out beside him, as certain about their future as she was about the stars overhead. And now he was building it. Frame by frame. Nail by nail.

Zach leaned back against the kitchen counter, glancing around the half-finished space. The wiring was done, at least. Hot water too. He was proud of the work he'd already done, all the sanding, framing, and painting. Zach was pouring everything he had into these walls.

He was going to order the kitchen cabinets next week. Maybe Madison would like to take a drive with him and pick them out...

Zach cursed under his breath and forced himself to mentally backtrack.

It was dangerous, letting himself hope like that. Because no matter how good it felt when she was in his arms, looking up at him like he was the only man on Earth... there was still a part of him that remembered what it had felt like when she'd left. And Madison had bigger dreams than Maple Falls.

He couldn't ask her to give those up. Not for him. Not for this house.

Still... staring at the blueprints pinned to the wall, he couldn't help it.

He could see her here. Standing in the kitchen, barefoot, laughing, maybe stealing hot biscuits straight from the oven.

Madison Kelly-Whitaker.

The thought hit him so hard, he had to steady himself against the counter.

God help him. He was already so far gone.

A familiar voice broke the silence.

"Knew I'd find you here," Liam said, sauntering in with a pizza box and a six-pack, like he owned the place.

"You keeping tabs on me now?" Zach asked, arms crossed as he turned from the blueprints.

"Nah, it's just that there's nothing to do, and I'm lonely," Liam said sarcastically with a smirk.

He set the pizza box down on a pair of sawhorses doubling as a table. "Take a break, have some pizza. I got it from Pino's with extra sausage and black olives."

Zach tried to wave him off. "Seriously, dude, I'm fine. You don't need to keep checking up on me."

Liam ignored him, cracking open a beer. "I don't know. No one's seen hide nor hair from you. It's like all you do is work and you know that's no way to live."

"Pot calling the kettle," Zach said, coming over and grabbing a beer.

"Fair." Liam grinned, chewing.

Zach drank in silence, staring at the blank drywall and scattered tools.

"So," Liam said between bites. "You gonna tell me what's eating at you? Or am I gonna have to guess?"

"Nothing's eating at me." Zach glanced over at Liam.

Their eyes locked.

That was enough.

Liam jumped up. "Holy shit. You and Madison hooked up!"

Zach shook his head. "I thought you'd have heard by now; it's all over town."

Liam grinned. "Here I'm thinking you're out here nursing a broken heart, and you've been off doing the dirty like a couple of teenagers."

Zach suspected Liam didn't know if he should be offended or impressed that Zach hadn't told him.

"Christ, man," Zach grumbled, taking another swig of beer. "It's complicated."

"Complicated my ass," Liam shot back. "You two've been complicated since the fifth grade."

Zach cocked his head and took another drink. He had to give Liam that.

"We're busy working on the inn ahead of the relaunch. We agreed to just enjoy each other's company for now, not think about the future," Zach supplied after swallowing. He'd already counted down the days. It wasn't many. Madison wasn't sure she was staying, which meant she probably wasn't. It ate him up inside.

Liam nodded slowly. "But you think she'll leave after that?"

Zach didn't answer, which said enough.

"I thought she was staying in Maple Falls... That's what—"

"C'mon, Liam, even you should know not to take gossip as word." Didn't matter if Zach might've allowed himself to hope just a little. He wouldn't admit it, not aloud.

Liam exhaled and grabbed another beer. "Look, you've never been casual about Madison. And you sure as hell know she's not casual about you."

Zach stared at the floor. "It's not just about me. Her career's in New York, not here."

Liam leaned against the wall, studying him. "And you're just going to let that happen without saying anything?"

Zach's jaw tightened. "What's there to say? She's got a life back there."

Liam shook his head. "No. She's got a choice between two lives. And you're scared she won't choose you."

Zach didn't answer. He just drained the rest of his beer and stared at the empty kitchen. Wishing he knew how to build something that could actually keep her here.

FORTY

MADISON

October 23rd

"I'm going to pretend you're dying to make a fall wreath and not just here to get the four-one-one on Mrs. C.'s letter," Gram said, giving Madison a knowing look as they got out of the car in front of Mrs. Humphrey's house.

"Of course," Madison replied with a fake grin.

"Oh, you're just as bad as Kit, pretending like she doesn't want my shortbread recipe." Gram leaned in and added in a conspiratorial whisper, "I'm not giving it to her either."

"You're terrible," Madison said with a smile. "But you're right. It's good to get out of the inn and out of my own head."

"I imagine that boy has you turned every which way but up. Well... maybe a bit on your back, too." Gram chuckled.

Madison's face instantly flushed, thinking about their plans for tonight. Zach had invited her over for dinner at the farmhouse. She had all sorts of sexy ideas involving him and his tool belt, right there in the middle of his half-renovated kitchen.

Gram patted her hand. "Now, dear, there's nothing wrong with a little hanky-panky. You and Zach love each other, I can see that well enough. And that's all that matters. Maybe this time things will end up right."

Madison wasn't sure how, though, seeing as she still planned on heading back to New York on November 1st.

At least, she thought that's what she was going to do. She'd been avoiding opening her work email, ignoring the growing pile of upcoming assignments. She had told her editor she was only taking three weeks off, and that time was almost up.

Madison soon had a decision to make, and she wasn't sure what she was going to do. Most of the time she tried not to think about it, much like her overflowing inbox. It's not like she hadn't been busy enough with the inn's upcoming relaunch to keep her mind occupied.

The front porch steps creaked beneath their feet as they climbed them, crafting tote bags in tow.

Mrs. Humphrey's front yard looked like a Halloween aisle had exploded at a home goods store. While the front of Mrs. C.'s home was known for its ornamental gardens and beautiful blooms, every square foot of Mrs. Humphrey's front yard was covered in decorations, including the porch rail, which was wrapped in orange and black garlands. Ceramic pumpkins lined the steps, plastic bats dangled from the ceiling, and a skeleton wearing a witch's hat sat on the porch swing, propped up by orange and black throw pillows.

"Well, there you two are, and just in time—the mulled wine is ready," Mrs. Humphrey said, taking their canvas tote bags so they could take off their coats. She had a built-in coat rack in her entryway, where the other guests had already deposited their coats and shoes.

Her schnauzer came forward, sniffing everything: their shoes, coats, pants. He was dressed for Halloween with an orange plaid vest.

Madison bent low and gave him a couple of pats. The pup danced in circles around her feet.

"Don't mind Charles; he's very excited with all our guests today," Mrs. Humphrey said as she led them down the hallway into her kitchen area. "Come along, Charles. Leave them be."

Surprisingly, the dog did just that, trailing after Mrs. Humphrey happily.

Mrs. Humphrey's kitchen, dining room, and living room were one long rectangle. The dining room table had circular wicker wreaths set out at each place setting. A handful of hot glue guns were plugged in on the center island, surrounded by bins and baskets filled with mini pinecones, wooden pumpkins, and spools of ribbon.

"I'll just put those leaves here," Mrs. Humphrey said, tipping the tote over into an oversized basket. The red, orange, and yellow leaves fluttered down. The woman gave the tote a shake to make sure every last one came out before folding the bag and setting it on the counter.

"Who wants some witch's brew?" Mrs. C. called out. She ladled the steaming wine from the crockpot into mugs. "It's my own special recipe—red wine, nutmeg, ginger, and apple juice."

"You know I want some," Mrs. Bishop declared from the dining table. She'd been organizing the ribbon, barely looking up when Madison and Gram had entered. "What do you think? Should I go with the striped orange and red ribbon or the glittery gold one?" She held two spools of ribbon up in the light, examining them. "Or what about brown? It has some shine to it." She picked up a third spool of satiny chocolate ribbon.

Mrs. C. handed Madison a steaming cup. "Don't bother answering her. She'll change her mind before you do."

Madison smiled, accepting the cup.

"You're right. I think I'll go for the checkered print instead," Mrs. Bishop said, selecting a thick cream and orange ribbon.

Mrs. C. raised her eyebrows as if to say, *See?*

Madison took a sip of the mulled wine. The warmth spread

through her body, taking away the chill she hadn't realized she'd carried in from outside.

At that moment, someone knocked at the door.

"Oh, that's probably Cassidy," Mrs. Humphrey said with excitement, hurrying over, Charles trotting close at her heels.

Madison turned to Gram, whispering, "Who's Cassidy?"

"No idea, dear," Gram replied cheerfully, reaching for a pumpkin cookie.

Before Madison could ask, Mrs. C. offered, "She's new in town. I think she's just passing through, but she looked so lonely at the bakery yesterday morning. Couldn't not invite her, now could I?"

Mrs. Humphrey swung the door open, and sure enough, in stepped a young woman bundled in a yellow pea coat and a bright green knit beanie, her blonde hair braided in two long plaits down her back. She carried an oversized canvas tote with a hand-painted sunflower on the front and wore a pair of thick red wool socks on her feet.

The woman looked unsure of herself, but she seemed to relax a little when she spotted Madison.

"Hi, I'm Madison," she said, stepping forward to shake the woman's hand.

"Hi, Cassidy."

"And this is Madison's grandmother, Edith—and you already know Mrs. C. and Mrs. Bishop. Rita from the chocolate shop will be here too."

Cassidy smiled nervously and reached into her tote, pulling out a small tin.

"I brought truffles. I wasn't sure if you needed anything, but I didn't want to come empty-handed."

Mrs. Humphrey wasted no time popping the lid off and inhaling deeply. A smile lit her face. "These smell heavenly. And plenty for everyone. Except for you, Charles," she said, placing the tin on the counter next to the rest of the snacks. The dog looked up expectantly.

Mrs. Humphrey fetched him a treat out of a separate jar so the pup wouldn't feel left out.

"You made these?" Madison asked, taking a bite and letting the chocolate melt in her mouth. She couldn't describe it, but something about the chocolate reminded her of the city.

Cassidy grinned. "Yeah. I trained as a chocolatier in Paris before moving back to New York."

Madison blinked. "Wait—New York? Whereabouts?"

"The Village," Cassidy said, setting down her tote. "My brother and his husband run a patisserie on Bleecker Street. I worked there before... well, before deciding to find a new adventure."

Madison's jaw dropped. "No way. La Petite Chocolatine?"

Cassidy's eyes widened in delight. "You know it?"

"I live two blocks over!" Madison said, laughing. "Their croissants kept me alive during my internship."

Cassidy grinned. "That was mostly my brother's doing. I specialized more in the chocolate side of things. Truffles. Caramels. Ganache, if the mood struck."

Mrs. C. clapped her hands. "Well, isn't that something? Small world after all."

Just then, Rita bustled in, cheeks pink from the cold, shedding her jacket as she spoke.

"Sorry I'm late. Maple pecan emergency. Long story."

She spotted Cassidy and smiled warmly.

"You must be Cassidy. Rita Matthews," she said, offering a hand. "Owner of the Cocoa Corner."

Cassidy shook it. "So nice to meet you. Everyone keeps saying I have to stop by your shop."

Rita's eyes twinkled. "And if you're a chocolatier, you and I definitely need to talk."

Cassidy laughed, pushing her hair behind her ear. "I'd love that."

The group got to work on their wreaths. As much as Madison wanted to talk to Mrs. C. about the letter, she didn't want to ask in front of everyone. The fewer people who knew, the better.

"Well, isn't that something?" Mrs. Bishop said, eyeing Madison's wreath.

"Oh, it's something alright," Mrs. C. chuckled.

Madison frowned. Even she could admit her wreath looked more like something from *The Nightmare Before Christmas* than a festive fall decoration. Cassidy's wreath, on the other hand, looked like it belonged on the cover of a craft magazine. Her bow was tied perfectly at the center, with looping ribbon and faux pumpkins placed just so. Madison was convinced she could've sold it for a hundred bucks at any local craft fair.

Meanwhile, Madison was trying to peel her elbow off the table, realizing too late that a dollop of hot glue had dripped onto her sweater and hardened instantly.

She tugged at her sleeve, hoping it hadn't left a mark on Mrs. Humphrey's table.

"Wouldn't be the first time someone's glued themselves to the table," Gram said with a sly smile.

Madison wished she'd kept that to herself.

"Better than setting your wreath on fire," Mrs. C. chimed in.

"Fire?" Cassidy asked, rearranging her wooden pumpkins.

"I remember that!" Rita laughed. "Edith wasn't paying attention to her ribbon, and someone had left a candle burning in the center of the table—you know, one of those big glass jar ones. The ribbon tail caught, and the whole thing went up in smoke! We ended up chucking it out the back door and hosing it down."

Madison glanced back at her own wreath. Surely it wasn't that bad.

"So, you and Zach," Mrs. Bishop said without warning.

"Who's Zach?" Cassidy asked, adjusting her wreath.

"Madison's ex-boyfriend, who she's recently shacked back up with," Mrs. C. said matter-of-factly.

"You want to watch out for these two," Madison said, turning to Cassidy, who laughed. "Definitely don't tell them anything about your love life. You could sneeze in someone's direction and they'd be planning your wedding."

"Don't worry, we're all just rooting for you," Mrs. Humphrey called from the kitchen as she brought a fresh plate of warm pumpkin cookies to the table. She set Cassidy's chocolates next to it.

As the afternoon wore on, Madison realized that while she had initially come over to learn about the letter, she now wasn't in such a hurry to leave.

She liked being in Mrs. Humphrey's kitchen, the scent of pumpkin cookies and mulled wine lingering in the air, the buzz of women laughing and teasing over their half-finished wreaths.

She liked the way Mrs. C. always had a quip ready, how Gram pretended to tsk, tsk at their comments, and how Mrs. Bishop kept sneaking truffles when she thought no one was looking.

For the first time in what felt like years, Madison wasn't rushing to be anywhere else. She wasn't refreshing her email. She wasn't checking her phone. She was here.

She felt rooted. She felt at home.

When everyone was finishing up their wreaths and getting ready to head home, Madison took a moment to pull Mrs. C. aside in the corner of the kitchen.

"About that anonymous letter..." Madison left the sentence hanging.

"I have it in my purse. Let me grab it for you. Oh—" Mrs. C.

paused mid-step and turned back to Madison. "Before I forget—Mayor Bloomfield got one, too. Poor guy went fishing just to avoid us nagging him about it."

"Are you serious? Why?"

Mrs. C. shrugged. "Just found out about it yesterday at the bakery."

"Do you know what it said?"

"I don't. You'll have to ask him yourself, dear. I'm sure he'll be back tomorrow."

Madison decided right then and there—she couldn't track down the mayor fast enough.

She unfolded Mrs. C.'s letter, and read:

Mrs. C.,

The Cinnamon Spice Inn has always been a part of this town's heart, just like you. George needs a bit of help now, even if he's too stubborn to admit it. Please consider lending a hand with the gardens. You have such a talent for it. It would mean more than you know.

Sincerely,

—A friend

Madison's throat tightened. The writing was careful, but there was warmth in it, too; again, it was like whoever wrote it genuinely cared about the inn, and about her father. Who were they?

She folded the letter back up and looked at Mrs. C., who was watching her closely. "And did you?"

Mrs. C. lifted her chin, eyes twinkling. "Weed the flower beds? Not yet. I told your dad I would stop by tomorrow."

Madison could only hope she wouldn't also try to persuade her dad to sell the place while she did.

FORTY-ONE

ZACH

It was probably a mistake, but Zach couldn't help inviting Madison out to the farmhouse. He wanted her to see the bones, see the potential—see where their future could lie.

He stood on the back porch, looking at the rows of old apple trees, some of their branches still heavy with fruit. The height of the trees rolled along with the hills, and beyond that, the far-off glimmer of the lake. He hoped she'd love the place as much as he did. That she could see a future here with him like she used to.

Zach might not have been able to cook a four-course meal, not without a proper kitchen, but he could grill, and he knew a mean chili recipe and one for cornbread casserole. Madison would like that. He loaded the Weber with five pounds of charcoal and started the fire.

He worked outside at the picnic table, chopping onions, celery, and jalapeños while the coals heated up. Once everything was in the pot, he made the cornbread casserole and set that on the grill, too.

A few hours later, after stirring the chili and checking the cornbread, Zach looked up and saw Madison bumping down the driveway in her dad's old pickup truck. Zach had offered to pick her up, but she'd insisted she had a ride. There was no need to give her directions—she'd been to his grandparents' house more than once when they were teens.

Her window was cracked just enough to let in the unusually warm fall air, blowing her hair back. Zach walked over and opened her door. Madison looked like a picture of perfection in her tight jeans, striped sweater, and thick wool socks peeking out over the tops of her hiking boots. She had left her hair down, wild—the way he liked it.

"Wasn't sure what you were making, but I hope a bottle of red goes with it," she said, grabbing the wine bottle off the passenger seat and handing it over. Zach took her hand, and the wine, and helped her down.

She leaned in and kissed him on the cheek, lingering for a moment.

"I've got a couple of glasses," Zach said. "Not fancy wine glasses, mind you, but something to pour this into."

Madison allowed him to lead her up the driveway. "I was wondering what you were making, seeing as last I heard you didn't have a kitchen."

"I've got chili simmering on the grill and cornbread. How's that sound?"

"Cornbread, huh?"

"Our pantry rendezvous inspired me." Zach winked.

It took Madison a moment to remember that she'd been searching for the skillet when they'd been locked in the closet together.

"Come on in; I'll pour you some wine and show you the progress," Zach said.

Zach had to force himself not to make excuses for why he hadn't fixed up the porch yet or why he hadn't painted the front door. But when you walked inside, the wood floors gleamed. He'd managed to sand everything down and re-stain them. He'd picked a warm light gray for the walls—a color he thought Madison would like. She could add pops of gold or blue to brighten it up or go with earthy tones like greens and browns to ground it more, like the trees outside in the summertime.

The staircase wasn't redone yet, nor the three bedrooms upstairs, but he'd made good progress on the master bedroom on the ground floor. He tried not to think about that either. But it was impossible not to picture her here, to imagine what it might feel like if she stayed.

"I can't believe how different everything looks," Madison said, taking a slow circle around the kitchen. "You took down a wall here?"

"I did. Opened it right up to the dining room."

The dining room and kitchen now had an open floor plan, but an arched wall still separated them from the living room and staircase.

"I like it—it makes it feel bigger." Madison walked over to the blueprints tacked to the wall and examined them. "Planning a big island, huh?"

"That's the plan." Zach laid out the space for her, showing where the farmhouse sink would be, the pantry, the dining room table, built-in shelves for cookbooks, and a corner for a writing desk. He didn't mention that in his mind, they'd be her cookbooks, her writing desk. He didn't want to push.

She nodded and smiled. "I can picture it all, and it's beautiful."

Zach had to fight the urge to tell her he was doing it all for her. Instead, he said, "Dinner's about ready. Let me pour us this wine, and we can take it outside."

Zach figured they could picnic, seeing as the weather was so nice. It was hard to tell from day to day what the weather would be—storming one day like the middle of summer, bright and sunny the next. He knew it would be snowing any day now. Christmas would be here before they knew it.

But not today. Today had turned unseasonably warm. You had to take those Indian summer days whenever they came.

He grabbed the blanket, and they took their bowls and wine out into the yard.

"Ever have a picnic in an apple orchard?" Zach asked.

"There's a first time for everything, isn't there?" Madison replied as they walked a few feet deeper into the trees.

"I'm surprised it's this warm. I was freezing earlier," Madison said, pushing her sleeves up.

Zach spread the blanket in the middle of a row. The trees still had their leaves, and a few apples still dangled high on the branches. The low evening sunlight played off the trees, casting warm shadows onto the blanket. The orchard smelled of sun-ripened fruit and woodsmoke from a distant farm.

It was quiet here. Peaceful. The only sound was a crow calling out above as it circled looking for a place to land.

"This is so good. Are you sure you're not a New York-trained chef?" Madison teased, settling in and taking a bite.

He grinned, stretching his legs out.

After a few moments, Madison shifted, plucking a loose apple leaf from the blanket and twirling it between her fingers.

"You never talked about fixing up this place. I never knew you wanted it."

Zach leaned back on his elbows, staring up at the sky through the gaps in the trees.

"I didn't know either," he admitted. "Not until it was almost gone. When my mom started talking about selling it, it hit me—this land... it's in my blood. The Whitaker roots run deep out here. I could feel it in my bones."

Madison nodded, understanding flickering in her eyes.

"I get that. That's how I feel about the inn. It's my family's legacy, you know?" Her voice tightened and she pressed on. "Mrs. C. said something about us selling it, and it just lit a fire in me."

"Can't imagine that," Zach said with a smirk.

Madison playfully shoved his shoulder but ended up gripping the muscle of his bicep. Making up her mind, she scooted closer, wrapping her arm under his and resting her head on his shoulder.

"Who would've thought that after all these years, we'd be sitting out here like this?" There was a wistfulness to her voice.

She slipped her fingers through his, their hands naturally intertwined, and in that moment, Zach felt like everything was right in the world.

He looked over at her and smiled.

"What?" Madison asked, picking her head up and gazing up at him.

"Nothing. I just want to remember this moment. How you look right here, right now." Zach bent his head low. His hand came up to cradle her cheek, and he kissed her softly.

He hadn't planned for it to escalate; truly, he'd just wanted to remember this moment, but Madison clearly had other things in mind when she deepened the kiss.

She pushed her weight into Zach, leaning against him until he was forced to lie back. Madison rolled over until she was straddling his lap. He kept his hands behind his back, bracing himself, but they were itching to touch Madison. He was restraining himself, but one word from her and he would break.

And then she kissed him. It was deeper this time, filled with all the years of need. His hand came up, sliding along her thigh, tracing the curve of her hip before slipping around to the small of her back. Her sweater hitched higher as he moved, and he let his thumb brush a line along the soft skin above her waistband, just enough to make her breath catch.

Madison leaned forward, forcing Zach further onto his back. She held his gaze, brushing her fingers down his chest, slow and deliberate. "I want *you*, Zach."

She unbuttoned his jeans and lowered them just enough

while kissing a trail down his abdomen. Her hand found him, hard and ready, before her lips did.

She stroked him as she took him fully in her mouth, and he was gone. He was hers. And she didn't stop. Not until he was groaning her name like a prayer, and the world fell away completely.

FORTY-TWO
ZACH

Madison sensed the storm before Zach did. One moment they were lying blissfully on the blanket underneath the trees, Zach returning the favor, and the next Madison was scrambling for her sweater, her pants, trying to get dressed as quickly as possible. Thunder rolled in seconds later, the sky flashing with light.

"It's okay, it's alright," Zach said, but Madison's eyes were wide. When Zach looked into the depths of them, he saw nothing but fear.

"You don't know that," she said, shaking her head, panic in her voice. "You don't know it's not a tornado."

Zach's heart dropped. It had been so long since he'd seen her raw with fear. He knew storms triggered her. They were never just lightning and thunder. They were memories of the tornado they'd lived through as kids.

"Madison, listen to me," he said, placing his arms on her shoulders. "Go inside. The farmhouse is safe. I'll be right there. You trust me?"

She nodded reluctantly but didn't move until Zach gently pressed his hand to the small of her back. "Go on, I promise," he urged.

Madison finally took off while Zach quickly threw on his jeans, grabbed the blanket, used it to bundle up the dishes and the rest of the clothes, and ran after her.

The rain started coming down fast and hard before he made it inside. It came in sideways, in thick sheets, and the sky danced with lightning every few seconds.

Inside, Madison stood in the center of the living room, shaking uncontrollably. The wind howled against the windows, and the rain followed.

"Hey." Zach framed her face with both hands, trying to ground her. "You're here with me. There's no funnel cloud, just some wind and rain. You're safe."

Outside, the thunder cracked, and Madison buried her face into his chest.

"I know it sounds ridiculous," she whispered. "It's just... every time the thunder hits like that, I go right back there."

"It's not ridiculous." Zach wrapped his arms tightly around her. "We lived through something terrifying."

Madison let out a shaky breath. "And I still remember the sound. The trees snapping. The store shaking."

Madison pulled back, eyes darting around the room like she was searching for trees about to crash through the ceiling.

"The trees are clear." Zach moved and grabbed a thick blanket off the back of the couch and wrapped it around her shoulders. He wished like hell he had more furniture in the room. He hadn't gotten around to it yet, but he would soon.

"Here, stand by the fire." Zach had a couple of dry logs in the hearth and a pack of matches in the kitchen. Even though they didn't need the fire for the temperature, he thought it might help calm her.

Madison sighed and pulled the blanket tighter around her shoulders. "I know I shouldn't be but..."

"But you're scared," Zach finished softly.

Madison nodded.

"Don't worry. Let me get the fire going, then I'll sit right here with you."

Zach prayed the old wood would catch. Once the kindling was lit, he ducked back into the kitchen and returned with a bottle of bourbon.

"Something for your nerves?" he asked, trying to lighten the mood. He pulled the cork out from the sphere-shaped bottle.

"Oh, the good stuff." Madison smiled, reaching up to take the bottle. She downed a gulp without hesitation and didn't even choke this time.

Zach took a sip and settled on the couch beside her, watching the flames lick up the logs. Madison shifted closer, burying herself into Zach's side, her arms wrapping around his waist, her head resting against his chest.

"You're okay," Zach whispered, rubbing her back. His hand moved in slow circles, his thumb tracing the curves of her back, trying to comfort her.

"So... tell me about New York," Zach asked. He felt Madison stiffen slightly against him.

"Why?"

"I've never been. Tell me what you love about it."

Madison thought for a moment. "Well... it's fast and exciting, and there are a million people. There's always something to do, you know?" She hesitated, then added, "Jo is there, too, plus some of the best food in the world. Don't tell Kit I said that."

Zach chuckled. "Do you think I'd like it?"

He hoped if he kept her talking, she'd forget about the storm raging outside—and so far, it seemed to be working.

Madison tilted her head, considering. "Maybe not forever, but it's a place you should experience even if just for a visit. It's definitely not charming, cozy, or quiet. Not really your vibe. But you could probably charge a fortune as a contractor."

"You're right about that. Half the time, I don't even charge anything." Zach grinned.

"I know," Madison teased. "What's up with that? Mrs. Bishop said you fixed her shelf and she paid you in cookies."

Zach shrugged. "A lot of people around here are on fixed incomes. Not a lot of money, not a lot of time. I've got enough of both. Seems like the right thing to do."

They didn't speak for a long moment.

"Do you ever miss the quiet?" Zach eventually asked, afraid of what her answer might be.

Madison stared at the storm outside. "More than I thought I would," she confessed.

Zach told himself he'd think about that more later.

He didn't admit it out loud, but he was surprised by how strong the storm had gotten and that it wasn't letting up.

"Want to help me with something?" he asked, leaning back to look at her.

"Help you? With what?"

"My grandma used to say stirring was the best thing for a nervous heart."

Madison raised a brow. "Stirring? Now?" She didn't know where he was going with this.

He stood and offered her a hand. "Apple butter. It's either that or I can offer you a round of bourbon strip poker. What'll it be?"

She laughed and took his hand. "As tempting as the poker is, I've never made apple butter before."

"I was afraid you were going to say that. Right this way, then."

The kitchen might have been in the middle of a renovation, but it was warm and smelled faintly of sawdust and whatever candle he'd lit earlier. A battered wooden crate of apples sat next to the back door, waiting.

Zach pulled it toward the makeshift kitchen table—a piece of plywood balancing on two sawhorses with two mismatched chairs tucked beneath it. He set out a cutting board, two paring knives, and his grandmother's old stock pot.

"She always made a batch when she was worked up about something," he said, pulling a mixing bowl from one of the storage boxes.

Madison stood across from him, rolling an apple across the table with her fingertips. "I knew I liked her."

"She was a legend," Zach agreed. "Not nearly as scary as people said. Unless you burned her biscuits."

They peeled in silence for a bit, the soft scrape of the knife against the wood and the steady fall of rain outside the only sounds. Madison's shoulders slowly dropped. Her breath evened out.

Good, Zach thought, watching her relax before him.

"You slice apples like a lumberjack," she teased, watching Zach maneuver his knife with less than usual finesse, seeing he was so caught up in watching her.

Zach smirked. "And yet, somehow, it still turns out delicious."

Once the apples were peeled and sliced, he dumped them into the pot, added a generous scoop of brown sugar, a heavy shake of cinnamon, and—because it was Zach—a big splash of bourbon.

"Was that... necessary?" Madison asked, raising a brow.

"Completely," he said. "Family recipe."

As the pot warmed on the stove, the scent started to spread. It was rich, warm, sweet, like fall had moved in and made itself at home.

Zach put Madison in charge. She stirred the butter slowly, leaning forward and breathing it in.

"This might be the coziest night of my life," she said, resting the wooden spoon against the side of the pot, and she looked back up at him with a soft smile. Zach swore in that moment, the storm disappeared. It was just them. The steam rising. The quiet comfort of something simple and safe.

"Did you really used to make this with your grandma?" she asked, breaking the moment. She turned back and picked up the spoon again.

Zach nodded. "Every year. She'd bring out her big stock pot and say, 'Fall isn't here until the butter bubbles.' I didn't even know what that meant, but I believed her."

They jarred the first batch while the second pot simmered, the lids popping as they cooled. Madison stole a spoonful before it was even fully set.

"Oh my God," she said, licking her lips. "That's incredible."

Zach grinned. "Yeah?"

"Better than Gram's jam. Don't tell her I said that."

"Your secret's safe with me."

Eventually, the storm let up, and the fog rolled in. The temperature had dropped twenty degrees, Zach was sure of it.

Madison looked up at him. "I didn't think I'd ever feel okay during a storm again," she whispered. "Thank you."

"You never have to thank me."

He reached out to tuck a strand of hair behind her ear. His fingers brushed her cheek. He didn't say anything. Couldn't say anything.

All he could do in that moment was pray. Pray that this time, she'd stay.

FORTY-THREE

MADISON

October 24th

The next morning, Madison woke before Zach did. She was curled up beside him in his king-sized bed, the duvet pulled up over her shoulder. The window had been left slightly cracked open to help air out the house. Outside, she could hear birds chirping and the wind whispering through the trees.

It was peaceful. And for a fleeting moment, she realized just how easy it would be to get used to this—to waking up next to Zach like this every morning. The thought both thrilled and terrified her.

Part of her felt like this was exactly where she belonged. What was she so afraid of? They could make it work, couldn't they? Build a life here, right in this very house. She could manage the inn, stay in Maple Falls, raise a family, grow old beside the man she loved. They used to talk about it, in the past. Everything they wanted. Two kids, maybe three. A dog, maybe a black Lab, to run around the yard. Everything they would one day have. They were young and certain their dreams would all work out.

But how could she walk away from food writing, just as her career was really taking off, with all the contacts she needed in New York? Her stomach twisted. She loved to write. She loved her job.

She forced the pain back, not letting it surface. She would figure out a different way forward for her career.

This time, she was choosing him.

Madison smiled, warmth blooming in her chest. Yes, she could do this—and more than that, she wanted to.

A ripple of excitement moved through her. What would Zach say if she told him she was ready? That she wanted to make it official, to fully commit?

Rolling over carefully, Madison smiled at Zach, still sound asleep beside her. Her mind buzzed ahead, crafting ways to broach the topic. Should she do something sweet? Something like the time she asked him to be her boyfriend in fifth grade—when she cut a heart out of construction paper, scrawled, *Will you be my boyfriend? Circle yes or no,* and slipped it into his backpack?

Or maybe it needed to be serious this time. Something real and heartfelt, the way this was real. The way her heart felt fuller, steadier, when she was with him.

She was still debating how to bring it up when her phone vibrated on the nightstand. She grabbed it quickly to silence it before it woke him.

Jo's name flashed on the screen, hearts decorating the contact ID.

Madison sighed in relief and slipped out of bed. Zach deserved to sleep in after all the long hours he'd put into the inn. She figured she'd call Jo back later.

But just as she was about to crawl back under the covers, her phone buzzed again—this time with a text.

Jo: Fancy envelope here, next-day aired. Looks important.

Fancy envelope? Was it another one of the mystery letters?

That thought was enough to have Madison quietly pulling on a sweater and slipping out onto the porch to call.

"What's this about an envelope?" Madison asked.

"Well, nice to hear from you too," Jo teased.

"Ha, ha—funny," Madison said, biting back a grin.

"All good over there?" Jo asked.

"Better than good," Madison's voice purred.

"Oh no, I know that sound," Jo groaned. "That means I'm going to be looking for a new roommate again, aren't I?"

Madison laughed nervously. "Let's just focus on the letter for now."

Jo sighed dramatically but relented. "Alright, alright. Do you want me to open it?"

"Yeah, go for it," Madison said, shifting on her feet as she listened to Jo tear open the envelope.

There was more rustling on the other end and then silence as Jo read through it.

"Okay, shut up—you are not going to believe this," Jo said, excitement bubbling in her voice.

"What?" Madison pressed. "What is it?"

"It's from *Plated*. They're offering you a full-time editorial position."

Madison's heart stopped. "What?! No way. That can't be right. *Plated*? The biggest food magazine in the country?"

"The one and only," Jo confirmed. "And hold on, that's not all—shut the front door—they want to commission you for a Maple Falls recipe book to go with it."

Madison's breath caught. "A what?"

"A recipe book," Jo repeated, her words spilling out. "Apparently you must have talked about Maple Falls when you interviewed last year?"

"Did I talk about Maple Falls?" Madison thought back to

the interview. She'd been so nervous, she'd practically told the panel her entire life story.

Jo continued, "They said your ideas about the cozy seasonal recipes, community gatherings—all of it—gave them the vision for a cozy cookbook series, and they want *you* to write the first one. They're offering a huge advance to lock you in."

Madison pressed a hand to her chest, trying to catch her breath. "You're serious?" she shouted before remembering Zach was still asleep.

"Dead serious," Jo said, and Madison could hear the grin in her voice. "Hold on, I'm texting you a picture of it."

The photo came through, and Madison stared at the number of zeros at the bottom of the contract. With that advance she could fully staff the inn, hire a manager, finish the renovations, and still have enough to ensure the Cinnamon Spice Inn would never close its doors again.

Her head swam.

"That's one hell of an offer," Madison whispered, staring at the screen.

This would mean red carpet events. Food festivals. Book deals. Travel.

But most importantly, she could ensure the inn's future, her mother's legacy. She could make sure her dad and Gram were happy and cared for in their old age. There would never be a question again about whether the Cinnamon Spice Inn would need to be closed.

But it also meant:
No Zach.
No Madison at the inn.
No cozy farmhouse mornings.
No orchard orgasms.
God, she would really miss those orgasms.
But it wasn't just about the sex. It was about the way Zach looked at her like she was the only thing that mattered. The way

he remembered things, like how she took her morning coffee, or that she was always cold. It would mean losing the man who kissed her forehead when she was half-asleep and tucked her close to him at night.

"Pretty amazing, huh?" Jo said, misreading Madison's silence.

"Yeah," Madison replied faintly, the weight of it crashing over her. "It's... it's unbelievable. Holy crap."

"Super proud of you. You deserve it!" Jo added.

"Yeah. Thanks. Listen, I've got a lot to think about. Call you back in a bit?"

"Yeah, yeah, of course. But don't think too long—I wouldn't leave them waiting to hear back from you."

"No, trust me, I know."

"Alright. I'll talk to you soon."

Madison ended the call and stared out at the apple orchard beyond the farmhouse. She had some serious thinking to do.

FORTY-FOUR
ZACH

The sheets were slightly tangled around Zach's waist, but the comforter was pulled high. His arm instinctively reached out for Madison—her side of the bed was empty but still warm. He took comfort in that, knowing she'd slept all night by his side.

He closed his eyes, imagining she'd just slipped off to the bathroom and would be back any second. His thoughts drifted to all the lazy, perfect ways they could start the day—wrapped up in each other, breaking in the bed properly, stealing a slow morning just for them.

The idea sent a rush of heat through him. He was already halfway hard just thinking about her smile, her soft skin, the way she curled up against him.

Zach was still fantasizing about what other surprises the morning could hold when he heard her voice coming in through the cracked window outside.

Jo, she was talking to Jo. She sounded surprised and excited at the same time. His brain struggled to catch up, still groggy from sleep, but the words "plated" and "hell of an offer" woke him up like a zap of lightning.

Zach lay frozen beneath the covers, staring up at the ceiling as her conversation continued. His gut dropped.

Of course. A job offer. The city. Her old life calling her back. It was like watching her slip away all over again—this time from twenty feet outside the window.

He fisted the sheets tighter, trying to get ahold of his thoughts. Just because she had a job offer didn't mean anything.

Don't be an idiot, he told himself. *Maybe it's not what you think. Maybe it's nothing. Maybe she'll turn it down.*

But he couldn't shake the ache settling in his chest. They hadn't talked about their future, not really. And if Zach was being honest, he hadn't really believed she would stay this time, despite what Liam had said. That's what pissed him off the most. He *knew* this wasn't anything long term, yet he couldn't help but get wrapped up in his fantasies whenever Madison was around. *Damn fool*, he thought. *I should probably get it tattooed on my forehead after this.*

Zach pulled the covers up to his chin and stared out the window, forcing his breath to stay steady. *Give her space*, he thought, trying to convince himself. *Don't push. Let her figure it out first. She'll talk to you.*

Moments later, he heard Madison's footsteps on the porch and the soft creak of the farmhouse door as she slipped back inside. She was moving quickly around the space, gathering her things.

Zach closed his eyes, pretending to still be asleep, wondering if she was going to even come in and say goodbye.

When her truck started in the driveway, he had his answer.

FORTY-FIVE
MADISON

Madison didn't wait for Zach to wake up. She wasn't sure what she'd say anyway, and her face would probably have given her away after the call with Jo. She needed to clear her head, get some space.

Before she left, she brewed a fresh pot of coffee in the farmhouse kitchen, just the way he liked it—strong, black, two sugars on the side. She found a scrap piece of paper by the fridge and scribbled a quick note.

Hate to leave early, something came up. Wish I could stay. I had the best night. —M

She hesitated for a second, heart twisting, then tucked the note next to his mug where he'd see it. Only then did she slip quietly out the front door, her breath misting in the chilly morning air. She'd see Zach later, and maybe by then, she'd have a clearer head.

For now, she had other things to focus on until she was ready to process the news about the job offer. Like her meeting with Mayor Bloomfield about the mysterious letter that had changed everything.

She'd called his office after leaving the crafting club and managed to squeeze into his schedule for 11 a.m. Madison wasted no time heading to City Hall.

When she knocked on his office door, Mayor Bloomfield looked up with a wide grin. "Ah, I was told you were my eleven o'clock."

"Yes. How was your fishing trip?" Madison asked, stepping inside and trying to keep it casual.

"Splendid, I tell you. Does my old bones good to get out on the lake every now and then. You'd think living here, I'd get to dip a pole in the water more often, but you'd be mistaken."

"I know how that goes." Madison smiled. "Sometimes you have to get away from everything just to enjoy what's right in your backyard."

"Exactly," he said with a knowing nod.

Madison always thought of Mayor Bloomfield as something of a grandfather figure to the whole town. He had an ear for everyone, never without kind words or a warm smile. It was no wonder he'd been mayor for as long as she could remember—people respected him, and he genuinely cared about Maple Falls.

"So, what can I do for you today?" he asked, folding his hands and leaning forward across the desk.

"I heard you received a letter... about the inn," Madison said carefully.

Mayor Bloomfield's grin returned. "Ah, that I did. And I'm guessing you'd like to hear all about it?"

"That would be helpful," Madison said, sitting a little straighter.

The mayor sighed, and his expression turned more serious.

"The letter asked me to look out for your dad, make sure he was doing okay. And, well, I'm trying to figure out the best thing to do. You see, there's something else you need to know."

Madison's stomach tightened. "Oh?"

He sat back, hands folded to his chest. "Even though you were living at home, which saved on living expenses, tuition was steep, and your parents still had to manage the inn."

Madison nodded slowly, dread creeping into her chest.

"So," he continued, "I helped them out. I bought the inn from them."

"You what?" Madison's voice rose, and she shot up from her chair, hands braced on the desk. The room tilted slightly as a wave of dizziness passed through her. "You own the inn?"

"Please sit down," Mayor Bloomfield said gently, reaching out a hand. "It was supposed to be a temporary arrangement, a secret between me and your folks, just until business picked back up, but it never did."

Madison sank back into her chair, feeling like she'd been hit by a truck.

"Your parents just wanted what was best for you," he said kindly. "But now—"

"Now what?"

"Madison, the inn isn't doing well. I'm bleeding money. George hasn't been coping with it and I'm wondering if it would be better for him to cut his losses now, too. Whoever sent that letter clearly knows he's struggling. So, unless it has a miracle turnaround with this relaunch you're planning, I'll have to sell it—"

"How much?" she asked quietly.

"Pardon?" He blinked.

"How much do you want for the inn?" she clarified.

"Oh..." He rubbed his chin. "Well, I suppose I'd let it go for what I paid for it."

Madison's mind spun. She thought of *Plated*'s offer—the generous salary, the career she'd dreamed of—and the

Cinnamon Spice Inn. Her family's legacy. The home she now knew she couldn't bear to lose.

"I'll take it," Madison said firmly. "I want it back. Just tell me how much it costs, and I'll make it happen."

Inside, she was already running numbers—figuring out how much she'd need to live on and how much could go toward paying him back.

The Cinnamon Spice Inn belonged in her family. And she'd make sure it stayed that way.

FORTY-SIX
MADISON

Madison held it together until she stepped outside City Hall. Above her, the bright autumn sun felt far too cheery for her mood. Her boots crunched on the fall leaves as she walked toward her father's pickup truck, her mind reeling with the revelation—her family didn't even own the inn.

She had come home to save her family's legacy, but it wasn't even theirs anymore.

Madison climbed into the pickup truck, slamming the door harder than she'd intended. Her thoughts spiraled. How had the day gone so wrong? She'd woken up that morning ready to tell Zach she was all in. Now... now she didn't know what she was going to do.

She drove around the lake on autopilot. She'd made this drive thousands of times, but today it felt like she was floating outside her own body. She drove past familiar landmarks: the community gazebo, the farmers' market lot where she and her mom would buy fresh bread and berries, the craft store.

Madison didn't want to head back to the inn—not yet. She didn't want to face Zach either. She was too confused, too torn up. Instead, she parked downtown, just a block away from the inn.

Around her, tourists and locals alike strolled up and down the sidewalks, smiling with to-go cups of coffee and shopping bags dangling from their gloved wrists.

She stared across the town square at pumpkins and hay bales artfully arranged for fall. Further down, a banner stretched across two lampposts: "THE CINNAMON SPICE INN GRAND REOPENING!" Gram must have ordered it.

Her chest tightened.

Everything her parents had sacrificed—their home, their savings, their security—they'd given it all so she could chase her dreams. So she could have opportunities they'd never dared to reach for.

And now, she had a chance to give it back. To give the inn back to their family. To finish what her parents had started, to honor every quiet sacrifice they'd made.

There was no choice, really. She had to take the job.

She had to save the inn. For them. For Gram. For every memory tucked inside those walls.

But that meant...

She looked down the street, where the trees blazed gold against the cloudy sky, where the lake shimmered in the distance beyond the rooftops.

It meant leaving this beautiful place. Leaving Zach. Because Zach would never leave Maple Falls. His roots were here. He'd said so himself.

The knowledge settled into her chest like wet cement.

She pulled her mother's old scarf tighter around her neck, trying to brace herself against the chill. But the cold wasn't just in the air—it was inside her, threading through her veins.

Before she could talk herself out of it, Madison climbed out of the truck and started walking blindly through the square.

The scent of pancakes and bacon from the café was warm

and familiar, but she barely noticed it. Her thoughts were spinning too fast.

Was she really going to leave Zach again? Her heart screamed, *No*, but her mind said, *Yes*. This was what she had to do, for her family.

She was halfway across the square when she spotted Gram stepping out of the bakery, a to-go cup in her hand.

Madison hesitated.

Part of her wanted to turn around, run back to the truck, and keep on running until the world made sense again.

But a bigger part, a braver part, knew she needed someone to talk to.

And Gram had never been anything but honest with her.

Gram lifted her cup in greeting, her face lighting up until she caught sight of Madison's expression. Her smile faltered, replaced by quiet concern.

"I've seen that face before," Gram called, voice light but edged with worry. "And it's never good."

Madison's heart twisted painfully. She felt like a little girl again—lost, unsure, desperate for someone to tell her it would be okay. To tell her what to do.

But she wasn't a little girl anymore. She was the one who had to make the hard choices now.

"I just..." Madison shook her head helplessly. She glanced back toward the bakery, where Mrs. C. and Mrs. Bishop sat gossiping over cookies like nothing had changed. Like the world wasn't tilting under her feet.

"I don't know anymore."

Gram stepped closer, wrapping an arm around Madison's shoulders. "Come sit with me, darling. We'll figure it out."

Madison allowed Gram to lead her to a bench under the largest oak tree in the square. The grand tree was full of vibrant yellow leaves that seemed to soak up the brightness of the sun.

"Now, tell me what has you so worked up," Gram said, taking a sip of her drink.

"I went to see the mayor." Madison let the statement hang heavy in the air.

The look on Gram's face said she knew exactly where this was going.

"You knew?" Madison asked.

"That your parents sold the inn?" Gram nodded.

"Of course you knew." Madison stared at the ground, feeling left out and lost.

"I don't think they meant to keep it a secret, not forever. Your parents did the best they could with what they had. They never wanted to make you feel bad about it."

"But I *do* feel bad," Madison said, her voice thick. "I feel awful. I feel like I never should've come back. If I'd stayed in New York, I wouldn't have picked things back up with Zach, and accepting this job offer wouldn't be so hard."

"Job offer?" Gram tilted her head.

"It's an amazing opportunity, Gram. Huge payday. I could buy back the inn, make my parents proud, fix everything."

"Except for you and Zach," Gram said knowingly.

Madison nodded, tears threatening to fall. "No matter what I choose, someone is going to get hurt, and not just me. But I owe it to my parents, don't I? After everything they did?"

Gram reached out and gently patted Madison's thigh. "Nonsense. This is your life, darling. Create one you love."

FORTY-SEVEN
MADISON

Madison knew the one person who might have answers was her dad.

Gram had meant well, trying to explain how things were back then. And part of Madison understood it. She really did. But another part couldn't shake the feeling that her dad should have trusted her enough to tell her the truth.

He should have told her when she first came home that the inn was no longer theirs. The truth left a knot in her chest. It was a tangled ball of gratitude, guilt, and grief that she didn't know how to process.

When she walked inside, Madison stopped and stared at the empty lobby. There used to be so much life here. Even if Barry spent most of his shift asleep behind the front desk, feet propped up and snoozing soundly.

Madison thought again about the *Plated* offer and realized she'd have enough money to keep Barry on staff and hire some new workers who might not mind working. Barry was as iconic to the inn as her mom's cinnamon rolls. It would feel good to have everyone here—back home.

Home. The word felt hollow with the realization that all this wasn't theirs anymore.

Madison found George out back, refilling Honey and Biscuit's water trough. Cocoa was nearby, chewing lazily on a stick.

"You want some fresh water?" he asked as the Highland cows ambled over. "Just be patient. There's a good lass. I'm almost done," he continued to say.

Madison's boots crunched on the gravel as she walked over, arms crossed, hugging herself. The sun was warm, but she still felt cold. She tried to clear her throat, but when her dad turned and smiled, the tears welled up before she could stop them.

George wiped his hands on a rag. "Madison, what's wrong?" He stepped forward, ready to help his daughter in any way she needed.

"Why didn't you tell me about the inn—about the sale?" Madison blurted out before she could stop herself.

George looked away and Madison instantly felt guilty. "I'm sorry, I was just blindsided by it, and I want to understand."

George looked up and met his daughter's eyes. "I almost did, the other night."

Madison nodded, remembering their conversation.

"But then I'd already talked to the mayor. Told him I planned on buying it back. No idea how, but it felt like the right thing to do."

Cocoa stood up and padded over to Madison, tail wagging low. Madison gave her a half-hearted scratch behind the ears as her dad sighed and stared out at the trees like he was searching for an answer.

"I was hoping you'd never have to find out. I didn't want to hurt you."

"What happened? I thought back then the inn was doing okay." Madison thought back to her senior year of high school and how it seemed like they were booked every weekend. Or maybe they weren't, and she just hadn't paid any attention. She'd been too busy going off with her friends, living life as a teenager without a care in the world. Maybe she should've paid more attention.

George rubbed the back of his neck, avoiding her eyes. "It wasn't overnight. People stopped coming. Folks take trips to fancy resorts now, not old inns like ours. And when you got into college, we knew we couldn't afford both—running this place and giving you the future you deserved."

Cocoa trotted over to George and leaned against his leg. George kept going. "Then your mom got sick. Everything piled up at once. We did what we thought we had to." Her dad looked away, hands on his hips. Madison saw that he was fighting to hold it together. It made her tears fall fresh.

"You should've told me. I could've taken out loans or tried for more scholarships. You guys shouldn't have made that decision without me."

"Oh now, you were still just a kid. Your mom and I wanted you to live your dream. We didn't want you stuck here fixing leaky pipes, never knowing what else was out there."

Both of them fell quiet. Madison couldn't help but notice how much older, how much more tired her dad looked now compared to when she was in college. He looked exhausted, and despite her frustration, despite the hurt at being left out, sympathy won out.

They stood there quietly for a moment, listening to the trees sway and the faint sound of a distant chainsaw from another property.

Cocoa scratched at her dad's pant leg for him to pick her up. He did so without a second thought. As he scratched her ears, he said, "The town's always been here for us. Maybe too much sometimes."

"Do you regret it, selling the inn?" Madison asked softly.

George looked down at Cocoa, as if he couldn't say the

words to his daughter. "Only when I realized I might lose this place—and you—forever."

At that, he did look up and met her eyes. Madison saw so much love in his expression, but there was sadness too. So much so that Madison's heart broke right in half. And she knew she'd do whatever it took to get the inn back in their family's name.

No matter what.

FORTY-EIGHT
MADISON

After talking with her father, Madison walked to the lake. The late-afternoon sun was beginning its descent, and the wind blew across the water, sending her hair back and rippling the surface. She shivered as the waves rolled in and the wind slipped under her sweater. Tucking her hands in her pockets, she stared out across the water.

So many memories were rooted here at the lake, at the inn. She thought back to her childhood, all the wonderful moments with Maurice, her mom in the kitchen, teaching her how to knead dough and make cinnamon rolls.

She'd played hide-and-seek with Zach and Emily, and a dozen other kids who came and went from the inn. The maple tree. The great room was full of memories—Christmas mornings, the big balsam fir dominating the room, and the fireplace crackling.

Every holiday, every birthday—everything had felt so magical, comforting, and cozy at the Cinnamon Spice Inn.

The memories turned bittersweet as the realization hit her all over again: her family had lost it. Madison pulled out her phone and stared at the text from Jo for the nine hundredth time. The job offer glared back at her. Her heart pounded as she reread the number.

But then her gaze drifted across the lake. Toward the apple orchard. The old farmhouse. Zach. The memory of his hands on her waist, the taste of apples and whiskey.

Madison's chest tightened, and she felt like she couldn't breathe. Taking the job offer meant leaving Zach, leaving the life she was starting to want again. The deep happiness she was just starting to believe she deserved. All she had to do was reach out and take it... but at what cost? The price was too high.

Was she strong enough to save the inn but lose Zach?

How was she going to talk to him about this?

The wind kicked up again, scattering more leaves across the path. She gripped her phone tighter just as it started to ring. "What, was your Spidey sense tingling?" Madison said, balancing the phone between her ear and shoulder as she zipped up her jacket. The air was definitely colder, cloudier, which matched her mood perfectly.

"Well, let's see," Jo replied dryly. "This morning, you were staying in Maple Falls forever, and now you've got a job offer. Knowing you, you're ping-ponging like crazy."

Madison sighed and shoved her free hand deep into her jacket, her boots crunching over the gravel scattered along the path. "I swear you know me so well."

She veered toward the lake's edge, where the wind tugged her hair loose from her scarf. Across the water, campfire smoke drifted lazily from the campground. She could see it curling up into the air. Somewhere, faint laughter echoed from a group of kids, and ducks quacked in the lake. It all felt so Maple Falls—and yet there was an ache behind it like she was standing between two lives.

"Talk to me," Jo insisted. "Unless you don't want to, and in that case, I'll leave you alone."

"No, you won't," Madison said with a smile. Her first real one of the day.

"You're right, I won't."

Madison slowed her pace, pausing near a bench where she and her mom used to sit with mugs of cocoa and people-watch. She leaned against the nearby birch tree.

"So..." Jo interrupted her thoughts, "let me guess. You're in love with Zach, aren't you."

"Yes," Madison whispered. She tipped her head back against the tree and closed her eyes.

"There it is," Jo said gently. "So, stay. Live happily ever after. There'll be other job offers."

Madison blew out a breath and kicked at a patch of gravel near the path. "I was going to stay... but here's the thing—I just found out my family doesn't even own the inn anymore. My parents sold it to the mayor to send me to college."

Jo sucked in a sharp breath. "Oh, Maddie. That's rough."

"I know. And that job offer would give me enough money to buy it back. You should've seen the look on my dad's face. He feels so guilty that he wasn't able to provide everything for me. I know he wants it back. *I* want it back."

"So what are you going to do?"

Madison started walking again, this time faster. "If it's the only way to save the inn and secure its future, then walking away from Zach now is the right call, isn't it?"

There was silence for a moment. Then Jo asked, "Do you want me to just agree with you?"

"Right now? Yes." Madison laughed bitterly. "Because if I do this, I'm doing it for my dad. For the inn. For my family."

"For you, too?" Jo asked softly.

Madison ignored that part.

"So..." Jo pushed, "you'll be back here in about a week?"

"Yeah. I'll stay through the grand reopening on Halloween, then head back."

As much as Madison tried to stay steady, her heart ached just thinking about it. She could already see it—handing in her key to the inn, leaving Zach behind, letting go of this happy small-town version of herself.

"Well, good talk," Jo said, clearly trying to lighten the mood. "I gotta run—I'm heading to the market to fix yesterday's oyster disaster. Let's just say thank goodness New York's most acclaimed food critic wasn't in town to get word of it," Jo said with a laugh.

It felt good to talk about work. Madison pushed for more details and let Jo take the conversation away—to life in New York, the restaurant, and all their mutual friends. The more Jo talked, the more Madison realized she was making the right decision. It was just going to be really hard... until she got back to New York. Then she could forget about everything.

She might have a broken heart, but her family's legacy would be restored.

She'd talk to Zach soon. She just couldn't face it right now. But she'd lay it all out, tell him why she was going back to New York, why she had no choice. She wouldn't leave the way she had before.

Only, maybe she wouldn't tell him *everything*.

Because she'd thought about it—asking him to come with her this time. Fighting for them, fighting for both the career she loved and the man she loved. But every time she looked at him, at the way he fit in here, at how he belonged to the orchard and the farm and the rhythm of this town, she knew she couldn't ask him to leave it all behind.

She couldn't be the reason he gave up the place that made him happiest, the place that felt like home.

And maybe that was what love was—wanting someone to be happy, even if it meant letting them go.

FORTY-NINE
ZACH

October 25th

Zach hadn't heard from Madison since she'd left the morning before, and it gnawed at him like a loose nail catching on everything. He told himself he was giving her space. She needed time. She had a lot on her mind. He didn't want to push her. But deep down, fear beat in his heart like a steady drum.

The sun was hiding behind the clouds when he stepped into the inn, toolbox in hand. The scent of cinnamon and coffee lingered in the air. Zach had been getting used to going back to the cabin, smelling of the inn, after a long day's work. It used to comfort him. Now, he wasn't so sure.

Zach spotted Madison right away behind the front desk. She was hunched over a stack of order forms, studying them, while Gram worked through the new computer software.

"Do I click here or there?" Gram asked, squinting at the screen and pointing with one finger like she couldn't remember to save her life.

Madison looked up and spotted Zach. She startled.

Zach tried to let it roll off his back. He smiled in return, trying to smooth her nerves.

It didn't work. Madison returned the smile, but it felt flat. Practiced.

"Computer training?" Zach asked, trying for lightness as he moved closer.

"I don't know what's wrong with pencil and paper. It's done me good for decades." Gram sighed and crossed her arms, clearly unimpressed.

"You click here first," Madison said, for probably the fifth time, "then you input the client's information," she continued, tapping the screen gently, "and then you click here to save it."

"I keep telling her I'm a lost cause, but she insists I'll get it," Gram added, picking up her coffee.

"You're not a lost cause," Madison replied, her voice softening in a way Zach wished it would've for him.

"Whatever you say, dear. I'm going to scoot out of your way and take my break." She winked and disappeared toward the office.

Zach caught the flash of panic in Madison's eyes before she ducked her head, and it hit him low, like a punch he hadn't braced for.

Zach shifted his weight and leaned forward, casually, trying to act like he hadn't noticed.

"Busy morning?"

Madison barely looked up this time. "Too busy. With the reopening coming up next week, there's still too much to do. I need to finish updating the branding. The designer I hired flaked on us. The website's a mess. And I haven't posted on social nearly as much as I should. I really need to schedule posts. It's a lot," she said, her pencil nervously tapping against a folder.

"Do you want to grab a coffee later? I just need to finish that second coat of stain out back…"

"I'm sorry, I wish I could," she replied quickly. "But I really need to focus on things here." Madison snapped her fingers, thinking of something. "Shoot," she said to herself before apologizing to Zach again. "Sorry, I just remembered I need to order towels and linens today or they won't be delivered on time." She gave a quick shrug but didn't meet his eyes.

"Alright then, maybe later."

"Yeah, sure." Madison feigned excitement. Zach hated that he knew her well enough to know that.

Zach nodded, jaw tight, and grabbed his toolbox. Madison excused herself and walked off in the opposite direction, files in hand.

Zach could practically feel the space between them widening with each step.

His stomach twisted. No matter what he told himself, she was slipping away.

A huge part of him wanted to go after her. To tell her that this time, he'd leave everything behind if it meant keeping her. That if she asked, he'd follow her anywhere. Even to New York. Even if it broke his heart to leave Maple Falls behind. That nothing mattered more than her.

But he couldn't go after her. Because if she loved him back, wouldn't she at least be trying to find a way to give them a chance?

So, he just stood there, in the gray zone once more. Praying that she would reach out, terrified that she wouldn't.

FIFTY

MADISON

Later that night, Madison and Gram were cozied up in the great room. Gram sipping spiced tea, Madison with her coffee, unwinding after one too many hours of computer training. Gram was right—maybe she should stick to pencil and paper. The new hires would probably pick up the computer more quickly, and it would be less stressful for everyone.

"Can't believe you're staying in tonight. I heard there was a dart tournament down at the tavern."

Madison looked up from the food magazine she had been skimming. "Oh?"

"Kit was getting a team together. I'm surprised she didn't ask you."

"Come to think of it, she did. It's just... there's been so much going on that I kind of like just staying in. You're not trying to get rid of me, are you?"

"Nope. In fact, I could use the company. Hank's been pretty busy too, but I'm hoping to catch up with him soon. What about you and Zach?" Gram looked over the rim of her teacup, bouncing her eyebrows.

"Can we not talk about that now please, Gram?"

"Hm," Gram said, narrowing her eyes.

Madison checked her phone and saw a new text from Zach: *Just saying hi. Want to hang out later?*

Madison stared at it, thumb hovering over the screen. For a second, she almost texted back something reckless like, *I miss you.* But instead, she tucked the phone under a cushion, out of sight.

"I don't know what's going on between you two, but you can't avoid him forever," Gram said.

"Don't worry, I won't."

Gram gave her a long, assessing look. "I suppose this means you're taking the job offer?"

Madison nodded. "I already have. I start in two weeks."

Gram gave her a knowing look. Madison forced a smile and changed the subject. "When's the next craft club meeting?" she asked abruptly.

Gram's eyes twinkled. "Oh, that won't be till next month. We only meet once a month. Maybe if you're back in town for a visit..." Her voice trailed off. "We're making snowmen this time, and I'm hosting."

Madison could picture it... Mrs. C. bossing everyone around. Mrs. Bishop keeping everyone full of hot cocoa and peppermint bark.

Kit would probably be there, and maybe Cassidy, too. Madison had heard a rumor the newcomer was thinking of staying.

It would be lovely.

But could she really live her life between two places?

"Maybe." Madison sighed. For the first time in a long time, the coffee in her mug tasted bitter.

FIFTY-ONE

ZACH

Zach pushed open the wooden door to the Kettle and was greeted by the usual chorus of laughter, clinking glasses, and the low hum of conversation. The tavern smelled like pizza, beer, and buffalo chicken wings.

Orange and black garlands were strung across the rafters, and a carved jack-o'-lantern glowed from behind the bar. At least no one was dressed in Halloween costumes. Not yet. He still had a handful of days until he could stay home with his porch light turned off. He'd never been a big Halloween sort of guy—well, except for that one year when Madison had dressed up like a sexy witch. He still remembered the fishnet stockings and purple velvet bodice she'd worn. Come to think of it, everything that year had been pretty fantastic.

He scanned the room instinctively, hoping, stupidly, that Madison would be there. Maybe Kit had convinced her to come out after all and he could "casually" run into her, like a guy straight out of some rom-com, standing around at a dart tournament waiting for his maybe-girlfriend to show.

But he didn't see her.

Zach claimed a stool at the bar and ordered a beer. He took

a drink and pretended to be interested in the bulletin board next to the register. There was a signup sheet for the Halloween trunk or treating at the community center, a reminder for the annual chili cookoff, and info about next month's seasonal craft club meeting. It had something to do with snowmen, and it was meeting at the inn.

That damn inn.

He took a slow sip, chest tight, trying to shake off the weight pressing down on him.

Behind him, Mr. Alders from the hardware store and Mayor Bloomfield were arguing good-naturedly about the best apple pie in town.

"Mrs. Bishop's crust is pure magic," Mr. Alders said.

"Ha! That's because you haven't tasted Edith's. You missed it at the festival. Hands down, the best!" Hank replied with a wide grin.

The mayor turned to Zach to get him to weigh in.

"Don't drag me into this." Zach knew better than to pick a side.

Both men groaned with a "Bah!" and waved him off.

Zach smiled weakly, too caught up thinking about Madison. He'd texted her earlier, hoping they could meet up like they used to, when everything between them made sense.

But she hadn't replied. She hadn't even bothered to brush him off this time.

Zach hadn't thought it was possible, but he felt even worse.

"You're pathetic," he mumbled, picking up and swirling his beer.

"She's not here," Liam said, coming up beside him with a dart in one hand and a beer in the other. "I already checked."

Zach grunted. "Didn't ask."

"No, but you're wearing that hopeful puppy look, so I figured." Liam shrugged.

"Don't you have a game to get back to?" Zach looked over his shoulder.

"Hey, Whitaker!" Kit called from across the room, her sleeves pushed up, dart in hand. "Thought you'd come crawling for a rematch."

Zach let out a forced laugh and made his way over to where Kit and a few locals were forming a team. The table was crowded with pint glasses, appetizer plates, and the unmistakable scent of deep-fried everything.

"Rematch? That was pool, and I'm pretty sure we let you win last time," Zach said, folding his arms beside her.

"Nuh-uh," Kit replied, smirking. "Madison beat you fair and square."

Zach nodded, trying to act casual. "Is she joining you tonight?" He kept his voice light.

Kit clicked her tongue, catching the subtext immediately. "Nope, said she was busy."

Zach nodded too fast, pretending like it didn't sting.

Kit's expression softened. "You two on the outs?"

"Nah," Zach lied. "Just... taking it slow, that's all."

Kit didn't seem to believe him, but she let it go. "Well, if you get tired of brooding, we've got room on our team."

"I'll let you know."

Zach returned to the bar and leaned against the counter as conversations buzzed around him. Kit laughed loudly across the room as Liam fumbled his next throw while someone at the next table argued about the merits of pumpkin beer versus hard cider.

Neither, Zach thought as he sat there, nursing his beer, scanning the door every time it creaked open, hoping Madison might still show up.

The room moved around him.

People laughed. Darts hit the corkboard. Drinks clinked.

None of it reached him anymore. Zach was too twisted up in his own thoughts.

He stared into the beer glass, thinking about the way Madison had smiled at him just a few mornings ago, tangled up in the farmhouse sheets.

When Liam walked over, trying to get him to join the next round of darts, Zach just shook his head. "I'm good, man."

Liam raised a brow but didn't push.

Zach's grip tightened on the glass as Liam walked away. He knew he couldn't sit here pretending anymore.

Zach tossed enough cash on the bar to cover his drink and then some.

No more chasing, he told himself, stepping outside. No more waiting for texts, no more hoping for surprise visits. Why should he offer to move to New York when she wasn't willing to even talk with him?

He shoved his hands deep into his jacket pockets, eyes fixed on the cracked pavement ahead.

As the wind picked up and rustled the branches overhead, Zach made a decision. He was done. He'd bury himself in work —finish the farmhouse, fix every loose board, every crooked shutter. That, at least, was something he could control.

And maybe if he kept his head down long enough, he'd stop thinking about what he'd just lost.

FIFTY-TWO
MADISON

October 29th

This sucks, Madison thought as she stared around the inn's lobby. The fall sunlight streamed in through the front doors, casting a welcoming glow over the newly polished floors. Everything was perfect—except her. She was a mess.

"What's that frown for?" Kit asked, walking briskly through the lobby, her arms full with a crate of butternut squash she was planning to turn into soup.

Madison blinked, startled out of her thoughts. "What?"

Kit set the crate onto the front desk with a soft thud. "Your face. You're doing that thing again where your eyebrows scrunch up like you're solving a murder mystery."

Madison attempted a smile, but it didn't quite reach her eyes.

"The inn looks great," Kit said, gesturing around the lobby. "I mean, really great. Zach did an amazing job."

She wasn't wrong. The place had come together better than Madison could've hoped. The dining room glowed with new light fixtures, the walls had been painted a cozy sage green, and the fireplace had fresh tilework that somehow made the whole room feel more alive. It looked like a real inn again. Like it was ready for the next chapter.

Madison nodded, her throat tight. Zach had done all of that, and she'd barely seen him the past four days. No phone calls. No text messages. No casual drop-ins or jokes about her caffeine addiction. Just... silence.

And she deserved it.

She tried to tell herself that it was easier this way. She could keep her mind on the inn's relaunch and postpone their conversation until that was over.

But even though she tried to stay focused, it hurt. Every inch of this place had his fingerprints on it—his hard work, his care.

Her chest squeezed.

Hopefully, when they talked, he would understand.

Hopefully, Madison would forgive herself someday.

Madison realized that Kit was still staring at her. "No, everything's fine. I'm just lost in my thoughts. Thinking about New York."

Kit gave her a long look. "You leave next week, right?"

Madison shook her head. "Thursday." She fiddled with a pen on the desk. "Grand reopening is Wednesday. I'll leave the next morning."

Kit leaned on the edge of the desk. "I'm really going to miss you, you know. You're going to come back this time, right? Pop in for a visit every now and then?"

Madison forced a smile. "Of course! I'll be back."

But even she didn't believe it.

Madison stood there a moment longer after Kit headed back to the kitchen. The quiet hum of the inn filled the space—the tick of the front desk clock, the faint rustle of the trees outside, the clink of dishes coming from the kitchen.

She needed air. She grabbed her sweater off the coat rack

and slipped her arms into the sleeves, stuffing her phone into her pocket without checking it. A walk. That's all she needed. Just a little space to clear her head and remind herself why she was doing all this in the first place.

Downtown Maple Falls had fully embraced Halloween. Shop windows were strung with orange twinkle lights and faux cobwebs, and plastic bats fluttered on thin wires whenever the breeze picked up. A skeleton dressed as a barista leaned against the café's door with a tiny pumpkin spiced latte in its bony hand.

As Madison walked past the bookstore, the familiar chime of the chocolatier's bell caught her attention. The door swung open, and out stepped Gram, bundled in her cranberry wool coat, holding a white box tied with black-and-orange striped ribbon. Right behind her was none other than Mayor Bloomfield, happily munching on a chocolate-dipped cookie.

"Well, if it isn't our favorite innkeeper," he teased, brushing cookie crumbs off his sweater vest. "Come to get into the Halloween spirit?"

"Something like that," Madison replied half-heartedly.

Gram raised an eyebrow, her gaze narrowing just slightly. "She's got that look again," she said to the mayor. "Come on inside. Rita's got a new truffle that might fix whatever that face is about."

Madison didn't protest. She followed them through the door, letting the aroma of chocolate, caramel, and just a hint of peanut butter wrap around her.

"Back so soon?" Rita asked, coming around the counter.

"I think Madison could use a couple of those new truffles of yours," Gram said knowingly. "Can we buy a few more?"

"No need. These ones are on the house. I need a few more taste testers to tell me what they think. Do you mind?" Rita directed the question to Madison.

"Not at all." Madison stepped forward.

Rita opened the display case and placed a chocolate square on a white napkin before handing it over. "It's a s'mores truffle."

"S'mores truffle?" Madison had had plenty of s'mores before when they'd had bonfires down by the lake in the summer, but she had never had one in a bite-sized chocolate.

"They're made with a graham cracker crust, marshmallow filling, covered in milk chocolate, and finished with a sprinkle of sea salt," Rita explained. "Tell me what you think."

Madison took a bite. "This is heavenly!" she declared, covering her mouth with her hand so she could talk.

"Aren't they delightful?" the mayor agreed. "You truly are a wonder," he said to Rita.

She blushed under his praise.

"We're sure going to miss you," Gram added.

"Oh no, are you leaving town?" Madison asked. Rita had owned the chocolate shop for as long as Mayor Bloomfield had been in office.

"That I am. I am retiring where the sun shines year-round, and I don't have to deal with any more snow!" Rita said with a smile.

"Florida?" Madison guessed.

"Mexico!" Rita laughed at Madison's surprise. "My girlfriend and I found a nice apartment not far from her son's family who moved there a few years back. We thought, why not!"

"Well, that's exciting! Maple Falls' loss, though," Madison replied.

"Don't worry," Rita said, her smile growing. She turned, motioning toward Cassidy, who had just walked in through the door, her cheeks flushed from the chilly air. "I'm leaving the shop in good hands."

Cassidy blinked. "What did I miss?"

"I'm just telling everyone how talented you are," Rita replied. "I'm happy to be turning over the keys to you."

"Oh, well, in that case." Cassidy bowed. "I'll do my best to live up to your reputation," she said sincerely. "It's really a dream come true."

Madison's heart warmed instantly. "That's amazing," she said, meaning it. "Welcome to Maple Falls."

Cassidy smiled wide and bright. "It feels right, you know? Like this is exactly where I'm meant to be."

"I bet," Madison said, trying and failing to sound as excited as Cassidy looked.

Madison glanced over toward Gram and Mayor Bloomfield. They seemed to be lost in their own little world. Gram looked carefree, leaning toward Hank while he looked at her like she was the best part of his day. There was something so easy between them. It was subtle but unmistakable.

A warmth spread in Madison's chest. She was happy for her grandmother, truly. For Cassidy, too. But it seemed everyone was finding their place in Maple Falls while she was getting ready to say goodbye.

Madison knew what she needed to do. She couldn't put it off any longer. She couldn't use waiting for the inn's relaunch as an excuse. She had to be brave, find Zach, and tell him the truth. All of it.

It was time to say the words she hadn't had the courage to face. Even if it broke both their hearts.

FIFTY-THREE
ZACH

Zach should have been freaking thrilled. The job was done. The inn was complete with two days to spare. He could go back to the farmhouse full time—which, by the way, was coming along beautifully.

Zach was back at the farmhouse, sanding the front porch. It was a perfect fall day—bright blue sky, trees blazing in gold and crimson. The scent of apples still lingered in the air. The fruit was riper now, like cider. The weather reminded him of the afternoon Madison had stopped by and they had snuck off into the orchard.

He shook his head, not letting his thoughts go there.

A breeze rustled the cornfields nearby, the sound just soft enough to make a person feel like the world had quieted down for a minute. But none of it settled him.

The only sound Zach cared about was the rasp of the sander, a low mechanical buzz that ate away the old wood. He worked it over and over the same spot until it was raw.

Zach was still fighting with the way Madison had dismissed him. One moment, she'd been lying in bed next to him, and the next, she'd got a phone call with that job offer—and she was gone. Just like that. Ignored texts. Clipped conversations.

The whole attitude pissed him off more than anything. Maybe if he held onto that anger, he could get past the hurt. Get past the blame. Be angry with himself for letting Madison get close to him all over again.

Zach fought with himself to quit thinking about Madison and focus on the work that needed to be done.

The inside of the farmhouse was even more put together. The kitchen cabinets were in, the flooring, the new appliances. The living room was repainted, as was the master. He had to gut two of the bathrooms and the bedrooms upstairs, but he wasn't in a rush. Not anymore.

What's the point if she's not going to be here? he thought.

Zach pushed harder, sanding the deck until his arms ached. The pain felt nice, in a way. It distracted from the ache in his heart. The more exhausted he got, the more detached he felt.

Zach glanced up in time to see Liam coming down the driveway. He got out of his truck and shut the door.

"What, no beer this time?" Zach ribbed him.

"I don't know. The way you've been up here alone, I was worried I might find you with a bottle of Jack sitting on the porch."

"You know that's not my style."

"Not usually. But Madison has a way of screwing with your head."

"Gee, thanks," Zach replied with a half-hearted chuckle and continued focusing on the railing.

"You keep going like that and there won't be anything left."

"If you've got something to say, why don't you just go ahead and say it?" Zach said, turning off the sander.

"I'm just wondering why you haven't talked to her. Why you're not even fighting for her?" Liam asked, tucking his hands into his pockets like it was just a casual conversation about football.

"Why should I have to go after her?" Zach snapped. "She knows how I feel."

"Does she? Have you told her?"

Zach looked off into the trees, past the orchard, down toward town. It was miles away. He couldn't see it, but he knew she was there.

"I just think the two of you should talk. And for what it's worth," Liam said, holding up his hand to stop Zach from interrupting him, "I'd tell her the same thing."

"I don't know," Zach deflected. "Maybe I should just sell this place. Head west. Work on someone else's fixer-upper."

"You're seriously thinking of leaving town?" Liam looked genuinely shocked.

"A change of scenery might be nice. I've lived in this town my whole life. Maybe it's time I saw what else is out there. Maybe Madison's onto something."

"Or maybe you should just talk to her," Liam said, turning and heading back to his truck.

If Zach had thought that would be the last of his visitors, he'd be mistaken because not two hours later, he looked up to see Madison driving up to the farmhouse.

Zach's heart stopped as he watched her through the front window, navigating the turn into the driveway. He steeled his resolve. So, she had finally found the courage to come and end things once and for all.

God, part of him wished they never had to have this conversation—that it was never going to come to this. But it was better this way, rather than another silent falling apart. He told himself he'd listen to what she had to say, thank her, and get on with it. No point dragging out the inevitable.

He didn't approach her. He waited for her to come up as he stood watching from the living room window. Madison seemed to take in everything—the porch, the new windows, the fresh paint. He'd done so much work since she'd been there. The house looked like a different place.

Madison's eyes softened, and just that one look made his heart do the same. *If only it were enough*, Zach thought to himself.

She knocked on the door and opened it, not waiting for him to answer. Zach stood there, sawdust on his jeans, sleeves rolled up, trying to pretend like he was focused on the built-ins in the living room.

"Didn't expect to see you," he said, turning back to hammer the boards into place, his expression unreadable. Or at least he hoped it was.

Madison continued to look around the room. Zach wondered if she noticed that the farmhouse walls were painted in her favorite light gray, or that he had built a cozy nook by the window where she could read her recipe books. Or even the fact that he'd put a hook by the door for her keys. He had built this house—remodeled it—for her.

Zach wondered if she realized that while she was pulling away, he was still there, building this for them. Again, he felt like the biggest idiot on this side of the Mississippi. There was something about this woman who twisted him up, made him do stupid things. Dream of the unattainable.

Madison visibly swallowed. "I didn't know you were making this our dream house."

So she did notice.

Zach shrugged. "It's just a house, Mads."

"It was never just a house." Madison's eyes filled with tears. "Listen... can we talk?" Her voice was soft.

"Why? What's the point?" Zach asked, tossing the hammer onto the shelf. "You're leaving, right? New York's calling."

Madison opened and shut her mouth, unable to speak.

Zach ran a hand through his hair. "I heard you on the phone, Mads. I've been trying not to ask because I already knew the answer. And then you pulled away. You didn't even give me the decency of a conversation, of trying to figure things out together. I thought I knew you better than that. I thought you cared about me more than that. But maybe I was always second to New York."

Tears trailed down her cheeks, but Zach didn't hold back.

"I thought if I made this house perfect, if I built something solid, you'd have a reason to stay. I thought if you knew how much I loved you—because dammit, Madison, I love you—I thought that would be enough to make you stay. I thought building a life here, carrying on your family's legacy... that you wanted that as much as I do. But one phone call and you drop me. Christ."

"I do want that," Madison said. "I just... I can't have it. And I don't know how to make you understand. There's just so much that you don't know. Zach, I—"

"And how am I supposed to know if you don't talk to me? You don't tell me anything, Mads."

Madison just stared at him like she was about to burst into tears.

This wasn't how Zach had thought this would go. He'd thought he'd give Madison a chance to talk, a chance to tell him the truth. He'd fight to stay calm. Rational. Because that's the kind of guy he was.

But not now. Not in the heat of the moment when everything exploded out of him in a way he'd never expected.

He pressed on. He had to. "I know you've made your decision, and you're headed to New York in a few days. I was willing to give up everything here and go with you this time, but you shut me out. You don't want a relationship with me, I get that. I love you, you don't love me. I just think the way you went about it is pretty damn awful. So, unless I've got it wrong, I think we're through."

Zach turned and walked out of the living room, through the kitchen, and right on out to the backyard. He didn't stop until he reached the apple trees.

It didn't take long to hear Madison get in her truck and drive away.

FIFTY-FOUR

MADISON

Madison drove away from the farmhouse, her hands gripping the steering wheel. She felt like crying, yelling, and turning back around all at once.

Seeing calm, steady Zach that torn up, seeing the pain on his face, had broken something open inside her. She'd come there with so much to say, things she needed him to hear. And his pain had struck the words right out of her mouth. She didn't know how to fix this, and yet she couldn't bear to hurt him anymore.

Madison drove around the lake once, then twice, before pulling over in one of the scenic overlooks. She stared out across the water.

"How did I end up back here," she whispered, "feeling like a kid again, staring at the same lake, still looking for answers?"

It was quiet, almost too quiet, but she didn't mind it. It was the kind of quiet that allowed her to think or at least try. She rested her arms on the steering wheel and closed her eyes.

She couldn't believe Zach had even considered coming with her. But she knew in her heart that would never work. She couldn't see him ever being happy in New York. He wasn't a city man and never would be. Madison loved him too much to do that to him.

Her mind wandered to the inn—baking cinnamon rolls, learning how to ride a bike in the circular driveway, taking pictures in front of the maple tree.

The inn had never been just an inn. It was her family's home.

And Zach had never been just a guy. He was *the one*.

Madison mentally weighed her two futures. New York City was fast-paced, filled with awards, travel, and recognition. Maple Falls was quaint, charming. It had Zach, cozy mornings, and her family.

One had everything she'd ever wanted. The other had everything she hadn't known she needed.

Madison smiled, thinking of the inn's grand front porch, the smell of apples baking in Kit's kitchen, and the sound of her dad laughing while Cocoa snored at his feet. She thought about Zach's hands, rough and steady. The way he'd built that house for her without ever saying a word.

It wasn't just that she loved him. It was that she loved the life she was starting to have with him, right here in Maple Falls.

Madison rested her head against her arms.

Maybe, just maybe, it wasn't too late.

There had to be a way to have both.

FIFTY-FIVE
MADISON

October 31st

The town turned out in full force in support of the inn's grand reopening—and at that point Madison didn't expect anything else. The weather was perfect for late October. It was warm enough that you didn't need a coat but cool enough for scarves and boots. The only person missing was Zach. Madison had told herself that she would seek him out later that night if he didn't show.

Mrs. C. was sampling everything to eat in the dining room, telling Kit what she thought, leaving nothing behind. "Don't let Mr. Alders sample your pumpkin pie—it'll top mine in his regards!" she said, going back for a second forkful. "I think you have a little bit too much cinnamon on those turnovers, but if I had a bit more ice cream, maybe that would balance it out. And you know I just love a good butternut squash soup. Yours is divine. You could probably sprinkle some toasted pine nuts on top if you wanted to give it a little extra kick."

Kit took all the feedback in stride, knowing deep down that her recipes were perfect as is. That was just Mrs. C.'s way—she always had to weigh in and give her opinion. Madison was coming to appreciate that, too. There was never a short supply of people willing to lend a hand, lend an ear, or give an opinion in Maple Falls—for better or worse.

Madison looked around at everything they had accomplished in the past few weeks. The inn looked completely magical. There were glowing jack-o'-lanterns on the front porch, apple cider barrels and hay bales out front, and a big Halloween wreath hung on the front door—courtesy of the crafting circle.

Bowls of candy sat in the entryway, and the smell of cinnamon rolls still clung to the air from that morning. The wooden floors gleamed, polished and clean, and guests chatted in the lobby with mugs of cider in hand.

Madison couldn't wait until tonight. Kids would come knocking, saying, "Trick or treat," in their adorable Halloween costumes. A few of them were already running up and down Oak Way dressed as superheroes and princesses. She might've even seen a zombie here or there.

Guests were steadily arriving, too. The inn wasn't sold out, but they were well on their way. Things were looking bright and up in all areas.

Except for one.

Zach.

After that day at the farmhouse, Madison had reached out, tried to tell him she was sorry and that she wanted to talk more—but all she'd heard back was radio silence. She didn't blame him. She had iced him out first and she was willing to take full responsibility for how she'd acted. She just prayed that Zach would hear her out. Give her a second chance... or maybe it was a third by now. Regardless, Madison had to be brave and ask him to take that chance on her, on them.

Madison moved through the crowd, smiling and chitchatting here and there. The place felt full of life. Cocoa was there too, getting plenty of pets and more than one dog biscuit. Visitors naturally filtered out onto the lawn, petting Honey and Biscuit and giving Aspen carrots. The animals were getting more affection than they had in the last six months—well, more than from just George, anyway.

Madison looked for her dad and smiled when she saw him chatting easily with Mr. Alders and Mayor Bloomfield. They were congratulating him on a job well done. George was quick not to take any credit. "I couldn't have done it without Maddie here. Well—Zach, Kit, Gram, the entire crew. You too, Mayor," her dad said, raising his cider in a toast to the man who had kept the inn going long enough to give Madison a chance to buy it back.

"There you are," Gram said, joining her on the lawn.

"What's wrong?" Madison asked more out of instinct than anything else.

"Well... I may have accidentally loosened the inn's porch railing earlier." Gram had the decency to pretend to be sorry. "Someone's on his way to fix it. Maybe you could patch some things up too?" Gram patted Madison's hand.

"You did not," Madison said with a smile.

"He won't dare ignore a call from me," Gram said, chuckling.

Madison knew she was right. Zach wouldn't ignore a call from Gram any more than he would ignore a call from his own mother. Speaking of which, Anita had arrived with a lovely bouquet of orange and white flowers. Madison had put them in a crystal vase and set them on the registration desk. It really brightened up the lobby.

Zach arrived just as Kit was starting to panic about keeping the guests away from the danger zone while the railing was still loose.

"If everyone could just come toward the back, that would be great. The railing is just a little unsteady," Kit said, luring people away with caramel-dipped apples and homemade kettle corn. She didn't have to tell people twice—the sweets easily lured them away.

Madison watched from a distance. Zach, with his sleeves rolled up, looked every bit like a small-town hero trope come to life. He wasted no time opening his toolbox and tightening the railing. If Madison didn't act quickly, he'd be in and out in less than five minutes.

"Hey," Madison said, approaching.

He looked over his shoulder with a head nod, then turned back, continuing to tighten the bracket. "Thought you'd left town already."

"Not yet. I want to talk to you." Madison looked around, realizing how many prying eyes were watching them. "Maybe someplace in private?" she suggested.

Zach allowed Madison to lead him down the path toward the lake until they were behind the honeymoon cabin, with the water stretched out before them. It was about as private as they were going to get, and it felt right—having this conversation with Zach in a place that meant so much.

"So, what did you want to say?" Zach asked, as if he'd rather be anywhere else.

"That morning, when I got the job offer, I needed space. I didn't know what to do, so I ran, and I'm sorry for that."

He shook his head, a humorless laugh leaving his lips. "You didn't just run, Mads, you disappeared. Just like before."

She winced. "I know. I know, and you're right. But it wasn't because I didn't love you. It's never been that."

He looked away. "You have any idea what it's like, watching you walk away? Wondering why I'm never enough for you to stay?"

Tears stung her eyes. "Zach, it wasn't like that. I found out my family didn't own the inn anymore, that they sold it to pay for my college. I thought I had to take the job in New York, get the inn back for them, for my mom's legacy—even if it meant losing you. I thought it was the only way to fix everything."

He looked back at her then, eyes burning. "You didn't even give me the chance to fight for us."

"I know." She swallowed hard. "And I'm so sorry for that. I thought I had to choose, but I was wrong. I talked to my new boss, and the job's going remote. I'll have to travel some, but I'm staying here. I want this life, Zach. With you. And the inn."

She stepped closer. "I'm in love with you. It's always been you; it always will be. Please tell me it's not too late. Tell me you can forgive me."

His gaze softened, but the hurt was still there. "How do I know you won't run again?"

Madison lifted her chin, trying to show her strength. "Because I'm done running. Because I love you more than I love any job or city or anything else. I'll fight for this. For us. For you."

Zach looked at her. Really looked at her. And then he stepped forward. "You're late," he murmured, "but not too late." And he kissed her, pressing her back against the cabin wall.

The kiss deepened, hot, urgent. Madison was suddenly very aware of exactly how little privacy the back of the cabin offered.

Breathless, she broke away.

"Inside," she whispered, tugging him toward the door.

Zach didn't hesitate. His hand found hers, and together they raced to the door, fumbling with it like two people who couldn't bear another second apart.

The door slammed shut behind them, and then he was on her again. He laced his hands through her hair and pulled her sweater up over her head, discarding it onto the floor without ceremony. She did the same with his shirt.

He kissed down her body—slow, unhurried, savoring. She gasped when his mouth found her breast, teasing her nipple with slow, lazy flicks of his tongue until she was writhing before him, clutching at his shoulders.

"You're driving me insane," she panted.

Zach chuckled low against her skin, the sound sending vibrations straight through her core.

"Good," he said, grinning wickedly. "Because you've been driving me insane for years."

Zach lifted Madison up and carried her effortlessly to the table, just like he had in her fantasy.

"I dreamed of us like this," she confessed.

"You did?" Zach arched a cocky brow. "When?"

"That first night back," Madison whispered, her cheeks flushing, but she didn't look away.

Zach's grin turned wicked. "And here I thought I was the only one losing sleep."

He set her carefully on the table, undressing her until she was bared to him.

"You have no idea what you do to me," he murmured, voice low and reverent. "Every time you smile at me, every time you look at me like you see the best parts of me... I come undone."

Madison's heart squeezed, her throat tightening with emotion.

Because she did see him. She always had.

"I don't want to dream anymore," she whispered, reaching for him. "I want this. I want you."

"You're not dreaming," Zach said roughly, leaning in and capturing her mouth in a kiss that was both a promise and a possession.

Madison fumbled with the button of his jeans, needing more, needing him.

When he was ready, Zach slid his hands up her thighs, gripping her hips and pulling her closer to the edge of the table.

Their eyes locked.

With one slow, deliberate thrust, Zach pushed inside her, filling her completely.

They both gasped because it was perfect.

It had always been perfect between them.

"God, Mads," he rasped.

She clung to him as he began to move, slow and deep, each thrust sending sparks racing up her spine.

The table creaked beneath them, but neither of them cared.

It was raw and real and so, so good.

Zach kissed her like he couldn't get close enough, his hands everywhere, grounding her and worshipping her all at once.

Madison met every roll of his hips with a little whimper that only made him move faster, deeper, driving them both higher.

The coil of pleasure tightened until she was shuddering around him, crying out his name.

Zach followed with a guttural groan, his body trembling with the force of his release.

She lay back on the table, breathing hard and laughing softly.

"What's so funny?" he murmured, still trying to catch his breath.

Madison smiled, a warmth blooming in her chest. "That first night, my dream was interrupted. I've been waiting for this exact climax for a while. And it was way better than any fantasy could have been."

Zach huffed a low, pleased laugh. "Good. I like exceeding expectations."

He leaned forward and helped her up. His arms wrapped around her, holding her close like he had no intention of letting go.

And for the first time in a long time, Madison believed it.

This wasn't a fantasy; this was real.

Him. Them. This moment.

It wasn't the start of something. It was everything.

FIFTY-SIX
MADISON

Madison didn't think Halloween could've been any more perfect—except for maybe later that night. She was going with Zach to the farmhouse, where she had a feeling she'd be spending a lot of her nights from then on.

Madison smiled with each step she took up to her bedroom, her body buzzing from the excitement of the day. Hundreds of costumed kids had knocked on the door, and the great room was full of laughter. She could hear her dad telling stories to a guest about years gone by, and Gram was giving an impromptu knitting lesson to a teen trying to make a scarf.

It was just the way things were at the Cinnamon Spice Inn. You arrived as a stranger, but you left as part of their family.

Madison pushed open her bedroom door and, for the first time since she'd been back, really appreciated all the cozy details of her childhood bedroom—the soft quilt, the twinkling lights still strung across the window, and even a few of her old recipe books left on the shelf.

Madison took a deep breath and caught the faint scent of apple, cinnamon... and something else. Something floral and soft.

Her mom's perfume.

I haven't smelled that in years, Madison thought. *But here it is—like she's here too, like she never left.*

When she opened her eyes, something caught her attention. It was an envelope resting gently on her bedspread, propped up against the pillows. The envelope was slightly yellowed, like the other letter she'd received—but this time, her name was written on the front in her mother's looping, familiar handwriting.

Madison just stared at the envelope for a moment before sitting on the edge of the bed and picking it up. Her fingers trembled as she opened it, withdrew the letter, and began to read.

Dear Maddie,

If you're reading this, it means you've found your way home.

I always knew you would.

Maybe not right away. Maybe not in the way anyone expected. I know it hurt you to leave things the way you did with Zach, and your friends.

But I knew you, my brave girl—you'd come back when the timing was right.

You've always been brave, even when you didn't feel it. I saw it in you when you were five, standing on that step stool to stir the cinnamon roll filling. I saw it again when you left for New York, heart wide open to the world and all its possibilities.

Bravery isn't always loud. Sometimes it's just showing up when you're unsure. Sometimes it's staying when it would be easier to leave.

This inn was never about the bricks and beams—it's about the hearts inside it. It's about the way your dad plays music in the kitchen on Sunday mornings. The way guests come back year after year because they remember how we made them feel. It's the laughter that echoes in the great room and the quiet peace that comes when the first snow falls outside those old windows.

It's home. And it's yours, if you want it. Wherever you are in the world, it will always be your home.

But listen closely, sweetheart: Only stay here if it's what your heart wants.

Your dreams will change and grow. That's okay. Just don't forget to check in with your heart. Don't chase a path just because it looks shiny. And don't stay out of guilt or fear. Stay because it fills you up, even when it's hard. Because you feel more like yourself than you ever have. Because there's love— real, messy, worth-it love.

I hope you read this with the windows open and the smell of something baking in the kitchen. I hope there's laughter in the house again. I hope you're surrounded by good people, the kind who remind you of who you are.

And I hope you remember this more than anything:

I am so proud of you.

No matter where you go or what you choose, I'll always be with you. Just follow the scent of cinnamon and listen for the wind—I'll be in both.

Love you forever,

Mom

Madison looked up and saw her grandma standing in the doorway with a smile on her face. "It was you," she said, looking at her grandmother.

Gram stepped forward, her hands folded. "Your mom wrote those letters before she passed, asked me to deliver them when the time was right."

Madison's throat tightened. "All of them? Around town?"

Gram let out a breath, a sheepish smile tugging at her lips.

"Almost all of them. Cocoa was all me. I saw how much your dad needed someone to take care of, and Cocoa needed someone to love."

Madison laughed, pressing a hand to her heart. "I should have known."

Gram's smile softened. "It wasn't easy, keeping this secret from you, Maddie. You've always been such a straight shooter, and I hated not telling you. And truth be told, when you showed up without warning, I was surprised, even though I'd just sent out the letter a few days before. I didn't expect you to come so soon." Her eyes sparkled. "But I'm so glad you did."

Madison nodded, swallowing down her emotions.

She looked back at the letter, her thumb brushing over the final words.

The wind blew gently outside, lifting the curtain through the cracked window. The breeze carried the faint scent of her mother's perfume.

Madison closed her eyes and let it move through her.

"I'm home," she said.

EPILOGUE

Madison stepped out of the Cinnamon Spice Inn with two large cups of coffee. The chilly November wind blew her hair across her face, carrying the scent of the never-ending cinnamon rolls coming out of Kit's kitchen.

Madison tucked deeper into her mother's emerald knit scarf. Christmas was just around the corner, and Madison couldn't wait. She'd already picked out the Christmas tree from Liam's farm, the one that would dominate the inn's great room, and she was just waiting until the day after Thanksgiving to unbox all her mother's holiday decorations.

She'd pull out all the stops, twinkle lights and fresh evergreen draped across the mantel, red and green throw pillows on the couches, her mother's miniature Christmas village on full display in the lobby. It would be beautiful, and Madison knew all the guests would love it. The inn's calendar had quickly filled up after the grand reopening. Every room was booked, and it would be a lovely way to welcome in the New Year.

This year's holiday season would be filled with joy, love, and zero pressure, unlike for the businesses selected for the Christmas

Countdown Competition. Madison was relieved not to have to participate in the decoration contest. She and Zach had worked hard enough that fall and were ready to spend winter's long nights cozied up in each other's arms at the farmhouse. They still had plenty of rooms in their new home to break in...

But that didn't mean they wouldn't pop into town and enjoy the festivities. Madison's money was on Cassidy and her chocolate shop to take the grand prize, while Zach was sticking by Liam's side and his farm shop. Sparks were sure to fly between the competitors. She'd bet money on it.

Madison was still thinking about the upcoming competition when she stopped to watch a couple pose in front of the newly planted maple tree, its red-orange leaves glowing in the afternoon light.

It had broken her heart when they'd lost the original tree, but this new one was strong, beautiful, and full of promise. Zach and Madison had planted it side-by-side, placing it securely in the earth where its roots would grow deep for years to come.

Zach joined her right on time.

"Hey." His voice rumbled low behind her, followed by the warm press of his hand against the small of her back. "The place looks great, but you look..." He let his eyes linger appreciatively as she handed him his coffee, voice dipping to a whisper. "Even better."

Zach's arm slipped fully around her waist as they started walking. "You did it, Mads. This inn, this life... you made it happen."

"We did it," she corrected softly. "We found our way back together."

Zach nodded, always more action than words. But then he paused near the tree. "I was so scared that you'd leave. That I'd open up and get gutted all over again."

Her breath caught. He rarely talked about his feelings like this.

"But I wouldn't change any of it," he added. "Not one damn thing. You've made me believe in love again. In building a real relationship. And as long as there's breath in my body, I will love you."

Madison turned toward him fully. "Zach..." Her voice caught, but she didn't look away. Instead she reached up, cupping his cheek, grounding them both in the moment. "I've been scared, too. Of messing it all up again. I know I can be... a lot."

Zach chuckled, reaching up and taking her hand in his own. "My very own firecracker."

"You light me up, but you also ground me." She leaned into him. "And every time I worry about being too much, every time I am overwhelmed, I think of you."

His voice dropped to a whisper against her ear. "We're both going to mess up, and that's okay. So long as we work through it together. And I don't want perfect. I want real. I want us."

She smiled through the tears. "And I will love you through every season, for the rest of my life."

A LETTER FROM HARPER

Thank you so much for reading *The Cinnamon Spice Inn* and spending time in Maple Falls with Madison and Zach.

Writing their story was a true labor of love fueled by a lot of strong coffee and cinnamon rolls. It was very much inspired by the cozy, quirky small town I'm lucky enough to live in. It's been so much fun to escape into the world of Maple Falls, and I hope you enjoy it as much as I loved writing it.

If you enjoyed the book and want to stay up to date with my latest releases, you can sign up for my newsletter at the following link:

www.bookouture.com/harper-graham

Your email address will never be shared, and you can unsubscribe at any time.

I'd also be so grateful if you left a review. Reviews make a huge difference and help new readers discover my books. And honestly, I would just love to hear from you. I hope *The Cinnamon Spice Inn* warmed your heart and gave you the perfect autumnal escape.

Feel free to reach out through Facebook, X, Instagram, or TikTok.

With all my gratitude,

Harper

KEEP IN TOUCH WITH HARPER

- instagram.com/harpergrahambooks
- facebook.com/HarperGrahamAuthor
- tiktok.com/@harpergrahambooks
- x.com/HarperGraham_

ACKNOWLEDGMENTS

I want to thank my editor, Rhianna Louise, for bringing Maple Falls to life. Her editorial suggestions are always spot on, and I've learned so much from working with her. You're brilliant, Rhianna!

To the rest of the amazing team at Bookouture—thank you for all the behind-the-scenes magic, your enthusiasm, and your unwavering belief in this series from the very beginning.

To my talented agent, Cindy Bullard, for making all the right connections and always having my back. I'm so thankful for the work you've put in.

To my husband for all the love and support a girl could ask for. Thank you for holding down the fort so I can sneak away and write my heart out. I couldn't do it without you.

To Libby, for asking me every day how the book's doing. And sending numerous GIFs of encouragement. You da best.

Finally, to you, the reader, thank you for taking a chance on this story.

Whether you've shared it with a friend, left a review, or simply fallen in love with Maple Falls alongside Madison and Zach, please know it means the world to me. Your support keeps these stories alive.

PUBLISHING TEAM

Turning a manuscript into a book requires the efforts of many people. The publishing team at Bookouture would like to acknowledge everyone who contributed to this publication.

Audio
Alba Proko
Sinead O'Connor
Melissa Tran

Commercial
Lauren Morrissette
Hannah Richmond
Imogen Allport

Cover design
Alexandra Allden

Data and analysis
Mark Alder
Mohamed Bussuri

Editorial
Rhianna Louise
Ria Clare

Copyeditor
DeAndra Lupu

Proofreader
Becca Allen

Marketing
Alex Crow
Melanie Price
Occy Carr
Ciara Rosney
Martyna Młynarska

Operations and distribution
Marina Valles
Stephanie Straub
Joe Morris

Production
Hannah Snetsinger
Mandy Kullar
Nadia Michael

Publicity
Kim Nash
Noelle Holten
Jess Readett
Sarah Hardy

Rights and contracts
Peta Nightingale
Richard King
Saidah Graham

RAISING READERS
Books Build Bright Futures

Dear Reader,

We'd love your attention for one more page to tell you about the crisis in children's reading, and what we can all do.

Studies have shown that reading for fun is the **single biggest predictor of a child's future life chances** – more than family circumstance, parents' educational background or income. It improves academic results, mental health, wealth, communication skills, ambition and happiness.

The number of children reading for fun is in rapid decline. Young people have a lot of competition for their time, and a worryingly high number do not have a single book at home.

Hachette works extensively with schools, libraries and literacy charities, but here are some ways we can all raise more readers:

- Reading to children for just 10 minutes a day makes a difference
- Don't give up if children aren't regular readers – there will be books for them!

- Visit bookshops and libraries to get recommendations
- Encourage them to listen to audiobooks
- Support school libraries
- Give books as gifts

There's a lot more information about how to encourage children to read on our websites: **www.RaisingReaders.co.uk** and **www.JoinRaisingReaders.com**.

Thank you for reading.